A PUNK ROCK FUTURE

a science fiction anthology

"Lean, whip-smart, and raw as a fresh gash in the mosh pit, these stories revel in the anarchic zeal of punk rock while rooting themselves in the black-glitter futurism of science fiction. Johnny Rotten may have sneered 'No future!', but *A Punk Rock Future* dares to scream otherwise."

— Jason Heller, Hugo Award-winning editor and author of *Strange Stars: David Bowie, Pop Music,* and *the Decade Sci-Fi Exploded.*

A Punk Rock Future © 2019 Steve Zisson

Published by Zsenon Publishing
Zsenonpublishing@gmail.com

Cover illustration & design by Eva Heaps
Interior design by Eva Heaps
Text set in Baskerville and Optima.
First Edition
ISBN (Print) 978-1-7337750-0-7
ISBN (e-book) 978-1-7337750-1-4
First Published in October 2019 by Zsenon Publishing

A PUNK ROCK
FUTURE

A SCIENCE FICTION ANTHOLOGY

Edited and with an introduction by Steve Zisson

FEATURING STORIES BY

Erica L. Satifka, Margaret Killjoy, Spencer Ellsworth,
Sarah Pinsker, Corey J. White, Zandra Renwick,
and 20 Others

Published by Zsenon Publishing

To all future punks, real or imagined.

☒   ☒   ☒

TABLE OF CONTENTS

INTRODUCTION

You don't want to read a lengthy introduction to *A Punk Rock Future*. I'll keep it quick, like a Dee Dee Ramone count-in, so you can get to all the great stories. They're fast reads. They're furious.

This is where it all began for me. I loved punk bands when I was growing up in the late 70s—The Clash and The Jam, as well as Boston bands from Willie Alexander and the Boom Boom Band to the Nervous Eaters and so many others. The Neighborhoods, of course.

During that time—the ancient 70s and early 80s—my love of science fiction and fantasy, particularly its punk variants starting with cyberpunk, also took off. So it was quite natural for me many years later to mash up science fiction and fantasy with punk rock. It's a combination that has been a long time in the making. Science fiction and fantasy literature is bursting with "punk" niches today, some of the latest being solarpunk and hopepunk. There's hope.

Before you get to the 26 short stories in *A Punk Rock Future*, I'm at least going to thank a few in particular who helped out along the way.

Erica Satifka for early encouragement and inspiration from her writing. Sarah Pinsker's stories for inspiration. Margaret Killjoy for timely advice and sending a story early. Aidan Doyle and David Steffen, both anthologists in their own right and fine writers, answered numerous questions. Spencer Ellsworth, too, for giving the book idea an initial nod and eventually a story.

The biggest contributor to the DIY ethos of *A Punk Rock Future* came from artist and assistant editor Eva Heaps. She did it all from the cover art and design, layout, inspiration, you name it. This is her book as much as anyone's. Dave Brigham, too, for stellar editing efforts even as he was starting yet another band.

Assistant editors brought a variety of skills and musical influences, including Karyn Korieth, Jay Kumar, Jay Breitling and Ric Dube.

We are thrilled by the range of stories in this anthology and hope you enjoy reading these visions of *A Punk Rock Future* like we did. It's your DIY project, too. Let's go.

Steve Zisson
Editor

TRIAL AND TERROR

Erica L. Satifka

Somehow, the van makes it most of the way through Iowa. Then it dies all at once, spectacularly, farting out its reserve of gas like an old man on taco night in the run-down nursing home his good-for-nothing children stuck him in after he drove the family sedan into a telephone pole.

Most of those things don't exist anymore. No nursing homes. Only a few sedans. And don't get me started on the lack of taco nights.

"Shit!" Frank yells, banging on the steering wheel. "Shit, shit, shit!"

Clementine, our bass player, smirks and snorts a little through her nose. "I don't think you said 'shit' enough times, Frank. Better say it again."

"*Shiiiiiiit,*" Frank moans, his voice the sound of a tugboat navigating through a soupy fog.

I open the door, which creaks ominously. "We'd better go find help. We passed a town around ten minutes ago."

Frank counts out numbers on his fingers. It takes a lot longer than it should. "But that's like a hundred miles!"

"It's seven miles," I say. "But it'll still take a while to get there."

"Dibs on staying in the van!" Clem doesn't even wait for an answer before flopping herself into the driver's seat.

Frank looks at her. I look at her.

"What? Someone might steal it."

"Let's go, Syl," Frank says to me.

I stick my tongue out at Clem and follow Frank down the dusty, corn-husk-strewn highway.

Our band's been on the road for five months now, spreading

the power of positive thinking across the Midwest after the Great Happiness Collapse. A few years ago, aliens from the constellation Cygnus temporarily tainted Earth's water supplies with pleasure-juice, a colorless and odorless shortcut to heaven. Then, just as we were all getting used to life under the drug, they cut it off, leading to a world-wide epidemic of rebound depression. One of the many imperfect cures for this huge downer was awakecore music, a genre Frank himself invented, which sounds a lot like a stray cat getting hit with a mandolin.

At this point in the game, Frank's mostly in it for the merch money. "Picture it, Syl," he says as we inch down the highway. "Mousepads with like, our logo on them and everything. I met a guy in Des Moines who found a whole warehouse full of blank ones. We can draw the logos with that puffy paint we use on the tee shirts."

I don't know what to criticize first: The fact that nobody uses computers anymore? That a mousepad with puffy paint all over it would be a very poor mousepad indeed? Finally, I hit on the most obvious fault. "That would require *you* not changing the name of the band every few months."

"I can't help that I keep thinking of better ones!" Frank leaps and grabs at the top of a speed limit sign. He doesn't even bend it, but from the way he starts to howl, I think he might have broken his hand.

"My hand!" He falls to the ground.

"You're a real idiot, Frank."

⌛   ⌛   ⌛

From the signs on the road, we are now entering Oskaloosa, Iowa. Low-slung buildings topped with drooping slate roofs line the banks of a slightly greenish river. From a distance it looks like pollution, but when we get closer I see that it's actually algae. Oskaloosa is a genuine cow town, not even big enough in the Time Before to justify a Cygnian recruitment compound.

We wade through the waist-high grass, me parting the greenery at the front, Frank limping behind even though it's his hand that's broken, not his foot.

"When we get there," I say, "stay at the perimeter. Be ready to run."

He wipes his face with the corner of his shirt, which hasn't been washed for the entire tour. "No, Syl. I'm going in with you."

"But you don't need—"

"Remember Peoria?"

I snort. "Of course I remember. That was only a few days ago."

"Remember how you went into Peoria to see if they had any supplies we could barter for, and then you didn't come back, and me and Clem had to come *get* you?"

I mow down a layer of grass with my forearm. "I'm surprised you convinced her to come on this tour at all. She seems like she doesn't even want to play the shows most of the time."

Frank glares at me. "You've never liked Clem, have you?"

"Of *course* I like her, it's just—"

He stops me short with his good hand. "Did you hear something?"

I strain my ears. Voices come from the direction of the town. We quicken our pace and round the bend to see a crowd of townspeople, who are surrounding a quartet of horses pulling ropes in four separate directions. In the middle is a dummy stuffed with straw. When the horses reach a certain point, the dummy explodes its straw confetti on the mostly blond heads. The crowd cheers.

"Hey, what's this?" I ask the random woman next to me.

"They're practicing drawing and quartering." She sneers. "You don't look like you're from around here."

"We're just passing through."

"This is what we do to criminals," she says, jerking a thumb at the horses. "And outsiders."

My stomach clenches and I reach for Frank, but he's already stumbled toward the eye of the crowd. He holds his trembling right hand aloft.

"Hey! Is anyone here a doctor?"

The Oskaloosans look up as a solid unit, their spooky pale faces like the glittering of evil stars. There's a generalized murmuring, and one of them holds up a mimeographed flyer. Then they advance on Frank like a wave. Like a *tsunami*.

I run toward him and start tugging on his sleeve. "I *told* you to stay back, Frank," I say, before the wave overtakes us both and I'm pinned choking on the asphalt under a solid four hundred pounds of cornfed Iowa flesh.

⧗   ⧗   ⧗

This isn't the nicest jail cell I've ever been in, but at least there are beds. There aren't always beds, as Clem and I learned the hard way in Indiana.

Frank paces the narrow room, a caged tiger. "Fucking *Iowa*." He kicks the brick wall and crumples to the ground with a shriek.

"Great job, Frank, now you have a broken hand *and* a broken foot."

"It's not broken," he says, hopping over to his cot and sucking back tears.

"We have to get out of here," I say.

Frank pulls at his hair with his remaining hand. "Clem will save us. She has to be getting worried by now."

Suddenly, whistling echoes down the long white corridor. A guard with a protruding beer belly presses his face against the bars. "Mealtime." He throws a handful of fun-sized candy onto the concrete floor.

"Wait!" I say, jamming my arm through the metal slats. "What are we charged with? You can't leave us in here forever." Technically he can, since the rule of law doesn't exist post-Cygnian invasion, but he might not know that.

"It's not up to me." The guard's hand creeps slowly toward his bellybutton and starts to pick it. "The judge will be here in the morning. You'll get a chance to plead your case."

"But what the fuck are the charges?" Frank asks through a mouthful of nougat. "When's our trial?"

The guard throws a balled-up piece of paper at us before lumbering off, and I uncrumple it to find a grainy picture of what might be Frank and Clem. Underneath them is a caption reading WANTED: MURDER.

"Murder?!" I pace around the ten-by-ten room, which isn't easy to do. "You didn't commit murder! How could you have committed murder, Frank? How?!"

He's a lot calmer than I think he should be. "Let's just wait for all the evidence to be reviewed."

"*What* evidence?"

Frank stares at his right hand, which is approximately twice the size of his left one. "Do you remember what happened in Peoria?"

"Well, apparently you and Clem *killed a guy.*"

He shushes me down, and nods at the other room where the guard is. "We might have. I don't know! It was dark! We were looking for *you,* Syl."

"This isn't my fault, like, *at all.*" I drop my voice; for all we know they've got the place wired. "Who did you kill, Frank?"

He beholds me from his cot, the moonlight turning his eyes into calm pools. "Some stranger. I thought he was going to hurt Clem, so I hit him with a rock. He fell down."

I shake my head. "Shit."

"But when I went to check on him, he was gone. Disappeared. Me and Clem searched for an hour, but he must have gotten away." He glances out the window at the full moon. "Guess he didn't."

"You didn't kill anyone," I say, even though that's exactly what it sounds like he did. "And even if you did, he was a sleaze, right?"

"Maybe," Frank replies, and I can tell that he's tired of talking about it.

I shift around on my cot until it's clear that the bar jammed into my lower back isn't going to get any less obtrusive. Then I paw through the candy, foraging for cheap calories. And after that I look over at Frank. It's impossible to tell whether he's asleep or awake. I fluff the candy wrappers into a makeshift pillow and settle myself on the narrow cot, timing my own breaths to the snoring of the guard. I do not sleep.

⧗ ⧗ ⧗

Or, maybe I do. At least that would explain why Frank is in the cell with me one minute and gone the next. I'm not *that* inattentive, even if I did get lost on the mean streets of Peoria.

"Frank!" I yell, cupping my hands around my mouth. "Fraaank!"

The pudgy guard bangs a truncheon against the jail-cell bars. "Pipe down in there."

"Yeah, because I'm disturbing *so* many people," I say.

"You're disturbing *me*."

I cling to the bars of the cell. "Where is my friend?"

"I sent him to get that hand patched up. We also have to interrogate you two. Separately, of course."

"Naturally. But I won't talk until I see that he's alive."

"Hell, lady, what kind of people do you think we are?" He throws me another pocketful of candy and saunters away, whistling.

"Certainly not the kind that believe in a balanced diet," I mutter. I scoop the candy up and stuff my face with Snickers and M&Ms, gagging on the sticky sweetness.

Did Frank actually kill someone in Peoria? It's hard to believe. Oh, I definitely think he'd try to kill someone who was threatening Clem, but he just doesn't have the upper body strength.

There's a conversation too far away for me to hear, and then the door of the jailhouse slams shut. A different guard comes into view. Her warm brown eyes are cold when she looks at me. She frowns at the drift of wrappers littering my cot.

"Clean that up, we're not your parents," she says.

"Well, we *are* wards of the state at the moment. You people locked us in here, so now you have to take care of us." I scatter the wrappers even more.

Her eyes graze me over from top to bottom. "Your boyfriend's in some deep shit."

"He's not my boyfriend. He's our vocalist and lead guitarist. We're in a band."

"Oh yeah? Are you any good?"

"We're terrible." I thread my hand through the bars. "I'm Sylvia. Syl for short."

The cop whips out her Taser and holds it over her right hand, which she slips into mine. "Bettylou."

"*Seriously?* Is this place a stereotype factory?" Her face twists up hideously and I make a conversational U-turn. "I mean, pleased to make your acquaintance."

"Your friend's in the interrogation room. We're chipping away his defenses, bit by bit." Her top lip curls.

I don't bother telling her that Frank doesn't *have* any defenses. "Are we at least going to get a fair trial?"

"You'll get *a* trial." She turns and walks away, her thick thighs straining the limits of her pencil skirt. My gaze lingers perhaps a little bit longer than appropriate, but it's been so long, and I'm only human.

Bettylou turns, gives me a nod, and winks. I guess she has something in her eye.

⧗　⧗　⧗

A few hours later, Frank is back in the cell. The cast on his hand resembles a Mickey Mouse glove, but one you'd see at an unlicensed off-brand amusement park in Delaware or somewhere.

I check to make sure that neither of the guards is around, then shuffle over to him. "How was it?"

"That guard fucking *tortured* me, Syl," he says. "He tried to force me to confess."

"Did you?"

"No," he says, and I'm a little surprised. "But he said it wouldn't matter if I confess or not. He said they want to make an example of 'city slickers from way out East'." He snuffles and wipes his nose with his cast. "I mean, who even *talks* like that?"

I ruffle his hair, because I'm not sure what else to do.

"Clem *has* to get here soon," Frank says.

"Yeah, maybe." I don't want to say the thing I'm thinking, that Clem's absence probably means something bad already happened to her. Best case scenario is that she met up with a better band.

"I love her *so much*," Frank says before bursting into tears.

I wrap my arms around him, and I even keep myself from flinching when he sneezes a fine mist all over me.

"There's going to be a trial," I say. "I've watched a lot of legal dramas in my day, Frank. They were on Channel Eleven all the time. I can defend you."

Frank's face scrunches up. "Shouldn't we hire a real attorney for that?"

I spread my arms wide. "You think anyone in this town is going to give us a fair trial? We're outsiders from way back East."

Truthfully, I don't think any amount of legal wrangling can save Frank. But a show will. Whenever logic fails, our two-chord, atonal music has always saved us from whatever scrapes we happen to get into. We don't understand the magic, but that doesn't stop it from working. It's worked in the past and it's going to work now. *If* I can get the right tools.

⧗   ⧗   ⧗

Just as I've lulled Frank to sleep, Bettylou arrives, clanging on our jail bars with a baton. "It's time for your confession, Syl."

"I have nothing to confess," I say. Frank stirs in my lap, and I maneuver away from him, leaving him on his cot.

"It'll be better for you if you do. The judge will go easier on you."

I walk over to the bars and do my best to loom over her menacingly, which isn't hard. She's a full head shorter than me, and I'm not tall. "We'll take our chances at trial."

She smiles. "Come to the interrogation room anyway. Who knows, might be fun."

Bettylou herds me down a dingy gray corridor toward a door so nondescript that I can't even describe it. She pushes me inside and I topple headlong over a migraine-orange plastic chair and surprisingly land on my feet.

"Did you see that," I say. "It was practically a cart——"

"Shut up for just one second." Bettylou swings me around, takes my head in both of her hands, and presses her lips against mine in a sweet Iowa welcome. I yank at the buttons of her blouse and then melt into her, the feel of her body against me a warm misty rain on a very dry desert.

Afterward, as Bettylou and I are spooning on top of the chipped and graffitied interrogation table, she whispers, "Take me with you."

"Yeah, you can come. But what I need to know now is what's really going to happen when the judge gets here. Will he give Frank a fair trial?"

Bettylou skates her fingertips through my hair. "The judge isn't a he. Or a her. It's an it."

Well, at least I'm not being inadvertently sexist. "What, is the judge a robot?"

"No, it's a computer."

"A *computer* is going to sentence my friend to death?!"

She flips around to face me. "It's not only a judge. It tells us how to set up the community and live our lives for maximum harmony. What to plant, where to find clean water, who to marry——"

I can feel my lips purse up at the last one. "But it's a *computer*, Bettylou. Frank has the right to defend himself in front of a jury of his peers."

"His chances are probably better with the computer in this town."

This, at least, I can't refute. "You can come along with us. I really, really want you to come along with us. But I need to save Frank. I *know* he didn't kill anyone, and if he did ... well, he didn't."

"How can we do that? The courthouse is surrounded. This is the trial of the decade."

I sit up and the interrogation table creaks under my weight. "Go get some instruments. Guitars, drums, whatever you can find. We're going to throw this town a hell of a show."

Just then, the door slams back on its hinges. Bettylou bolts upright and smooths her skirt down.

It's the male guard. "This investigation is a little unorthodox, sergeant."

"I–uh, don't think I can crack her."

The guard shrugs. "Don't matter. The judge is here. That boy is gonna be drawn and quartered before sundown." He shuts the door.

"Double time on those instruments, Bettylou." I slide off the table and give her one last kiss. "I have to go stall that trial."

⌛   ⌛   ⌛

The courtroom is packed, but I haven't taken a shower in so long that the crowd parts around me, leaving me a nice empty space in the rows of seats.

A surly bailiff manhandles an even surlier Frank into a wooden cage standing next to a delicately filigreed dining table. The bailiff shoves him into it in such a way that Frank falls on his broken hand. Frank screams, then snaps at the bailiff like a rabid ferret.

"I fucking hate Iowa," I mutter under my breath.

A hush descends over the crowd. Two people dressed all in black, a man and a woman, carry an ornately painted box to the table and open it, revealing a laptop from the Time Before. The bailiff steps forward.

"All rise for the Honorable Patricia J. Atkinson, Supreme Judge of the Quad Cities Region. Court is now in session." The bailiff grins at Frank and draws a finger over his own throat.

A noise rattles from the laptop's speakers, sounding like a human cough filtered through wax paper. Then a gravelly, oddly accented voice begins to speak. "Please enter the nature of your problem."

The male assistant dressed all in black types into a remote keyboard placed on his lap, and the woman helpfully narrates. "This man, one Frank ... " She looks over at our beaten-down vocalist. "Hey, you got a last name?"

"Carnage." It's lame, but at least not as incriminating as his last stage name, "von Murderkill."

"Frank Carnage, an outsider, stands accused of the killing of an unknown victim last Thursday, at approximately 11:47 p.m., as witnessed by drone camera in the vicinity of Peoria, Illinois. Mr. Carnage, how do you plead?"

He shrugs. "Does it matter?"

I stand up. If Frank isn't going to defend himself, I sure as hell will. "He pleads innocent, you worthless computer slave."

The typist taps it in. "I shall now hear the evidence of the prosecution," the computer wheezes. "For a sore throat, try a spoonful of apple cider vinegar."

The male guard who'd tortured Frank only a few hours ago steps to the front of the courtroom. Apparently, Oskaloosa can't afford a separate prosecuting attorney. He holds up a flash drive. "I have on this disk video footage showing that Mr. *Carnage* here threw a rock at an unknown victim near the abandoned Cygnian compound in Peoria. The place wasn't *totally* looted; its security system was still functional. I believe you'll be pretty convinced." He slides the flash drive into the side of the Honorable Patricia J. Atkinson and plants a smug smile on his face.

The laptop's screen judders a few times, then its voice settles into a low purr. "Affirmative."

"But where's the *body*?" I yell. "And what kind of Cygnian compound goes unlooted for so long? This could all be some massive conspiracy." Visions of a detective's crazy wall enter my head, and I mentally plot a world-spanning scheme that will stall this trial for at least as long as it takes Bettylou to return with the instruments.

Something inside Judge Patricia whirs up. "State your name, Unknown Human."

"My name is Sylvia," I say, "and I'm in a band."

"The *greatest* band," Frank sputters out.

"A pretty okay band," I reply.

"Be that as it may," the jail guard/prosecuting attorney says, "that doesn't excuse murder. And who are you to speak for this man? You don't look like an attorney. Or smell like one."

I weave my way forward; the crowd dutifully parts ways for me. "I've known Frank four years now. We've lived together, we've been on the road together, and now we've been arrested together. And if you're going to accuse him of killing a person, then you're going to need better evidence than that."

Patricia J. Atkinson's screen flashes. "This will be a good season for corn."

I think back to all the endless hours of legal dramas I'd been exposed to when I worked at the Warsh 'n' Dry right after dropping out of college. "Your Honor, this is America. And in America, we have rights. Certain *inalienable* rights. Like, the right to be judged by a jury of one's peers, and not an old Dell computer with a scraped-off decal on its back. Also, a speedy trial. Speaking of speed, did you know cheetahs can run over sixty miles an hour? Wow, that's fast. Cheetahs live in Africa, where Toto blessed the rains." I hum a few bars from a barely remembered song. How long does it take a person to find some musical instruments in this town?

"You'd better be going somewhere with this," says the guard/prosecutor, "and not stalling for time."

The beach ball on Patricia's screen starts spinning again. "Does the defense call a witness to the stand?"

I gaze absently around the room until the guard/prosecutor coughs into his hand and checks his non-existent watch. I'm about to tell the computer-judge that I rest my case when Frank gestures wildly from his cage at the front of the room.

"You put *me* on the stand, Syl. That's how this works."

"I need to speak to my client," I say. I hunch down next to Frank. "I'm not sure this is a good idea. You said you might have killed that guy."

"It might not have been a guy. Maybe it was a woman."

I roll my eyes. "You're the worst client ever. But Bettylou's not back yet, so we don't really have a choice." I flag the bailiff over.

"Who's that?" he asks, but there isn't time for me to explain.

Frank perches on the rickety wooden chair between his cage and the Honorable Patricia J. Atkinson. He's chastened, like a little boy who's been caught with his hand in the cookie jar.

"Mr. Carnage," I say, pacing back and forth, "where were you on the night of the supposed 'crime'?"

"In Peoria. I was looking for you, Sylvia."

"I know," I say softly. "Was anyone with you?"

"Yes, my friend Clementine Disruption. She plays the bass."

"Objection!" says the bailiff. "Irrelevant."

"Overruled," drones the judge. "The next partial eclipse will occur on June 24."

"Thank you, Your Honor." I lean against the judge's table. "Mr. Carnage, what was your state of mind at the time of the purported 'incident'?"

Frank rubs his bare hand against his casted one. "We were scared. We thought you might have gone to the Cygnian compound, so we started there."

"I was looting the houses and the mall," I say. "I never went near the compound. You know those places freak me out."

"I'm glad you didn't," he says. And then he starts talking.

As in most cities over a certain population limit, there'd been a deserted Cygnian compound in Peoria, the building where the aliens prepared ten percent of humanity for a one-way trip from Earth to Cygnus. But from the wreckage left behind, it was clear that this one had been overtaken by the rejected humans of Peoria at one point.

Frank and Clem had picked their way through the compound, on the hunt for both me and anything that would be useful on the tour. And then they'd found him. Or her. The victim.

"It was dark, no moon at all. Clem said she felt like something had been following us. I laughed it off, but then we saw him." Frank wipes the back of his hand over his eyes. "The person or whatever."

"Please take a moment if you need to. Can we get some Kleenex over here?" I ask this of the bailiff, but he doesn't budge.

Frank barrels on. "He was on the pleasure-juice. I could tell that by the way he was staggering. It freaked us out. There wasn't much flesh left on the body." He sinks his face down into his good hand, looking glum. "I think he was part of the ten percent of people the Cygnians were supposed to take, but he got left behind when the raid happened. He was hungry. And he was coming for Clem. I *had* to do what I did, but I'm still sorry."

"You should have alerted the authorities, *son*," the guard/prosecutor says, "instead of taking matters into your own hands."

"*What* authorities?!" Frank rocks back in the chair and I brace myself for its collapse.

I decide I've had enough. Instead of objecting, I step back in front of Frank, hip-checking the bailiff. "You didn't do anything wrong, Frank. Stand up for yourself for once in your life!"

"It's over, Syl," Frank turns toward the open laptop, as if personally addressing whatever ghost powers that machine. "I'm ready to accept my punishment. The drawing and the quartering or whatever. But before I die, I have something I'd like to say."

"My charge is down to twenty percent," the judge says. "Please plug me in."

Frank takes a deep breath. "What I did, I only did to protect the woman I was with, Clementine. She means everything in the world to me. And when I saw that zombie—"

"*Alleged* zombie," interjects the bailiff.

"Shut up, man. Anyway, like I was saying. I shouldn't have done it, but I'd do it again. I'd walk over broken glass for that girl. I'd drink molten glass for her. I'd ... do a lot of things that don't involve glass. The point is, I love her. If you're going to kill me, I want it on the record that I died for love."

A tiny silence hangs over the courtroom. It feels, almost, like

applause is about to burst out. Then Patricia J. Atkinson opens its
stupid computer mouth.

"I find the defendant guilty. Commence the drawing and
quartering."

The bailiff whoops and grabs Frank's cast-hand. The judge's two
assistants take his legs. They hoist him into the air and my world turns
sideways.

"*Stop!*"

The voice that says this is low, sultry, and can't be mistaken for
anyone else.

"Clem!" Frank and I yell her name simultaneously.

A guitar in each hand, Clementine Disruption strides forth on her
hot pink, four-inch-high heels. Her dreadlocks flow behind her like a
nest of amplifier cables, and the makeup she concocts from the shells
of dead beetles doesn't look as bad as it usually does. Behind her is
Bettylou, hugging a tattered cardboard box. She smiles at me, and I
give her a little wave back.

The bailiff doesn't know whether to hang onto Frank or reach for
Clem, and while he stands there deciding, Frank wrests himself out of
the meathead's grip. The judge's lackeys scuttle away.

"I heard what you said," Clem says to Frank. "Every word of it."

"And?" His eagerness is painful to watch.

Clem glares down everyone in the courthouse. Not even Patricia
dares to speak. Then she takes Frank's head in her hands and kisses
him deeply, the guitar strings sproinging as they're mashed between
their bodies.

"Let's hit the road, baby," Clem says.

The guard/prosecutor half-coughs, half-belches. "If you were
here for that pathetic little declaration of love, you heard the verdict.
This man is guilty, and we intend to draw and quarter him as per the
town charter."

"We're leaving," Clem says, "but first we're giving you the show of
your life." She hands a guitar to Frank.

"I can't play," he says sadly, holding up his busted paw.

Clem hands it to me instead, even though I always sound like I'm playing with a broken hand. Bettylou takes a microphone from the box, gives it to Clem, who then hands it over to Frank. It's not plugged into anything, but it makes him seem about three times as confident. Though that still isn't much.

"I don't see what *any* of this has to do with the issue at hand," the guard/prosecutor says.

But the audience of attentive Oskaloosans has tired of their kangaroo court, and I can feel the supernatural pulse in the air that lets me know our one weird trick will work yet again. Clem bangs together a set of homeless drumsticks she'd pulled out of Bettylou's box above her head and then tosses them aside.

And we play.

I thought we'd start off with "Electrify Me," which is the closest thing we've ever had to a hit single, but Frank launches into a power ballad he wrote after the next-to-last time he and Clem broke up. He addresses only Clem when he sings, not the crowd.

"Why is this working?" Bettylou whispers to me, confusion stamped on her pretty little face.

"I don't know. But it always does. Roll with it."

Bettylou shrugs, takes a child's ukulele from the box, and plucks out a melody that perfectly complements Frank's nasal whine. At least we have one talented person in the band now.

When the song is over, the Oskaloosans stand and cheer, stomping their feet and throwing useless gobs of money at us. Frank scoops a few of the bills up and mops his forehead with them. Clem pounds out the opening bassline to our danciest number, and even though they can't possibly know what song we're playing, the crowd erupts in delight.

The guard/prosecutor is nowhere to be seen. Some people just don't like music or magic.

We play until the sun sets and the air grows cold. We run out of our own inventory of songs quickly, so Frank launches into a medley of commercial jingles from the Time Before. The audience shouts out the choruses before he does.

"I feel ... " Frank croons.

"Like chicken tonight! Like chicken tonight!"

By the end of the set we've resorted to improv, making up goofy songs about the audience members, who reluctantly file out one by one, all tuckered out from the most exciting thing that's ever happened to them. When the last of the Oskaloosans begs off, we repack everything we can in Bettylou's box and start out on our seven-mile trek to the van. We step over the sleeping forms of the judge's assistants, who cradle the Honorable Patricia J. Atkinson in their arms.

Frank flings open the courthouse door and we all stand face to face with the guard/prosecuting attorney. The gun in his hands is cocked and aimed, though not at Frank. He's pointing it at Bettylou.

"Sergeant," he says, the barrel of the gun only slightly trembling. "For aiding and abetting this man and his two accomplices, you are in violation of—"

"Oh, give it a rest, Zebediah."

Frank shields Clem with his body despite the fact that he's three inches shorter than her when she's in those heels. I do my best to cover Bettylou. "We don't want any trouble," Frank says.

"Then maybe you shouldn't have killed anyone, Mr. *Carnage.*"

Bettylou reaches around me and grabs at the gun. "Oh, this thing doesn't even have bullets; we haven't had bullets since—"

The shot fires right on cue, and I swear I can feel it zing past my cheek on its way into the building. Two loud yelps cry out, one after the other, followed by a sickening crash.

We all rush in, even though the four of us could have used this opportunity to scramble for the van. The two assistants stand over a smoking hunk of plastic: the former Honorable Patricia J. Atkinson, now forced into an early retirement.

"What did you *do?*" the woman stenographer says.

We all stand in an uncomfortable silence for at least thirty seconds. Then I say something, because *someone* has to say something. "You're free now. You're all free. It can't tell you what to do anymore."

Of course, they never had to listen to the thing in the first place, but I don't remind them of that.

"But we don't *know* how to run a town," says the other lackey. "Or how to judge the innocent and guilty alike."

"You'll learn," Frank says. "Everyone back in Pittsburgh, where we're from, learned how to get along after the pleasure-juice."

The two assistants seem skeptical, and so am I. They'll either learn or die trying, and I hope dearly that it's the former.

"Let's go, gang," Clem says.

⧗   ⧗   ⧗

We grab a few gallons of gasoline and a spare fan belt from one of the townsfolk who'd been there for the show.

"I was so excited I wasn't able to sleep," she says. "How did you ever create such glorious music?" We drag Frank away before he starts yammering on about music theory.

The van is untouched, although Clem had left the driver's side door wide open. We stack Bettylou's new instruments in the back next to my disassembled drum kit. You can never have too many instruments, especially when your lead vocalist is the kind of guy who likes to break them when he's had an especially good—or bad—performance.

The sun is up, and there's a whole new day ahead.

Bettylou picks up the fan belt and gets to work. "You're good at guarding prisoners, playing music by ear, *and* fixing engines? Be still my heart." I put my hands around her waist.

"What else can you do?"

"Just those three things." I wait for her to smile in jest, but she doesn't.

Frank claps his hands together, then winces. "So, where are we going next?"

"Texas," Clem says.

"Wyoming," Bettylou says.

"I want what she wants," I say, twining my fingers through Bettylou's.

"Let's just wing it," Frank decides, and without a map, that's kind of what we've been doing this whole time on tour. It's not like state borders really exist anymore. Location is a state of mind.

We pile into the van. Bettylou drops her head onto my shoulder and sighs contentedly.

"I only have one question," she says. "What's the name of this band? Bands have names, right?"

There's an uncomfortable silence as Clem guns the engine, which rattles to improbable life. Frank takes a swig from our communal bottle of homemade hooch and rests his cast on the door handle.

"That's a really good question," he says, launching into storytelling mode.

And that's what we listen to for the better part of the day, on our way to decharted territory, the four of us against the world.

ABOUT THE AUTHOR

Erica L. Satifka is a writer and/or friendly artificial construct, forged in a heady mix of iced coffee and sarcasm. She enjoys rainy days, questioning reality, ignoring her to-do list, and adding to her collection of tattoos. Her debut novel *Stay Crazy* (Apex Publications) won the 2017 British Fantasy Award for Best Newcomer, and her short fiction has appeared in *Clarkesworld*, *Shimmer*, *Interzone*, and *The Dark*. She lives in Portland, Oregon with her spouse Rob and an indeterminate number of cats, and is currently at work on more stories involving the band from "Trial and Terror."

WE WON'T BE HERE TOMORROW

Margaret Killjoy

I turned thirty yesterday, and the thing about being part of a teenage death cult is that you're not supposed to turn thirty. It was a personal failure on my part—the kind of personal failure that meant the ghouls of New Orleans were after me.

The night air was alive with usual white noise of gunshots and fireworks, and I stalked the cemetery, bouquet in my hand, past row after row of people who died young. Some were at rest in their own aboveground tombs, others had been crammed into mausoleums. No one ever seemed to ask why so many gutter rats and punks were buried in relative luxury in a private graveyard within city limits. We humans are a relatively non-curious species on the whole.

I laid thirteen white roses on Deidre's grave. Deidre didn't like flowers, but I like flowers. What she liked doesn't matter, because she's dead. Dead and eaten.

Everyone I've ever loved—really loved, not like the requisite and insincere love of child for parent—was laid out within one city block's worth of marble and cement.

Janelle Miriette Thompson, 1990-2009. The girl I came to New Orleans for, who broke my heart by deciding she was straight after all. She died drunk on a freight train before I had the chance to forgive her, before I had the chance to tell her I knew there was nothing to forgive.

Erica Freeman, 1988-2013. The next straight girl after Janelle. We stayed friends. We played in three bands together, the last one was Dead Girl. Suicide. On stage. Blood on the crowd. I haven't forgiven her.

Jorge Jefferson, dead at twenty. Marcel Smith made it to twenty-four. Damien Polanski, twenty-eight. Robert, Lance, Heather, Maria. Twenty-three, each of them. Suzi Hamilton and Suzanne Lanover never saw twenty.

Deidre Hanson, 1992-2018. I was so sure she was straight that she had to hit on me for a year before I let her kiss me. A year is a long time for people like us, the ghoul-sworn. We finally kissed down on the levee, at a place called the end of the world. We were old then already. I was twenty-four, and it was her twenty-third birthday.

She spent her twenty-third birthday with me, with just me.

Two days after her twenty-sixth, she died in a house fire at a party in the seventh ward along with two other people—one ghoul-sworn, one just unlucky enough to hang out with the doomed. I would have been at the party, but my truck wouldn't start and my bike had a flat and I was feeling lazy. So she'd died without me, and the ghouls put her here, and every year on the anniversary of her death they're back at her corpse for another little bit of her soul. A knuckle here, a femur there.

They eat bones, and they live forever, and Deidre was dead, like all of us ghoul-sworn were supposed to be while we were still young and our essence was still strong in our marrow.

There I was, alive. It wasn't long until dawn, until the ghouls would rise with the sun and haunt me, hunt me. Already, dogs were howling. Already there was light on the horizon.

One day soon, I'd be dead and the words Mary Walker were going to be carved into stone. People go to New Orleans to die. I didn't want to die anymore. I had to get going. I had to track down ghosts and rumors of those who'd escaped.

I left the flowers for Deidre.

Fuck you, Deidre.

Fuck you for dying.

It was Janelle who offered me the bargain. I hadn't been in the city for more than a week, and she and I'd been crashing on the roof of an abandoned grocery store. That place is a Whole Foods now, might get torn down by Bezos tomorrow. I've outlived every derelict building I've ever known.

"Y'all go hard, down here," I told her, after an evening that involved stealing drugs from a dealer, consuming those drugs, trying and failing to steal more drugs from the same dealer, and a roving party that moved through the darker bits of the city with a generator and a sound system in a shopping cart. Revelry had followed us like a cloud overhead. Dancing, debauchery.

Sobriety was creeping up on me unwanted, like a fever, and I wasn't entirely sure how we'd made it back from the party to our tarped-off overhang on that rooftop. I was eighteen. I don't know how to describe being eighteen, but you either remember it yourself or you might live long enough to know.

"You want to hear why?" Janelle asked.

"Yeah."

"We can't go to jail."

"What?"

"It's gonna sound crazy," she said.

"Bitch, I was born for crazy."

"Worse than that. I can't tell you everything unless you join us."

Whatever she was going to say, I already knew I was going to go along with it. I thought the sun shone out of that girl's asshole. I would have followed her into a wood chipper. Oh, to be eighteen again.

"What's it involve?" I asked.

"A permanent get out of jail free card—cops will look the other way, the courts will look the other way. In exchange, you gotta die before you're thirty."

"Like, someone will kill me?"

"Not unless you turn thirty."

I didn't expect to turn thirty anyway. The way the world was and is, who does? Survival didn't really seem possible, so I refused to prioritize it.

"I'm in."

That morning, as a ketamine hangover started in on me, Janelle took me to meet the ghouls for the first time.

⌛   ⌛   ⌛

The hot winter sun bore down on me, but I kept my hood up as if a ratty black hoodie offered me any sort of anonymity or protection. In the kangaroo pocket, I fingered my revolver. Snub-nosed. Shit for most purposes. Good for killing someone point blank. Good for killing myself.

I walked through the upper ninth and everything was weathered wood and smiling people. Somewhere in the distance I heard the horns and drums of a second line. This is a city that knows how to celebrate death.

Whenever the ghouls were gonna catch me—when, not if, because I was too much a coward to hold that Smith & Wesson to my temple—they weren't going to kill me as much as they were going to let me die.

I've been to their dungeons. You live to twenty-five as ghoul-sworn and they tap you for work down there sometimes, probably just to remind you of their power, probably just to remind you to get on with dying.

They were going to hang me from chains and they were going to cut me open and remove every bone from my body, one by one. They were going to crack me open to the marrow. They were going to let me watch.

It wouldn't work to run—the ghouls own the legal system, inside and out. As soon as I'd turned thirty, they'd set me up as convicted of every crime they'd ever got me off. Once I got popped, there'd be someone in my cell willing to take a full pardon in exchange for a knife in my guts.

I turned the corner and saw the levee, all handsome and full of birds. A few dogs ran off-leash while a few happy people passed a bottle on the grass. My finger found the trigger and I know it's bad form but I let it sit there. No safety on that thing besides the hard pull of a double-action. I needed to die. I didn't want to die.

They live forever and I was only going to live a few more minutes or hours or days.

A seagull landed on a concrete ruin. Under its feet, in red spray paint, someone had tagged "the devil let us." I stopped and watched that bird, because it was beautiful, because it was worth the risk. After some time, it flew off, and I went back to walking.

⧗   ⧗   ⧗

Desmond lived in a little fortress of an apartment in the heart of a massive ruined factory, up on the fourth floor. If you want a view of the water, or of the city, or really just to see the sun or the sky at all, you've got to leave that safety and walk a hundred yards across trash and needles and rubble to look out any windows. Desmond says the privacy is worth it.

Desmond is only twenty-two, but he's been sworn for a decade already. He's second generation. His mother hanged herself when he was fourteen. I gutted his father in an alley because I blamed him for his mother's death. I might have been right.

Ever since, Desmond has been one of my best friends.

He undid about fifteen locks and alarms and active defense systems to let me into his place. At least three or four million dollars in stolen lab equipment were barricaded inside.

"Didn't think I'd be seeing you again," he told me, from where he lay on a ragged couch. His pupils had eclipsed the brown of his eyes, his black skin glistened with sweat despite the relative cool of the room. I wasn't sure what he was on, but then again I was never sure what he was on. A vape pen dangled loose in his hand.

The whole place was bathed in dim lavender light. Even the

dozens of LED indicator lights had been modified to glow pale purple. The walls were wallpapered with flatscreens. Most were broken, some were playing a Cary Grant film.

I perched on a milk crate stool across from him.

"What do you want, dead girl?" He didn't turn his face to look at me. "You can't hide out here; won't work out for either of us."

"You give a shit about danger?"

He took a drag and let out a cloud of vapor. It smelled like jasmine. Desmond scent-coded his drugs, but I didn't remember there being a jasmine one.

"I guess not," he said.

His hands dug into the ragged upholstery, tensing and releasing of their own volition, and he gasped as something coursed through his veins.

"I can give you something to get out for good," he said, after his body came back under his control. "Painless, euphoric even. Dani took some last week, said it was pleasant. Before she went under."

"I'm not trying to die," I said.

"Life is a death sentence."

"Not trying to die."

Desmond turned his head, and only his head, to look at me. His eyes seemed to glow in the light. "It's too late, dead girl. You know that, right?" He turned back toward the ceiling.

"Averi got out," I said. Averi was an old genderqueer punk who'd haunted ghoul-sworn bars, talking to no one. Two years back, twenty-nine years old, they'd disappeared. I hadn't seen their grave and I hadn't seen them in the dungeons.

"Dead in the swamps," Desmond said. "Gators gotta eat too."

"That's not what I hear," I said. "I hear you deal to them sometimes. I hear you know where they are."

He took another drag and convulsed and filled the room with the scent of flowers.

"When did you go coward?" he asked.

"Wanting to live makes me a coward?"

"No. Wanting to live makes you a hopeless, idiotic optimist. Going to ground makes you a coward."

"It's that or what, just die?"

"Go out like Terri."

Terri Williams, 1973-2002. She set fire to a Marigny ghoul house in the middle of the day, then opened up on everyone who came out of the building with an impressive assortment of fully automatic weapons.

"Terri Williams is why we know you can't kill a ghoul with fire or bullets," I said. She was also why we knew there were worse ways to die than having your bones removed and eaten in front of you.

"Got to have been satisfying, though, for a minute. When she thought it was gonna work."

"The only way to hurt them I can think of is to starve them out." We all assumed they'd go hungry without us, though there wasn't any proof.

"If they ain't eating you, they'll be eating someone else."

He took another hit. This time, the convulsions kept going for a full thirty seconds.

"You gotta try this," he said, offering me the vape. "Doesn't have a name yet. It's a fast-acting upper. Shuts down your motor control. Intense while it's happening, but fuck, when you come down, you come down solid. Feel like yourself."

"I'm good," I said.

"Live a little," he said, then smiled at his own joke.

"I'm good."

"Here's what you do," he said. "I got it figured out. You let me kill you, which, let's be real, you should let me do anyway because you killed my dad. Only fair. Then ... there's an old cement mixer in here. I'll encase your body, drop you into the river. I get to kill you, you get to die, and ghouls don't get to eat you. Everyone's happy. Except the ghouls. Fuck them."

"Just tell me where to find Averi."

"You *really* don't want to find Averi. As a friend, trust me. Just die."

"You don't fucking get it," I said.

Desmond shot upright, so fast it was like a movie skipped some frames. He held a pistol, aimed at me. "Dead girl, you're the one who doesn't get it."

"We're friends," I said, in as calm of a voice as I could manage. Adrenaline started my heart racing, and I knew a panic attack was on its way. If I lived that long.

"We are," Desmond agreed. "I'm not killing you. You killed yourself a long time ago, when you swore a pact with demons. This is just me helping another friend not make a rash decision."

"Shooting someone is always a rash decision." The panic attack hit, like a wall of sound, and it made me question my resolve. Death felt preferable to panic.

"Three," he counted.

He raised the gun in both hands and aimed it at my temple. For a man stoned beyond reason, he held it steady. I wanted to vomit.

"Two."

I still wanted to live. I tensed my legs under me.

"One."

I sprung at the ground. He fired; missed. My ears rang. I shot upright; closed on him. Wrenched the gun from his hand. Held it to his temple.

"Hey, dead girl, we're friends." He spoke loud, like he could barely hear himself, which was probably the case. My ears rang.

"Tell me where to find Averi," I said, just as loud.

"I won't tell you anything when you've got a gun to my head," he said. "Matter of principle."

He was right.

I dropped the mag and cleared the chamber.

He lifted his vape pen, and I flinched. He took another drag, a tiny one. His hands clenched and unclenched.

I sat next to him on the couch, and he passed me the vape. I took a hit, and my panic intensified for a second before it dropped away entirely. I was as calm as I'd ever been. Sometimes that's the way through panic, same as danger: don't hide from it. Embrace it.

"Averi's in the swamps," Desmond said. "And they're not dead."

⧖   ⧖   ⧖

The character of a city is shaped as much by the wilderness around it as it is by its architecture. The character of a city is shaped as much by its closest wildlife as it is by its rulers. New Orleans is as much a city of cypress and cormorants as it is of shotgun houses and ghouls.

I cut through the swamp in a stolen canoe, the white noise of traffic and people replaced by that of water and wildlife.

Averi lived in a hunting shack, built on piers, disguised from all directions by trees. I parked at their dock, climbed a few stairs, and knocked at their door.

They answered in aviators, a Real Tree punk vest, and tight black pants. They looked exactly like I'd seen them, perched at the bar, every night for years.

Except they were paler than I remembered.

And they had a shotgun pointed at my belly.

"Fuck you want, Mary Walker?"

"To live," I said.

"Go away."

"How'd you do it? How'd you survive?"

"I ain't survived for shit, not yet. I've only got a year on you."

"That makes you the oldest ghoul-sworn I've ever heard of," I said.

They couldn't hide their pride when I said that.

"Look, can I come in? Just talk to you?"

"We can talk out here." They stepped outside and closed the door. There were no windows.

We sat on the dock, feet dangling over. Their fingernails and toenails were painted the blue of dead flesh. They spent a good moment lost in thought.

"Maybe we can help each other," they said.

We'd never been friendly, Averi and I. Averi hadn't any friends as long as I'd known them. Rumor said they lost most of theirs in a gang fight and just never bothered finding new ones.

"So why the swamps?"

"You know they're afraid of water?"

"What?"

"I've spent the last two years studying the fucking things. Learned an awful lot. They need sunlight to function . . . they're not just cold-blooded, they're un-blooded. They're afraid of water not because they'd drown—they can't—but because if they run out of energy down there where the sun can't reach, it's over for them. Torpor, forever."

"You're in the swamps because if you see them coming, you sink their boats."

"Bingo."

"That's it, then? Just hide in the swamps by yourself? Only come out at night?"

"Let me tell you how you stay alive, Mary Walker. You cling to life. You claw at it until your fingers bleed. You tell yourself, every time you take a breath, that you're going to live to take another one. That you will live forever, no matter what it takes. No matter how much it hurts, no matter how much you hurt anyone else."

"You sound like a ghoul." In the distance, some animal called out, like a human quietly screaming.

"They weren't always ghouls. They became ghouls, each of them individually."

"How?" I asked.

"You know how. The marrow of the ghoul-sworn. There's more to it than that, but mostly it's the marrow of the ghoul-sworn."

"All the ghouls were once ghoul-sworn? How can that work?"

"I don't know," Averi said. "It's the chicken and the egg. Chickens, though, they eat eggs."

Averi was going to try to kill me. They were going to try to eat my bones. I put my hands in the pocket of my hoodie and felt the revolver.

"I've told you how I survived," Averi said. Their shotgun was in their lap, and they rested their hand on the grip. "Now, you can help me."

For a half second, I considered waiting for them to move, to prove their intentions.

I didn't.

I drew the revolver, held it to their throat, and pulled the trigger. The wind caught the mist of blood and brought it to my face. I couldn't hear anything in the wake of the blast.

Their eyes drew open wide and they started to lift the shotgun, because they didn't know they were dead already. None of us know when we're dead already.

I stood up and kicked them into the water, and they sank.

⌛   ⌛   ⌛

"You were right," I told Desmond. It's usually best to lead with the apology.

"You want me to put you down?"

We sat on the roof of his squatted factory. The moon was waning in the sky above us. I couldn't see many stars—not as many as I'd seen paddling out from the swamp with a stack of Averi's notebooks piled in the canoe—but the lights of the city are stars of their own. Each one holds mystery and the promise of life.

"No, not that part," I said. "You were right about not clinging to life so desperately. That's the ghoul's life. I'd rather I wasn't caught up in any of this shit at all, sure, but I'd still rather be ghoul-sworn than a ghoul."

"That's my dead girl!" Desmond said. He took a drag from his pen. The air smelled like rose.

"What's that one?" I asked.

"Basically just speed," he said. "Has a worse comedown than

speed though. I'm still working on it. You want a hit?"

"You're not selling it well."

"So what's the plan? If you're not gonna let me kill you but you're supposedly not afraid of death anymore."

"Let's kill ghouls," I said.

"How the fuck do you kill ghouls?"

"You've got a cement mixer, right?"

"Yeah . . . "

"It's not me we're going to drop into the river," I said.

"I like the way you think, dead girl."

"Stop calling me dead girl."

"I'll stop calling you that when we're dead. Which . . . sounds like it'll be tomorrow."

"Yeah, that's about my guess."

"If we're dead tomorrow, want to get wrecked tonight?"

I took one long last look at the stars of the city.

"Yeah," I said. "Yeah I do."

ABOUT THE AUTHOR

Margaret Killjoy is an author, musician and anarchist with a long history of itinerancy who currently calls Appalachia home. When she's not writing, she can be found organizing to end hierarchy, crafting, or complaining about being old despite not being old at all. Her books include *A Country of Ghosts* (Combustion Books, 2014) and the Danielle Cain series (Tor.com, 2017-). She blogs at www.birdsbeforethestorm.net and says things @magpiekilljoy on Twitter. Killjoy produces dark electronica as Nomadic War Machine and atmospheric black metal as Feminazgûl. Killjoy is a Shirley Jackson award nominee for *The Lamb Will Slaughter the Lion*, published by Tor.com.

EXOPUNK'S NOT DEAD

Corey J. White

Downtown vibrates with sub-low frequency, churning Jack's guts alongside the anxiety he knows will only quiet with booze. The frame of his exoskeleton buzzes as he stomps closer to the source of the sound—metal humming to the kick drum thump coming up through cracked asphalt. Red paint flakes like dandruff; underneath the paint, steel rusts.

Jack's is a basic demolition exo: limbs attached to a sturdy hydraulic frame lacking any armour plating. He floats within the exoskeleton's torso, dangling on a battered harness with haptic converters aligned to his musculature. It's airy inside the machine, its canopy open to the elements. A breeze from the bay rolls over Jack's bare arms, carrying the salty smell of rotting seaweed.

Jack checks the flyer one last time, worried he might turn up at the wrong place—as though that distant clamour could be anything *other* than a punk show. The flyer's proper old-school, photocopied onto thin sheets of yellow paper:

EXOPUNK (WRECKING) BALL
OLD CITY HALL
DOORS OPEN 8PM

The city council was voted out a year ago, but even a democratically-elected governmental algorithm needs time to implement changes. At first, police had patrolled the grounds, protecting it while the city tried to find a buyer, but once enough of the walls had been torn open for the copper piping, they pulled out. The official demolition starts Monday, but after tonight's gig, with all the exopunks from the highlands dropping in, half the job will be done.

Jack rounds the corner and joins a procession of skels thudding up the street. Seeing his people, the knot of tension in his guts unravels. Even in his nine-foot-tall exo, the goliath city hall building looms threateningly: graffiti spots the stone façade like bruises, masonry already crumbling as decay sets in.

A broad wall of noise slams against Jack's chest as he stomps into the old building. The air is hot and humid, thick with competing scents of sour sweat and spilled beer.

The band on stage is lit up bright, high above the thrashing, glinting mosh, and plaster dust rains from the cracked ceilings with every heavy beat. Exos fill the pit: classic twelve-foot clankers slamming among sleeker SOTA rigs, while armoured bouncers look on. The pit is already three feet below the rest of the floor, marble tiling and cement foundations churned up as the opening acts hype the crowd.

Jack points his exo at the bar jutting from a hole bashed into the walls; behind the bartenders, empty office cubicles are filled with trash and drug detritus. He gets in line and forces his exo onto the balls of its steel feet so he can see over the heads in front of him.

"Nice ride."

At the voice, Jack pivots inside his skel. The guy has a thick, black beard around an easy smile. A thick mat of hair crosses his broad chest, visible through tears in his replica cosmonaut suit. He hangs inside his exo's frame, looking almost weightless—very 'stranded in space.'

When the guy starts to grin, Jack realises how long he's been staring without saying anything. His cheeks burn. A rat-king of nerves tangles in his stomach, but it's a good nervous, a 'cute guy is talking to me' nervous.

"Thanks," he says, finally. "It's a hand-me-down; was my older brother's."

"Makes sense; you don't see too many guys our age in one of the classics."

Jack laughs, just a single throaty 'Ha'. He knows his beat-up Ward-D2 isn't really a classic, but he can see a pick-up line for what it is and still want to be picked up, can't he?

The next song starts, and decibels soar like courier drones. Jack pushes his exo toward the bar as the line moves.

"Did he go into engineering?" the punk-onaut shouts.

"What?" Jack says, leaning forward in his harness. The chat-link light inside his exoframe blinks, and Jack hits the switch.

"Your brother," the other guy says, his voice tinny through Jack's audio system: "did he go into engineering or something?"

"Yeah, *something*," Jack says; he doesn't say that 'something' was prison. "My name's Jack."

"I'm Ramón, and no, I hate The Ramones."

Jack chuckles, then sees he's almost at the front of the line. "What are you drinking?"

"Cider."

Jack gets flustered at the bar and orders two ciders, though it's normally too sweet for his tastes. He takes one of the canisters and hands it to Ramón, then slots the other into his exo's rehydration unit as the band on stage finishes their set.

"Thanks," Ramón says. "I'll get the next round."

Jack drinks from the tube strapped inside the head module and the cider slides down his throat, thick, saccharine, and cold.

"Wanna go up the front?" Ramón asks.

"Hey, ho, let's go," Jack says, and beams at his own joke. Ramón rolls his eyes but smiles.

Exopunks drop into the cratered pit, their eyes eagerly following members of the next band as they walk out on stage; *Mucus Mary and the Moist Mothers* spray-painted on a bedsheet hanging on the rear wall.

The guitarist and bass player wear their instruments inside their skels and the singer has the microphone mounted to her exo's head. The drummer's exoskeleton clunks and thuds as it interfaces with the drum machine—twelve limbs flexing and stretching as she gets a feel for the gear. She counts in and the band erupts in a vicious car crash. The pit surges, sending dirt and cement chunks into the air where, Jack swears, they hover for a full second, held in place by the singer's banshee screech.

"I love this band," Ramón yells.

Jack thrashes to the sound and his shinbones shudder every time his exofeet jackhammer the ground. As the stage lights sweep over the crowd, the fog of cement dust around him and Ramón glows.

Ramón drops into the pit and before Jack can think twice he's done the same. Jack slams the head of his exo into the wall of the pit and Ramón joins him while Mucus Mary wails and squeals. Jack screams and euphoria seeps into his veins, as warm as the cider is cold.

He gulps a mouthful of air and dust as he wraps his lips around the rehydration tube. The dust gently scratches his throat as he swallows. Dust lines his nostrils too—if he gets a spot on the official demolition crew come Monday he'll be wearing respiratory gear, but right now, he doesn't care. His lungs could rot inside his chest and it would be worth it to be here tonight, drowning in noise, surrounded by the only thing that ever made sense to him. Study hard, they said; yeah, thanks for the debt. Get a job, they said; fuck you, there aren't any.

Jack dances harder, his suit's haptics fighting him as it struggles to keep up. The only truth Jack ever found was in punk rock: music that's dirty, fast, and over so soon, just like life.

The band starts another song and Jack stops dancing to take a drink. Ramón's chest hair glints with sweat and Jack imagines slipping his hands inside the cosmonaut suit so the hairs curl around his fingers. But Ramón doesn't catch Jack's overt gaze; his attention is elsewhere, watching three skinheads in archaic getups using their massive exos to tower over some kids in shiny-chromed rigs.

Jack's chest rattles—not from the noise, but the fight-or-flight thump of his heart. Ramón takes a step forward and Jack's mind is made up for him as he and Ramón push through the crowd.

"You fucking better not be here Monday," one of the skinheads says, thumping one kid's rig with a clenched exofist. "Those demolition jobs are for us. You want work, go back to Iraqistan."

"Hey," Ramón yells.

The three boneheads turn; identical triplets with their shaved heads and faces: babies that got big, but never grew up.

Jack's fear gives way to anger as he glances past the skinheads and sees the young punks cowering. They look like honour roll kids who miraculously discovered good tunes in the banal suburban sprawl. But that's the exopunk ethos: *anyone* is free to work if they've got a rig, and *anyone* is free to wreck if they've got that fucking fire in their belly.

The music lulls and the lead bonehead yells new slurs at Jack and Ramón. Far up front on the stage, Mucus Mary points into the crowd as her band breaks into a new song: a frenetic stampede of noise. A chorus joins in as Mucus Mary screams, "Nazi Punks Fuck Off!" It was a classic before Jack was born, and it's the one song every decent punk band knows, even if they never want a reason to play it.

Jack freezes as Ramón steps forward and grips the lead skinhead's rig in both exohands. The bonehead tries to break Ramón's grip, but he locks his exo's hands in place, unhooks his harness, and throws himself forward. Ramón grabs the collar of the bonehead's bomber jacket and buries a fist into the fucker's nose. Blood pours into his mouth, hanging slack.

Jack stomps close, barring the other Nazis as they try to get at Ramón. His hydraulics shriek with the effort of holding them back, a sharp screech that pierces his ears as more punks push in towards the scuffle.

Plaster dust underfoot glows purple—security moves through the crowd riding black security rigs, all sharp angles and blacklight LEDs. Ramón disconnects his exo and Jack pushes him back before standing with an impromptu line of exopunks, blocking Ramón from the bouncer's view.

Jack points and yells, "Get these Nazi fucks out of here," shifting his exo to stay between Ramón and the bouncers. Jack can't see the bouncer's face inside the armour, but the exo bobs in acknowledgement, and he hijacks the three boneheads' suits and leads them out of the pit.

Jack turns to Ramón, gingerly poking his knuckles with his left hand. "You okay?"

"I heard something crack, just hope it was his nose and not my knuckle." Ramón shivers and Jack feels it too: the drop of adrenaline leaving his body.

Jack unclips his harness and climbs out to stand on the frame of Ramón's rig. He slips inside Ramón's exoskeleton and buries his fingers in Ramón's coarse beard. "Want me to get some ice for your hand?"

Ramón lets out a deep breath, then looks up from his bloody hand, his eyes a deep brown, speckled with orange. "It'll be fine," he says.

Jack leans in, sour-sweet breaths coalescing in the moment before their lips meet, Ramón's tongue wet and hot against Jack's.

Jack smiles. "You really gave that guy a *Blitzkrieg*—"

Ramón cuts him off with another kiss, a longer one that only stops when they get jostled, the crowd slowly gaining momentum after stalling for the fight.

"Make another Ramones joke," Ramón says, "and that might be the last time I kiss you."

Jack kisses Ramón again while his heart beats double-time. His mouth tastes sickly sweet with dead apples and probable regret, but he doesn't care. This man might break his heart, but it would be worth it to be here tonight.

"What's the matter with your exo; we need technical support?" A bouncer stands beside Jack's abandoned exoskeleton.

"No, it's fine," Jack yells.

When the bouncer sees Jack inside Ramón's exo, he shakes his head and smiles. "Don't leave it empty on the dance floor, alright fellas; it ain't safe."

Jack almost laughs at 'dance floor', but he nods and climbs back into his exo as the bouncer walks off chuckling.

They get lost in the music again; moving with the crowd like every exo in the joint is linked. Sweat soaks through Jack's clothes as they yell and stomp in a circle of exopunks; he grins whenever his eyes catch Ramón's.

When Mucus Mary is done, she and the Moist Mothers leave

stage to a mushroom-cloud of cheers from the pit. Ramón leads Jack to the edge and they jump out of the crater. Jack pauses to take in the sweat-slicked revellers panting for breath and the exos knocking together with the clank of punk love; the bliss that follows an epic mosh.

Standing close enough to Ramón so that they can lean out of their exos and touch, Jack asks, "Are we gonna get another drink?"

"I only really came for Mary," Ramón says, "so I was gonna go home."

Jack frowns, and Ramón laughs.

He pinches Jack's chin and says quietly, "I was hoping you'd come with me."

ABOUT THE AUTHOR

Corey J. White is the author of The VoidWitch Saga–*Killing Gravity*, *Void Black Shadow*, and *Static Ruin*–out through Tor.com Publishing. He studied writing at Griffith University on the Gold Coast, and is now based in Melbourne, Australia. Find him online at coreyjwhite.com.

MAKE AMERICA SK8

Zandra Renwick

This isn't really a story the way you've been taught to think of as a story. There isn't a shit-ton of action, unless you count skating around town and moving furniture and writing letters. There isn't a bad guy or supervillain or even much adversity, unless you count this fucked up society we all do our best to struggle through, some days more successfully than others. There are no explosions or touchdowns or showdowns or sex scenes—there's not even a spectacular pay-off at the end, unless you count people coming through for each other, leaning on each other and doing their best not to get ground up in the machine of things outside what they can directly control.

This is just me, telling you, how it happened that I got the best job in the world, made new friends and hung out with old ones, and did my small sideways part to sustain the loose assortment of people and things and places that make up our immediate universes, which we call Community.

If that's not enough story for you, according to some hazy set of rules handed down from who-knows-where exactly who-knows-when like other arbitrary societal Shalls and Shall Nots and Musts and Must Nots, then I guess you don't have to bother reading the rest.

⧗   ⧗   ⧗

Back then I was between squats and looking for work. Freecycle Nation was hiring, so Dodi told Skittles and Skittles told Angel and Angel told Charlie and Charlie told me. Word of mouth has always been the people's free information highway, and that day it was at its finest, alive and well as anyone could see. So I slicked my fin and grabbed my board and booked my ass down to the warehouse district to see our town's matriarch of mosh, Lizzie Longboard, and get her to give me that job.

I found her in the rooftop garden she kept over the flat narrow warehouse tacked to the back of her ugly old one-time church building, with the halfpipe built squashed up tight against the rear. Silhouetted in morning sunlight, the long rambly structure looked from the side like some weird square brutalist dragon: the spiked churchtower for the creature's head; the long Freecycle warehouse for its squat body; the sweeping halfpipe for the serpent's curved tail, flipped up at the back end, with a fluttering anarchy flag flapping from the tip.

Lizzie squinted up at me from the tangled tomato plant she was soaking with a hose from a rainwater barrel, and in her famous busted-griptape voice said, "Hey kid. Keep your big goofy-footed feet out of my lavender. Please."

Lizzie may or may not have known my name despite having seen me skate the Ugly Church ramp a billion times on a million different afternoons, but she called everybody kid no matter who they might be or how important they thought they were. She was ancient as dirt and sweet as raw honey and still able to cop more air than any young pup and most of us older ones. She'd run Freecycle Nation out of her ugly church for six years, ever since the Smackdown—which nobody outside corporate mainstream news called the "Housing Arrears *Crackdown*"—left pretty much all of us with no place to live. We'd been a townful of renters and, worse, mortgagors, forking over money to vampire banks each month for places they'd rigged so we'd never own them. In hindsight, it's hard to believe pretty stories—or sad stories, or scary ones—could trick you into forever paying a faceless, pitiless entity to sell "your" house to you month after month, year after year, a relentless economic bloodletting you'd never escape. Just ask my mom. Or my brother. Or my grandparents. Or all their neighbors.

One thing about the Smackdown was it set us free. No formal renting anymore, no mortgages, not in our town, not anyone I knew.

We'd all turned to squatting or camping, or occasionally pooling funds with friends for legit temporary digs if we got too homesick for things like clean showers and private refrigerators. Lizzie Longboard, the sole genuine public taxpaying landowner in our community, had saved us.

"Heard you had an opening at Freecycle Nation," I told her, making sure to keep my big wrong-way feet on the right side of her garden edge. "I'm here for the job."

She studied me from under the mop of her snow-white dready mohawk—or, more accurate, she studied my skateboard. A thing of beauty if I do say so myself. My pal Mikey painted the deck for me custom, and I'd traded a month of hard labor for the trucks. I'd gotten wheels out of the deal too, but those never keep their new-car smell long, and I'd been beating the streets for a job. Our town's asphalt ate rubber like stomach acid eats lining.

Finally she looked me in the eye and said, "You like tomatoes, kid?"

There's only one sane answer to that, when someone's holding out a sweet little tomato the size of a marble and the color of rubies: "Shit yeah."

She handed me one and popped another in her mouth and we stood chewing, savoring, squinting at each other in the early morning sunshine already turning too hot for comfort. "It's not easy, working here," she said. "You got to keep all the little grommets in line down on the ramp—"

"Of course."

"—And you got to coordinate volunteers each day for the Freecycle warehouse, make sure people play nice picking goods up, dropping shit off—"

"Natch."

"—And you'd be asked to help with the booked acts sometimes, make food runs for rock-n-rollers, be able to ignore or what you might call tactfully navigate difficult requests, obnoxious behaviors—"

"Can do, boss."

She broke off. She knew who I was, despite not calling me by name. Like all skaters, Lizzie was a pretty good judge of the locals she skated with, and already knew everything she needed to: I showed up when I promised; I treated people with respect; I didn't have a temper; and I landed more tricks than I flubbed. I'd been trying to keep chill, but was excited as fuck to land this dream of fucking dream jobs staring me in the face and daring me to bail.

"You do understand this gig pays mostly just room and board," she told me.

"Plus skate time," I reminded her.

She had an awesome grin, super-white teeth cracking her sun-leather face, setting off highlights in her tufty white 'hawk. "Skate time, for sure," she agreed. "And whatever fresh veg we can scrape out of this patch of dirt. Hell, you even get a share of the take from shows we book, if there's any left after the band, sound people, security staff and everyone else gets paid. Fundraisers, community events, any donations first and foremost go toward keeping this place alive; you'd be second-to-last out of all us motherfuckers lined up to get cash money for anything we do here."

I didn't have to ask who the last person to get paid was. I knew it was Lizzie. I said, "You probably got a million people showing up asking for this gig. But I can't even count the times these last six years you gave me food when I was hungry, a chair when I had no place to rest, blankets when I was cold, clothes when all I had was rags to wear. You never asked a dime out of anyone who didn't offer it, and you kept this community afloat when everyone said it was drowning. If I never get a penny working for you, I'll still give it everything I have and be glad to do it. I *owe* you and the Ugly Church and Freecycle Nation. This place ... " I swept the hand not clutching my deck out across the rooftop, a gesture that included the warehouse, the ramp with its raggedy flag at the far end. "This place saved my life."

I tucked my board under my arm and held out my hand for a shake. She peered up at me, probably old enough to be my grandmother and still skating more vert than locals a quarter her age. Her expression turned grim. "Would you still want the job if I told you I might lose this whole place? If I told you we have to raise an amount of cash this month that makes me too sick to my stomach to say out loud?"

"Especially then," I said, no hesitation.

Her grin didn't come back, but she took my hand. We shook, griptape burn to griptape callus. "Okay kid. Scram for a couple hours. I'll get your room ready by lunchtime. Glad you like tomatoes."

It was hard as shit not to hug her. But I've never once seen a living soul hug Lizzie Longboard and I wasn't going to be the first to find out what happened if you tried. I shook her hand too vigorously for either of our comfort, unable to stop, all my chill gone. "You won't be sorry."

She tugged her hand back and waved me away, lifting her hose from where she'd dropped it to shake. "I know I won't. Now scram. And kid?"

"Yeah?"

"I didn't need a million people showing up for this gig. I only needed one, as long as it was the right one."

Her grin had returned. I laughed and pumped the air with a triumphant fist before turning and practically flying my deck all the way across town to grab my few possessions and tell Charlie to tell Angel to tell Skittles to tell Dodi I'd landed the raddest trick of all time.

⧗   ⧗   ⧗

I'd never worked the Freecycle warehouse floor before. I mean, yeah, sure, I'd logged volunteer hours at the Ugly Church same as every other local, usually building ramps, helping little grommets with their ollies, or gleaning usable items off the streets, lugging in stuff someone might want from the squats or temporary digs of friends and strangers. I'd repaired furniture once or twice too, perfectly good tables or chairs or beds wanting a bit of amateur carpentry to be good as new for the next people wandering in needing furniture. Anyway, it was a trip working the other side of the equation, showing anybody who walked in the big warehouse roll door how to find what they were looking for, what they needed. Shoes, toys, books. Bedding. Bike parts. Yarn. Lumber. The cool thing about Freecycle Nation was it had two simple rules: 1) take only what you need; and 2) treat everyone with respect. Everything past that was just karma and vegan gravy.

Lunch with Lizzie had been awesome, except for the little problem she'd hinted at earlier, which she'd described to me in more detail. Charlie was helping me move donations from the alley side of the Ugly Church to the attached warehouse where we sorted everything and set stuff aside for cleaning or repair.

"Nothing but a bunch of majorly F'd-up politics," he said, grabbing one end of a slightly more-than-less used sofa while I got the other. "Bloody F-ing political, is what it is."

"Yep," I agreed. "One-hundred percent political, for sure." My grandma used to tell me *political* had been an empowerment word in her day. *The personal is political!*, she used to say, pumping her fist in the air—a move I totally stole, I'm not ashamed to admit. My Gran was awesomecredible; she got it when I told her *politics* and *political* had become dirty words. It made her sad, though.

Charlie nodded for us both to heave the sofa into the air. "I mean, all that shidoodle about paying back taxes on the door take from every show the Ugly Church ever give and the—" he grunted, shifting the sofa's weight in his scrawny arms. "What she call it again?"

"The property taxation value-add of warehouse and other exterior structures."

He snorted. "Any F-ing tax man want a ramp in his backyard, I come build him one *cheap*. Exterior structures my skinny arse."

We crab-walked the sofa to the fixit area so some other volunteer with an eye for fine detail and more skill with a thread and needle than either Charlie or me could spruce it up for its next owner. On the count of three, we plunked the sofa down between an unstrung hammock and a wrought iron chair with a bent leg. "So you'll help get the word out?" I asked him, dusting my hands on my pants.

"'Bout the benefit show tonight? Hells yeah, I gonna help. I gonna get that word so far out it'll be orbiting U*ranus*, man. We gonna fill this ugly old church to the F-ing eyeballs, you hear?"

I knew Charlie would be good as his word. He was a local, like me, and had been around long enough to remember when the place was still full of bibles and the parking lot filled with Sunday drivers instead of skate ramps and little corrugated tin shacks keeping sun off used freecycle garden equipment, beat-up canoes, roofing shingles, the occasional rowboat or non-running motorbike.

He grabbed his deck and I echoed his goodbye nod before going to find others who might be good at letting people know about the benefit show. I trusted the people's free information highway. When I was little we'd had phones for such shit, before that bubble collapsed like all the rest. After that the only thing you could trust was word of mouth, which worked exponentially better with every mouth you got flapping. I'd spent all afternoon—between accepting donations alley-side, directing volunteers to one department or another, and return-ing waves from my buddies dropping into the vert and flashing me thumbs-ups—telling everyone that tonight was the night they needed to come give back to the place that had given so much to them, to all of us, these last six years.

And they'd come. I knew they would. They'd bring friends and friends of friends and grandmas of friends. They'd bring their spare change to contribute, and those who could would bring their dollars, and the few with a bit more would bring more dollars. And the bands would donate their time, and so would the sound tech, and the locals would volunteer to work the floor, work the door, make sure every-body got along and remembered their manners. . . .

But it wouldn't be enough. At lunch Lizzie had told me how much cash she had to raise, calm and collected, handing me a roast-ed tomato on grilled homemade tortilla with ground rosemary and a pinch of salt, and I knew every local in town could take hammers to their ceramic piggy banks and return every bottle and dig between their freecycled sofa cushions and it *still* wouldn't be enough to save the Ugly Church and Freecycle Nation from getting stolen by corporate-shill municipal authorities and handed to the highest bidder, churned into rubble and reborn as some commercial operation puffing up the coffers of some faceless inhuman conglomerate with more rights and less responsibility than any human born in my lifetime.

Good thing I had a secret weapon.

⧗   ⧗   ⧗

I thanked our volunteers and closed up the warehouse for the day. Lizzie was off making arrangements for that night, getting bands lined up and making sure sound and safety and everything else was in order to accommodate the thousand-plus people I expected would turn out for the benefit with their pockets and fists full of change and dollar bills, whatever they could spare. I grabbed my board and locked the Ugly Church gates on my way out, caught in a dizzying moment of excitement and gratitude to think this was my home now.

I skated the few blocks to the old Distillery warehouse, went around and banged on the small side door, three short, three long, like all the locals do to get Mook to open up and let them in.

Mook answered the door in a vintage speedo swimsuit, a see-through raincoat, and fuzzy slippers. "'Sup, buddy?" he said. "Come on in."

Mook called people buddy the way Lizzie Longboard called everyone kid. In a weird way it worked in both scenarios; practically everyone *was* a kid compared to Lizzie, and Mook treated everyone like a buddy.

Also similar was the way they both took care of lots of different people, providing basic needs to individuals and the community in ways no one else could or would or did. Difference between them was that Lizzie did it out in the open, using her home as a depot to store, process, and redistribute community goods and assets, keeping things local, helping us all help each other by giving what we could, taking when and what we needed, having a place to meet and congregate and stay connected. Mook's methods were less obvious: the Distillery was where anyone without anyplace else to go ended up until they got back on their feet, which for some people was, literally, never.

Walking through the enormous warehouse was like navigating a puzzle maze of blanket lean-tos and cardboard forts and beaded curtains draped over poles suspended from the old iron rafter struts overhead, a whole tent village under one huge roof. Communal kitchen, rainwater showers—the Distillery wasn't glamorous, but it had served as temporary home to nearly every one or another of us at some point since the Smackdown. Those who lived there longer smoothed the way for those who came later. Everybody knew Mook had lived there longest, and had his own private room in the old manager's office at the back. But only I knew Mook was a secret millionaire.

I'd known Mook since the first day of kindergarten, back when kindergarten still existed and politics hadn't killed public schools yet. His parents were pretty cool, loopy artist types who'd managed to sell real estate when selling was good and been smart enough to jump ship when it suddenly wasn't. The Distillery was one of many places they'd bought back when speculators still thought the warehouse district would boom like in other, more popular cities than ours. Massive urban condo overload knocked the teeth out of that bubble, but not before Mook's mom and dad made their mint and developed a taste for country life.

But Mook was a local, and skating was our world. He wasn't interested in rusticating, so him and his parents agreed to disagree about him going with them. He wrote them letters each week—honest-to-shit handwriting on lined paper *letters* in envelopes he folded himself, with his goofball ink sketches in the margins alongside descriptions of sweet tricks he'd landed that week or funny things he'd seen—and they paid all the Distillery's taxes and utilities. Past that, he took care of himself—and a lot of other people, too—never accepting cash money no matter how much his parents offered him, urging him to invest. He did his part to keep the community alive, anonymously, without anyone knowing how or why there was always food in the shared Distillery pantries, always running water for the toilets and uninterrupted electricity no matter how many people were living under the one wide flat warehouse roof, eating, cooking, sleeping, making babies, sometimes dying. Community was all Mook cared about. That, and skating.

I propped my board against the wall next to Mook's and flopped on the low boxy couch me and him made years ago from plywood salvaged off the first ramp we built together, back in his parents' garage. And then I told him how he could save everything he loved most, community and the best halfpipe in town, and how finally he had a worthy cause for a small portion of what his parents kept insisting was his share of the family wealth. That's another cool thing about Mook's parents: they always counted their child as an equal partner, saying he was integral to their family dynamic and entitled to invest a third of the family money however it made the most sense to him.

Mook got out his old-fashioned fountain pen and lined paper right away, super excited to write his parents, and to have figured out—so long as I promised not to publicly expose his stealth wealth—where he wanted to invest at last.

⌛   ⌛   ⌛

I'd like to say the benefit show was amazing. I'd like to say everything went off without a hitch and the bands were stellar and people had the times of their lives and we raised a boatload of cash.

Not exactly. It was hot as hellfire that night and people complained about not getting enough water. The lineup Lizzie managed on short notice wasn't exactly A-list, though anyone who could turned up to rub out a mini-set. Pitching Hectic played (neo-post-feminist thrash metal), and Accomplice Of The Slain Quotation (on the goth side, but super nice). I wasn't personally a huge fan of Agile Probe or Unwashed Nozzle, but both knew how to get a crowd rolling. Correlated Catfish And The Monologues happened to be passing through town, so that was cool. The Venture Crapitalists, Cock

Reform, Empty Residentials—yeah, there was a lot of aural chaos, and not always the good kind. The music was loud, which is crucial, but it's a sad truth the best bands get out of this town fast as they can, go to other places where the general public has money and actually pays to see shows. That's every band's dream, right? To get paid for their art instead of eternally trading it around for not much more than food and sex and admiration.

We also had our first potluck barbeque going on while the bands played, and that went okay, until Lizzie had to shut down the grill to stop the squabbling over who got to use it next and whether meat was allowed to touch veg. My euphoria lingered over getting to live and work at the Ugly Church, helping Freecycle Nation keep on keeping on, but though I spent the benefit show floating high on that cloud I was also taking mental notes, figuring out how to run the grill next time so people wouldn't fight over it, how to make sure the kiddies had at least a few designated responsible types to keep watch over them and a separate place to hang out where they wouldn't get trampled by careless exuberant locals. I told myself there was a learning curve. I was learning.

But for the most part, it was a successful gathering. People got to eat, bands got to play, the moshing was friendly and everyone got to skate and no one went hungry and nobody got hurt outside the regular few dozen hard-bail scrapes and bruises at the ramp, and Mook's arm on a slam. He'd have a swellbow for a week and it would hurt him to laugh too hard but we'd all been there, and would be again. It was a good day, the way I remember it.

There were a lot of good days, after Mook's money came in and we got help, along with a committee we formed together with Lizzie and a couple others, from some downtown professionals—recommended by Mook's parents—about how to use the funds for community infrastructure, to support the way Lizzie and Mook and others had been propping up what they could, but using sustainable models. The whole point was to switch over to allowing us to prop ourselves up, the whole neighborhood, practically the whole town, support the people who live to live here and not bleed it dry for far-away interests. We'll never be totally safe from outside politics, or from the corporate predators always circling around looking for weakness and blood. But we're safe for now, and we have each other.

I warned you up front this wasn't going to be a story the way you might be looking for. I've run Freecycle Nation for twelve years now, since Lizzie retired and passed her longboard down to a promising member of the next generation, a girl with braids so blonde they're almost as white as Lizzie's dread 'hawk. She passed the Ugly Church keys down to me, as well as her tomato and rosemary garden. My tortillas never taste as good as hers, but Dodi told Skittles and Skittles told Angel and Angel told Charlie and Charlie told me that he thinks they were much improved at our weekly community potluck gathering last Sunday, the best batch I've made yet.

I'm pretty happy with that, though I'll keep trying to improve my tortilla finesse along with my vert ramp skills. Outside community, all the rest is karma and vegan gravy.

ABOUT THE AUTHOR

Under various mash-ups of her full name, Zandra Renwick's fiction has been translated into nine languages, adapted to stage and audio, and optioned for television. She spent formative years in Austin, Copenhagen, and Toronto wearing ripped fishnets and sneaking into punk clubs. She currently lives and writes in Ottawa's historic Timberhouse, a heritage residence in the heart of Canada's capital city. Find her on Twitter @zandrarenwick.

THE KEY

Michael Harris Cohen

Christmas, like every day in the joint, runs like clockwork. Joyless. Predictable. Dulled tinsel snakes the chow hall bars, the same artificial tree droops at the end of the chow line. Same shit every year except for one. The year they put gift boxes under the tree, the only year they did. The year Louis found what they held, how they held what all us prisoners wanted. Want.

That year, like all the ones before and since, our warden popped up on the big screen as we ate. Thin hair slicked back, dark eyes squinting at the camera, I never bothered with his face, not anymore. It's memorized. Instead, I always gazed past him, to his office view of blue skies and green hills. To air that didn't smell like three hundred dismal cons, benched in a cafeteria.

The warden cleared his throat and rolled out the holiday speech: "You're not numbers in cages. You are men. With pasts to amend for, futures to dream of . . . " All delivered in the swaying tones of a sermon, as inevitable as the thin-sliced, 3-D-printed ham we gulped down each time he delivered it. Thirteen times for me. Old-timers had heard it twenty or more. I don't know how they didn't choke on their fake ham, trying to swallow those platitudes. Anyhow, that year was the last time Louis had to endure it.

Louis was fresh off a jumbo stretch in solitary for thumping a Dominican. The kid lost three teeth and an eye for sassing Louis about his neck tattoo—an ink Jesus nailed to a busted clock face.

Louis was skinny as a stick but punched like a jackhammer, and he moved dead speedy if you even sneezed weird. That Dominican kid had been green and puffed up. He'd let nerves and pride run his mouth. Bravado chatter that cost him the price of seeing the world in dimension. *Así es la vida.* No prostho-eyes for cons. We're lucky to get sterile staples for our shiv wounds.

I'll never forget the sound that kid made, a yowl like some tortured dog, as Louis thumb-gouged his eye. Or the look on Louis' face as he did it, a big-ass grin, like maiming a guy was just some goof. Just messy kicks.

Still, in the holiday spirit, I guess, they'd released Louis in time for the Christmas dinner. He blinked in the fluorescents, three down from me in the chow line. Two months in solitary is no cakewalk. I'd seen men cracked from a week. Louis looked sickly, skin the color of a nicotine stain, thinner even than usual. Crazier than usual too. His eyes pinballed the room like he couldn't quite take it in—the other cons, the pacing guards, the clatter of forks and trays, that ugly tree.

Louis was a triple-lifer, doing all day for trying to blow up the Greenwich clock with a gang of Anachronists. Yeah, the Greenwich 7, he was one of them. I'd noted the 5150 in his eyes when I'd first seen him. He had the kind of crazy that makes a sound if you listen close, a power line's hum of tight-coiled danger. We were the only two punks on the cellblock but I steered a bus-length clear. We'd only talked twice.

The first time, we established our different tastes in music. I was old school—Black Flag, Circle Jerks, Germs—bands long dead, though still illegal, acts my grandpa had turned me on to.

Louis was only about Dystopica. Yeah, the Anachronist band where the lead singer, Rigor Mortis, killed himself and his bandmates onstage—cheap theatrics, IMHO. A flashy, tacky joke. Though the government took them seriously, especially after the Greenwich bomb. And that whole Anachronist notion of there being no time, trepanning themselves to step out of the illusion, mega-deranged shit.

Louis had chugged their Kool-Aid. Along with the tattoo he had the trepan scar on his forehead, the divot of a true believer. Like every Anachronist I've ever met, Louis was barely in this world. Always popping in and out of the moment. Off and on. Here/Gone.

Timeshifting, Anachronists called it. I called it *what happens when you drill a hole in your fucking head*. Standing in line that Christmas Day, head lolling, eyes rolling, Louis looked more Gone than ever. Fully stirred from his months in the hole. KO'd by the crazy-stick.

His lurching gaze at last fixed on the gifts under the tree. His eyes bugged. The tray in his clenched hands went epileptic. He mumbled something. Low at first, then louder and louder. The same two words, over and over.

"The key. The key. The key."

The guy next to him stepped back, lips pursed, nagged by Louis' reedy chant.

"What key?" he said. "Man, what the fuck are you jawing about?"

"I'm telling you," Louis said. "THE key. Key to time."

The other man shook his head but Louis had warmed up, locked on and leaned in. Close enough to kiss the guy, noses almost touching, but loud enough for the whole line to hear.

"Brother, it's in that box," Louis ranted. "A Christmas surprise. Key to the trap. A hole out of this hole. That big box under that phony tree. See it? Red ribbon tied 'round it, glowing like a whip of fire."

My second and last conversation with Louis had been about drugs. He'd discovered I was in for selling digishrooms and laughed in my face.

"Those silicon fungi are for pussies," he'd said. "I need a longer ride."

He'd rolled up his sleeve and shown me the dead members of Dystopica. Rigor Mortis and the others. Their tattooed faces like balanced quarters on his forearm, green ink that glowed. It was a trip tattoo. A 24/7 ink infusion of DXT. The only one I've ever seen up close.

"Gotta break through," Louis had said. "Break time or it's breaking you."

Dystopica lyrics. I'd smiled and nodded but he didn't smile back. His eyes ran my face like I wasn't there, or I was but was something other than me. A lizard. A demon. A possible threat he might stomp.

After that, I'd kept my distance. It was simple prison math: Trip tattoos + a penchant for violence = mayhem.

I avoided even eye contact. Just like the other man did in that chow line. He'd run the math. He turned away, wiping Louis' spittle off his face. He stared ahead, facing the steam tables, ignoring Louis. The man minded the cook as he ladled gravy. The man had removed himself from the conversation. Because in prison, curiosity fucks you up.

But I couldn't stop staring as Louis rattled his tray on the counter, as mashed potatoes spattered the floor. Soon, we all stared. Because Louis was shouting, and the 300 forks of the dinner shift paused. Our eyes volleyed back and forth, between the guards and Louis as he monkey-mouthed, his voice squawky, accusing.

"Thickness brothers. Deep thickness. This place poisoned your blood. No vision but your next bite. Stuck in the illusion of doing time when you're done in by it. Freedom under your nose and you're too *thick* to see it! Too *dense* to seize it!"

He hammered his fist on the tray, splashing holiday dinner on his blues. A 6/8 drum beat of cheap metal, that weird time signature of Dystopica's one-minute screeds, loud, as it was dead quiet otherwise.

Everyone knew it was coming.

The guards knew. They started from different sides of the room, four of them, leisurely drawing stun-batons. One frowned. He was probably thinking ahead, to punching out and curling up with an eggnog. Maybe watch a skyball game. Maybe strap into a cyberfuck. Instead he was here. Caged. Like all of us.

Louis bolted and made for the tree. He dropped to his knees and tore at that big box, grinning like a kid, till the first guard cracked him over the shoulder. Calmly, Louis stood up and punched the guard in the throat, laying him flat.

I remember a feeling passed through the chow hall. A tense current, from con to con to guard and back. Louis had crossed the line. Jumped the fence that runs between everything. Hitting a guard, fucking him up, he'd tipped order to chaos. After that, anything was possible. All of us knew it. One chucked tray, one animal howl, one chin check—a single punch, and the whole room would tip over. In that moment we could tear the fence down. Flip the script. *Riot.*

Instead, we watched as Louis crouched back to the box and tugged at the red ribbon. All of us spellbound, like we had to know too. Curious of insides and secrets.

He had the ribbon free when the next guard, eggnog boy, cracked him in the mouth with his stun-baton. Louis' teeth spilled like a broken necklace, though still he grinned, cackling as he spat a cord of gooey red on the floor.

I've always wondered what he saw. Tripping balls, smiling up at that guard, then slowly standing, long arms swaying, ready to brawl whatever beast stood before him. Did he know what was happening as the other guards piled in? As he went under, buried beneath black-armored rage and stun-batons, what did Louis see?

I'd seen the guards work men over plenty. Sometimes it seems the frustration of having to beat a man urges them on, works them up. Plus he'd hit one of them and, unlike us, they were as one. All for one.

The chow hall stood silent except for the thumps of shock-rubber on flesh. Our heat wave had cooled, the moment for riot here and gone. Again, we were just 300 separate men, all without pity. All thinking *let the guards get it out of their system, then we'll be okay. Get it all out.*

I shifted my attention to the fake tree. Its aged plastic drooped, ornaments dull and chipped. I wondered, do they even make those anymore? Even my folks had a Holo-Tree the year I got busted. My dad couldn't stop turning it on and off. The decorated pine stretched to the ceiling, then vanished, all with the push of a button.

"Now you see it. Now you don't," he'd kept saying.

When they finally carried Louis off, out cold, face tuned-up beyond recognition, he still clutched that red ribbon in his fist. It trailed behind like he was a kite the guards were trying to get off the ground. Then it snagged on a table corner and slipped from his hand.

One guard stayed, eyeing us, breathing hard. He picked up the box Louis had half unwrapped and stared at it. Then he stripped off the rest of the paper with one swipe. It was a jumbo, laundry-soap box. *Tide.* The kind my grandma used to use, before phosphates were illegal.

Like a magician, the guard raised the box and shook it by his ear. He gave us a wide-eyed, cartoon stare. He shook his head in disbelief. He whistled amazement. Then he punched through the cardboard top and upended the box. We waited. An old lifer coughed. A dozen shoes tapped.

Stray soap flakes spun to the floor, like the beginnings of snow, and nothing else. No one said a word, not even the guard. He didn't have to.

We returned to our ham slices and tasteless potatoes. Talk restarted. Slow, then dialed up to a normal drone.

Later, the warden popped back on the screen. He didn't mention Louis. He wished us a Merry Christmas and read a Bible passage. He wiped his reading glasses and tucked them away. His image flickered to black. Blue skies and green hills gone again.

Louis transferred to a minimum joint. Word is, he eats through a straw and moves in a wheelchair, rolled out to the lawn twice a day. Sun in face, blue skies above, no longer netted up. Free, the word is.

But that Christmas we didn't know. That Christmas the guards, like always, handed us 3-D printed candy canes and marched us back to our cells. Usually, some sucked their canes down to brittle shivs and joke stabbed their buddies. Usually, the Christmas corridors were stuffed with laughter and clowning. But not that year. That year, we filed back to our cells like monks. The fresh smear of violence had quieted us. And something else, Louis had broke the routine, at least for an instant. A proper Anachronist act. That earned respect. A moment of hush.

I don't think about Louis that often, though I've got plenty of time for it. Ten years left for selling digishrooms. Two more tacked on for contraband—six nanodots of DXT. It's simple math: Twelve more Christmas speeches. If the warden lives that long. If I do.

I'm still an old school punk, now and forever. I'd never drill a hole in my head. Though sometimes I catch myself humming a Dystopica tune. I don't know the name of the song or most of the words, some-thing about: "Clocks have hands and faces … a prison designed just for you." That's all I remember. Though at night, when that song riffs in my head, eyes closed, I see Louis. Skinny as Jesus on that busted clock. Grinning like a mad fool.

Or I see a key. Glowing, like it's cut from red neon, hanging right there.

Probably it's just a DXT flashback or wishful thinking, but when I see it, the light in the dark of my head, I almost believe. That time is an illusion. A lie. A thing we can shift and escape from. Time's brittle arrow snaps.

Twelve years can pass like seconds.

Eyes squeezed shut, crisp air fills my lungs. Blue skies and green hills ahead for a moment. I'm free.

ABOUT THE AUTHOR

Michael Harris Cohen has work published or forthcoming in various magazines and anthologies including *F(r)iction*, *Black Candies*, *Fiction International*, *The Dark*, *Catapult's Tiny Crimes*, and *Conjunctions*. He is the winner of F(r)iction's short story contest, judged by Mercedes Yardley, as well as the Modern Grimmoire Literary Prize. He's received a Fulbright grant for literary translation and fellowships from The Djerassi Foundation, OMI International Arts Center, Jentel, The Atlantic Center for the Arts, and the Künstlerdorf Schöppingen Foundation. His first book, *The Eyes*, was published by the once marvelous but now defunct Mixer Publishing. He lives with his wife and daughters in Sofia and teaches in the department of Literature and Theater at the American University in Bulgaria.

GHOSTS ARE ALL OF US

Spencer Ellsworth

Dek knelt over the dead squatters' bodies.

Hazy white Martian sunset painted the folds of their tattered out-suits. Through the viewscreen of the suit, she caught sight of a face turned purple from lack of air, of teeth in prominent gums, lips peeling back.

She turned her comm off, touched the first body's heart, and then the second, and said the Squatter's Prayer.

"To freedom on red sand." She put a fist to her own heart. "Fuck the Provs. Up the squats."

Sanch's grinding voice intruded on the one-way comm. "What you saying there? Bendicionés to these raisins, who tried to make it with no positioning equipment?"

She flipped her comm on, then thought better of it and flipped it back off. No use wasting explanations on Sanch. Positioning equipment meant the Provs could find you.

Squatting had been a good life, once. Couple habs stitched together out in the middle of Martian nowhere. Lots of beer, solar when you could get it, stolen batteries when not. Cram as many people in a hab as you could and play until you were three minutes from losing air, suit up quick and then scatter. They played classic, battery-killing amps and electric guitars, a massive drain on air and power, just to rub in what they stole from Provs in their domes.

The music got on the feeds and got famous. People all over the solar system cranked up squat rock.

The players died, went to prison, and got their shit repo'd.

"Tomátela a tú for the silent treatment."

Dek kept ignoring Sanch as they cut the bodies out of the suits and flushed them into the organic-matter vat, and then the suits into the spare parts bin. More lives wasted, on a planet that supposedly didn't waste anything.

Clambering back into the cab chamber, Dek found, suddenly, that her arms wouldn't work. Like lifting cinderblocks. Like she just needed to sleep, or cry, or both. Like numbness had her.

"Tú echas panza, old woman?" Sanch asked, watching how slowly Dek peeled her suit away, exhausted by the effort just to get one arm out. "Getting fat?"

"Just getting old, a qué." Even that hurt to say.

"You should be happy," Sanch said. "You got a hab. I've been on a waiting list four Earth years now, sleeping in the shelter."

"I am happy," Dek lied, "just—"

Sanch, not listening, punched the display on his handheld. "Look at this shit, a qué! You're famous!"

"What?"

The display leapt three-dimensionally off Sanch's handheld. Lars Urson, the new favorite son of the Mars Dome Consolidation Party, tall and square-jawed like a fucking statue. The scroll read: *Urson claims favorite band is Sand & Nothing, prompting claims of tone-deafness. The "squat" music movement opposed tiered resourcing within domes, the cornerstone of Urson's party, which has created a super-wealthy class of domes on Mars.*

It cut to a feed of—"Fess?" Dek said. The woman onscreen, ragged kinky hair cut short, glared a black furious stare at the camera. *In a statement on behalf of the band, Fatima al-Abdul, singer and bassist, said, "Urson and his party are everything that Sand & Nothing fought against. The Provincial Sphere Plan cuts resource in the domes unequally in favor of free-market economics, as we pointed out in songs like 'Ghosts.'" People still die out there.*" Fess put a fist to her heart.

Dek smiled, a thing she hadn't expect to do today. Fuck the Provs.

"Fuck yeah, yee!" Sanch said. "'Ghosts!' Love that song!"

"I want to hear this," Dek snapped.

Another news scroll: *Urson offered thirty million in resource credit to the band if they were willing to reunite for his birthday party, a resource-heavy soirée in the elite Golden Dome.* A soundbite from Urson scrolled through with his gleaming smile.

Again, there was Fess. *I wouldn't do it for a private planet.*

"Right on, Fess," Dek said. "Stay angry."

"Thirty million?" Sanch asked, as he turned the cab on. "For one gig? That would set you up! You could build a whole hab dome and invite all the old squats!"

Dek didn't answer.

"Thirty million."

Dek sighed, and the heaviness in her chest came back, the momentary relief from the sight of Fess gone. "We'd have to find Sides, and no one knows where they fucked off to. Probably dead."

A moment later, Dek's port buzzed.

⌛   ⌛   ⌛

Dek sat in her hab, one hand tight on the water bottle. Just water. The depot'd had been out of consolidated grain and protein, so she couldn't even distract herself by the joke of "cooking" it with a few meager spices into a slightly tasty sludge.

The black mood was worse. A whole fucking planet sat on her shoulders.

"Ayrah feek, you old kalb," Dek muttered, swigging the water. "Get fucked. You can do this."

She pressed the button.

Three faces popped up on the screen.

"Dek! You made it!"

Fess, despite her anger on the news broadcast, looked much happier than a social worker had a right to. Her full neck tattoo, faded on her brown skin, crawled up from a sweaty old shirt that read *Olympus 50k 2155: Mars Runs To Beat Addiction.*

John, even more than last time, was swimming in resource. Wore the nicest sunglasses Dek had ever seen, puffing on a vape that probably had real marijuana in it, in clothes that might have had some actual flax or cotton in them. John had made a pile of money playing in a new band that definitely wasn't squat.

And Sides.

"Shit, Sides!" Dek said, and found herself breaking into a smile, despite the sight. Sides was rail-thin, smiling weakly, showing even fewer teeth than they used to have. Only their face, which meant they were using a handheld. "Shaku maku, cabrón! Where you been?"

"Here and there. Keeping clean, insha. Had some trouble for a while. How's parole?"

"Fucker! You would ask!" Dek laughed. "Pinche Provs never forget. But I'm done. Waited my five years and got a private hab last month."

"Dek," Fess said, "you see that asshole talking about S&N on the feed?"

"Oh yeah."

"Saw that," Sides said, their voice trembling.

"He can kol khara," Fess spat. "Only way I'd play a show for him would be if he were outside the hab in only his skin."

John spoke up, taking a long drag. "Sexway played the mayor's inauguration and that kalb was there. Tried to talk to me about squats. I told him where he could stick a drumstick."

"Oh really, John?" Fess said, with a barely concealed eye-roll.

"Much as I could. Was a paying gig."

Awkward silence ruled the feed. Shit, now Dek was nervous. "We don't forget, a qué," she said. "For the squats. Freedom on red sand."

All four of them touched their hands to their hearts. "Sand & pinche Nothing."

Dek smiled. For a moment, she wasn't depressed, nervous, or having a booze fit; she was just nineteen again in a squat hab out under the Martian sun, sweat pouring down her back as she played her guts out.

And then Sides spoke up. "Actually, shevs, I'm in a little trouble."

⧗   ⧗   ⧗

The sounds of "Underground" died, echoing off the warehouse walls.

"No dá. We're gonna have to tune down," Fess said. "I can't get up in that register anymore."

"He'll do us proper." John lifted a drumstick to point at the black-suited guy sitting in the corner.

"Sounded great, S&N," John's roadie said, smiling. "Este bueno. Like no time has passed at all. I'll just be a minute with your guitars."

"The beat was tight. I can see how you actually make a living at this shit, John," Fess said, as if the words had been dragged out of her. She handed her bass to the roadie. "You're sounding good too, Dek."

"I played like shit," Dek said, taking off her own guitar. Her fresh calluses ached at the tips of her fingers.

"It was good, wallah. Now, Sides." Fess gave a weak smile. "Not so good."

Sides, even skinnier than they had looked on the display, shook their head. "I don't think we even need that solo."

"The solo that *Crush It Mars* called 'the best fifteen seconds in squat?'" John tapped his drumsticks together idly. "That'd be like 'Complete Control' without the opening riff, kalb. We'll run it again, in the new key."

"I can't do it," Sides said. "I ... my hands shake. Maybe Dek can learn the solos."

Dek exhaled heavily. "Sides, I'm no fucking soloist."

She caught the look between Fess and John.

"We could bring in my guitarist Ren," John said. "She knows the parts ..."

"No ringers," Fess said. "That's in the contract. Sand & Nothing, original lineup for these fucking Provs. They'll scan for guitar implants that can run it."

Sides's face screwed up in an angry scowl Dek hadn't seen in twenty years. "Ya rab! Fucking Provs. We only played full-band to drain the batteries and skeev them off!"

"Sides, this gig is because of you," Fess said, her anger audible.

"This whole shitfest is because you need money!"

"Give us a minute," Dek said to the other two. "Outside."

She took Sides by the arm and they walked outside.

Overhead the dome shimmered, control points gleaming and microsolar shining. Beyond that, the endless low-pressure dust of the Martian sky. Fresh printed buildings made a solid grid down the line of this dome, with a few trees marking the public square. "Dusty day."

Sides was looking at the ground. "You ever see the ghosts?"

Dek nodded. "Not myself. They're out there, though." There wasn't a squatter alive who didn't believe in the ghosts.

"I see them all the time," Sides said. "Not the aliens, the old ones. I've only seen those, a few times. But todas las días, Dek, every fucking day I see the squats."

Dek nodded. "Mala leche, Sides."

"Everyone who died—whose hab sprung a leak, who didn't get back through the dust cloud, who took too much shine and choked on their puke in an out-suit ... " Sides knocked their teeth together, a creepy sound in the open air. "I see them all the time, Dek. All the time." Sides shrunk down, clutched their head. "I can't fucking play when I see them and I see them all the time."

"Sides, habibi." Dek put an arm around her friend. It was silent, the only sound the endless background hum of air recyclers. "I have depression."

"Que?"

"I feel all sad and heavy and stupid all the time," Dek said. "I take the pills and I go to the gym four times a week, and still every fucking day it's ... fucked."

Sides nodded, choking back a tear. "Pinche brains."

"Bad enough, some days, that I would take a walk suitless just to get rid of it. Enjoy some fresh Mars air, ya know?" Dek's throat was tight. Tough to talk about this shit. "There's still folk trying to squat, and most days, we find them dead out there. They turn off their positioning gear and then starve trying to navigate back to base. Or they accidentally rad their brains out trying to create a radiation shield and

... I clean them up. It's mal work, Sides, muy mal. I asked for this duty, because someone should be there to say the Prayer. I'm starting to think if I did things different—if I weren't always out there looking at the dead—it'd go away, ya know? But then I think I couldn't live with myself. I'd forget them."

"Ayrah feek to the Provs. They fucking did this to us."

"Yeah," Dek said. "I'm wondering how much of it I do to myself, though. And ... god damn, Sides, I miss the old days."

Sides nodded. "Remember Jen?"

"She knew how to get in a pit."

"Trace and Spence. Old Rat, remember that fucker?"

"Cabrón drank me under the table every night." Dek squeezed the bony arm she'd put one hand on. "I'm glad you're alive, habibi, even if you owe those smuggler assholes money. I kept thinking I'd get the call, do the prayer for you too."

"I see Rat," Sides said. "I can see him right now." Sides buried their head in Dek's chest. "I see them all the time!" They sobbed. "All the time!"

Dek rubbed her friend's back, didn't say anything while Sides cried for a while. Finally, Sides put their head up and said, voice trembling with sobs, "I can play the rhythm parts, Dek. Just don't ask me to fucking solo."

"All right," Dek said, trying to ignore the feeling settling on her shoulders. "I'll learn to solo."

⧗   ⧗   ⧗

The stage stretched across a wide square in Urson's garden.

A garden, on Mars.

This garden would have cost fifteen times what any public park cost. Trees glimmered, bright with the oxygen coming off their leaves, in neat rows. Flowers, actual bright yellow and pink flowers, lining the walkway. Behind them, a buffet table and open bar stretched the length of the stone walk.

Looked like a picture from Earth, except that right beyond the line of trees, the edge of the dome shone. Olympus Mons was turning to a stark gray shape in the sunset, beyond the wide open desert.

"So much resource it makes me sick," Fess said.

"Steak and lobster," John said, holding up a chunk of a weird bug-looking red thing. "You gotta try some. Once-in-a-lifetime experience. This stuff's even wild-caught, all the way from Greenland."

"No comiendo araña!" Dek said, shaking her head.

"You eat cricket flour every day!"

Dek adjusted her guitar over her gut. It had been a good three weeks. Work had given her unpaid leave, enough time to learn the solos under the tutelage of John's roadie. Her small share of the thirty mil would cover that time not working, and set up a little retirement, although that would just mean more fucking time with the black moods.

Still, even with Fess and John sniping, even with Sides's shirking and having to learn those pinche solos, Dek had smiled more in the past two weeks than she had in years.

Today, she could hardly feel the weight.

Except tomorrow it'd be over. She'd go back to cutting poor dead raisins out of their suits.

Dek turned to her left. "Sides, back me up. You don't just suck out a spider's ass——"

"Pissing resource on sand," Fess snapped, interrupting their conversation. "Putas need to take a walk outside the dome."

"Sand and fucking Nothing!" Lars Urson looked even shittier in person. His suit was spotless, a one-piece real linen-and-cotton black design with intricate folds down the front. His white-scrubbed smile seemed ready to pop off with *Wealth follows the builders, designers, the brave. This is why capitalism must be the driver behind dome-building.* "Shaku maku, bros! I've waited my whole life to be in your pit!"

"People in hell wait for ice water," Fess said.

"Knew you'd do it, yee!" Urson drank from his flight of champagne. "Who says no to thirty million?"

"It's gonna be thirty-five, we have to keep talking."

Urson just grinned. "This is gonna be a great pit!" He wandered off.

Fess spat after him. "Let's get this the fuck over with."

"We're not supposed to start for ten minutes," John said.

"I want out of this shithole!" Fess said. "Play!"

John sighed and tapped out the four-beat intro to "In Shadows."

The audience of evening gowns, one-piece Mars-style suits, Old Earth-style tuxes, saris and kilt-ons rushed up the stage. Made-up faces beamed and a bunch of dudes in tuxes—in *tuxes*—started a circle pit.

Fess practically screamed the last verse into the mic.

When we rise
The Martian sun will burn our eyes
Fist corazón
Out of your shadow we own what we own!

The band snapped to a stop on the last beat. And Fess screamed the verse again, a cappella.

Dek exchanged a look with John, who shrugged, and mouthed, "Buen solo." And then they were into "Underground."

The evening-dress-clad circle pit kept on moving. Dek shook her head, and focused on playing the solos. No one seemed to notice when she fucked up.

Halfway through the set, Fess turned around. "Yallah shabaab, prontissimo," she said, motioning for them to move faster. "Get this shit over with."

"We gonna do 'Ghosts?'" John asked. "Never decided that."

"Yes we did. You were smoking. We're not cheapening the memory—"

"'Ghosts!'" someone in the crowd yelled. "Play fucking 'Ghosts!'"

"'Ghosts!'" Others took up the call.

John grinned. "We're pinche committed."

"No dá," Fess said, and launched into the bass intro for "Breathe

Slow," which, with its sludgy, tromping beat, had some of the audience calling all the harder for "'Ghosts.'"

"One fucking song left," Fess said when they finished. "And then, finally—"

"Yo!" Lars Urson, now drunker, stumbled up to the stage. "Airless as fuck, S&N! But you signed a contract to go till nine."

"Ayrah feek, asshole—"

Urson waved his hand, sloshing his shot glass. "Not my fault you started early. Play fucking 'Ghosts' already!"

Fess ignored him and went through "Bullet Caro" and then "In Shadows" again. Then she shouted, "That's fucking it!"

The audience booed and started up a chant. "'Ghosts!' 'Ghosts!' 'Ghosts!'"

"Fess, we have ten minutes left," Dek said.

Sides's hands were trembling on their guitar. "Shevs, I . . . we have to get the money, we have to. The smugglers . . . they know where I am now. We have to."

"Not playing it!"

"Fess," Dek said. "Habibi, we're doing this for Sides, all right?" She stepped forward, leaned into Fess. This close, she could feel Fess's hot, angry breath. The same air she'd shared in a hundred shitty habs, once. "Fess," Dek said. "I don't want Sides to be another ghost. Let's just play it."

"Damn it, Dek," Fess said. She finally turned to the microphone and yelled, "All right, you pieces of shit, we'll play 'Ghosts.' Hope you kick each other to death in the pit. Calavera no chilla!"

And she launched into "Ghosts" before John even finished the count-in.

Look what you have done
Hadhih alsahara'
The corks we can't pop from our rum
Your deaths are so cara!

"Ghosts," of course, had one of Sides's toughest solos, and it went on for a good eight minutes, just to fuck with an audience expecting short songs. Dek was preoccupied with the octave leaps and bends and hammer-ons when John shouted, "What the fuck!" and missed half a verse, the drums stuttering and stopping.

"John, damn it!" Dek kept playing, and Fess kept singing.

All of us are ghosts!
All of us are ghosts!
All of us are ghosts!
All of us are ghosts!

And then Fess stopped, right when she was supposed to scream. "Fucking qué a qué what the ..."

Sides let out a sob. "I'm sorry," Sides said. "I'm sorry! I didn't mean to bring them!"

The audience screamed.

Dek looked up from her solo and saw the ghosts.

The lights in the garden illuminated the trees, the bushes, and reflected off the faint glimmer of the dome. Right on the other side of the dome, they waited.

There had to be two hundred of the old squats out there, in open Martian air.

Their faces, black eyes shining in the dark, staring. Their out-suits torn and tattered. Their fists on their hearts. Purple, shriveled faces from lack of air, sweating in radiation sickness.

Ghosts.

Dek recognized Spence, and Trace, and there was Jen, standing still for the first time, the little tweak. And Old Rat, his silver tooth gleaming.

Fess sobbed into the microphone.

And Dek put a fist to her heart and started the chant. "Fuck the Provs! Up the squats!"

The ghosts echoed her. No one should have been able to hear

them through the dome. But they spoke loud and clear, and Dek and the band with them. *To freedom on red sand.* Fists went from hearts to the air. *Fuck the Provs! Up the squats!*

The rich crowd scattered. Some ran back to the house. Others walked off into the trees.

Urson was the only one left after a while, standing there and staring at the ghosts.

Slowly, he walked toward the huge dome barrier, until he stood just on the other side from them.

Old Rat stuck a hand through the dome and Urson, confusedly, touched it.

Dek would spend a long time trying to explain it, and never be able to. Old Rat yanked Urson right through the wall of the dome like he was pulling the fucker into the pit.

The lights in the garden flickered, and the Martian night covered them …

And then they faced an empty garden, nothing but the haze of a dust storm beyond the dome.

Sides fell to their knees and started sobbing. John came around his drums and just stared.

After an age, Fess said, "That cabrón was our meal ticket."

"You think they'll claim breach of contract?" John asked.

"Oh, those rich putas will do whatever they can," Fess said. "Losiento, Sides. We'll get your money somehow——"

"Shit on this," Dek said, and for the first time in a long time, she was angry. Not depressed. Not heavy.

This planet was fucked.

It had taken her friends.

It was taking Sides, a piece at a time.

The weight wasn't depression. It was anger, anger so long under the depression for so fucking long that it sprayed up like a broken water main. "We need money? We tour." She motioned to where the ghosts had stood. "We've got one audience already. We need to show the system that they're listening." She yanked her guitar off, threw it to the stage. "I'm sick of feeling nothing, feeling like shit because there's too much to feel so my fucking brain shuts down. We get our shit together, we tour, we show these pinchecabrónes."

"Talked about that, Dek. We need someone to front the cash—" Fess said.

"Fuck that shit," John said. "I got money. Only a bit, but it's enough to get us on the road, even if we'll be skint out there. We do it. Maybe we come out the other side, maybe we don't, but enough of playing it safe." And for the first time, he sounded furious, too.

Dek turned to her friend. "We'll get your fucking money, Sides. The right way."

Sides, without words, got up, and put their arm around Dek.

They fell into a band huddle, heads pressed together like they were in a pit so crowded they couldn't move away. The only weight was the press that came from leaning against each other.

That was a weight Dek could stand.

ABOUT THE AUTHOR

Spencer Ellsworth is the author of the Starfire trilogy, which begins with *Starfire: A Red Peace*, and the Victorian fantasy *The Great Faerie Strike*, from Broken Eye Books. His short fiction has appeared in *Lightspeed Magazine, The Magazine of Fantasy & Science Fiction,* and *Tor. com.* He lives in the Pacific Northwest with his wife and family, works at a small tribal college on an Indian reservation, and would really like a war mammoth if you've got one lying around.

THIS NEXT SONG IS CALLED PUNK ROCK VALHALLA

Izzy Wasserstein

Like most of my tattoos, they seemed like a good idea at the time. On the back of my left hand, the Norse rune Algiz, life. On my right, the Hebrew word Maveth, death. What can I say? I was eighteen, playing guitar *terribly* for a local punk band, and trying to make peace between the traditions of my Jewish mother and my Nordic father.

They weren't my most embarrassing tattoos, but they were the ones that got me killed. The fucking neo-Nazis that jumped me were very clear on that, condemning my blasphemy. They also called me a whore and a cunt and every anti-Semitic slur in the book. For a few moments it was all weirdly affirming. Piss off Nazis that bad, and you've done something right in your life. Then the pain took over and I just wanted it to end.

It was a long time before it did. One moment I'm bleeding to death in the alleyway behind Liberty Hall, and the next I'm standing before a massive tree, so big it blots out the sun, the tangled branches stretching endless. Strange snuffling noises came from far above me.

"Huh," I said, eloquently.

"Well said."

I whirled to find the speaker, tall and gaunt, wearing a battered gray suit, his face complete with eyepatch. The trucker's hat might have thrown me, but the ravens didn't leave much doubt.

"Oh fuck," I said. The raven on his right shoulder cawed derisively.

"Not quite the reaction I was hoping for," Wodin said. I was still trying to deal with the facts that the afterlife was real, and it was a

Norse one.

"Whatever you're going to do, get it over with," I said, gritting my teeth. Those Nazi fucks had been super clear about their views. They'd sent me to their god, and here I was.

A hint of a smile crossed Wodin's lips. "Do? I'm going to have a conversation with you, then you're going to go on your way." As if to emphasize this, he walked past me, putting his weight on his staff, and then settled with a groan against the trunk of the tree. "There. Much better. Sit?"

I sat. He was a hard man to say 'no' to, and it had dawned on me that I wasn't in pain anymore.

"You're not here to make me suffer?" I asked, and both ravens laughed this time.

"Why would I? You kept the faith in your own way."

I struggled to see signs of deceit, but didn't find any. If the Allfather was lying to me, I had no way of knowing it.

"Then ... where am I?"

He rolled his eye. "I thought it was obvious. At the foot of Yggdrasil. I hope you'll indulge my flair for the dramatic."

I decided I needed to ask better questions. "What am I doing here?"

"You're here so I can tell you what's next."

I blinked, waited. I'd spent a lot of time on the road between gigs. I was an expert at passing time.

"You're no fun," he said. "What's next is Valhalla, of course. Where the brave will live forever and all that."

"Isn't that for warriors?" I said.

"You had more than your share of fights, woman. And you think we don't want bards at the party?"

I caught myself grinning. I'd written a song about an afterlife without amps not being worth having.

Wodin grinned, showing his yellowed teeth. "Now you're beginning to understand me."

"But aren't we on opposite sides?"

His grin soured, and the two ravens rose from his shoulders, cawing with obvious anger. "You think just because some racist trash know a few runes that they're my people?"

"Sorry," I said hurriedly, putting my hands up. "They were ... very insistent on that point." I felt my face twist into a grimace at the memory.

"You're forgiven," he said. "They certainly went to great lengths to convince you."

I stared at the tattoos on the backs of my hands, thinking. This still felt like an elaborate trap, but there was something tugging at the back of my mind.

Oh.

"My body," I said. It was impossible to tell if Wodin winked or blinked.

"I told you, woman," he said. "If anyone hates those bigots more than you, it's me." He saw me as I am. I was in my body, not the one I'd been stuck with through a torturous, testosterone-plagued adolescence. The body I'd made peace with. Claimed. Scarred. Mine.

"I believe you," I said quietly.

"Good," he smiled and pushed himself to his feet. "Valhalla awaits." He paused, knelt to study my face. "I'm sending you to paradise, yet somehow you aren't happy about it."

I was relieved that he wasn't the God of Blood and Soil, but he was right about that. "I was murdered by fucking Nazis," I said. "I don't want paradise. I want blood."

Blood, blood, blood, the ravens called, and settled again on his shoulders. He leaned closer, the ancient lines of his face inches from mine.

"Blood," Wodin said. "Blood, I understand." He tilted his head to one side and one raven bent close as though whispering. "Ah," he said. "I will ask her."

"Valhalla awaits," he said. Or I can send you back to ... settle accounts. You'll be different, something like a Valkyrie, and you'll be able to take vengeance in my name."

"What's the catch?" I said. I wasn't a total fool.

"It will hurt," he said. "Being reformed as my warrior, and then just the pain of living. It will hurt a lot. You'll be giving up on paradise for pain and a chance to balance the scales."

I thought of the agony I'd just experienced, those long minutes when death wouldn't come, the evil leering bastards above me. It wasn't a tough decision.

I gave Wodin my answer. He smiled. Only much later did I realize he had expected me to take his offer. He turned to the raven on his right. "Muninn," he said. "Go with her. I want to remember their faces."

Wodin was right. Being sent back felt like having every molecule in my body torn apart and recombined. I've never regretted it.

They were still kicking the shit out of my old body when I returned, Muninn on my shoulder and a big fucking spear, naturally, in my hands. They looked up and up and up at me, and I'll admit, their expressions were fucking satisfying.

As I brought the spear down, I was pleased to note that my tattoos had returned with me. Life and death: like I said, seemed like a good idea at the time.

ABOUT THE AUTHOR

Izzy Wasserstein is a writer of poetry and fiction. Her work has recently appeared or is forthcoming from *Clarkesworld*, *Apex*, and *Fireside Magazine*, among others. Her most recent poetry collection is *When Creation Falls* (Meadowlark Books, 2018). She shares a home with the writer Nora E. Derrington and a variety of furry companions. Reports that she is actually a cyborg fox remain unconfirmed.

ELECTRIC TEA

Marie Vibbert

I came home in the watery dawn, exhausted from waitressing all night. As I eased my bike against the porch railing to chain it up, a neighbor who had never said two words to me before leaned over his chain-link fence. "Hey, Sue, right?"

Tsui. I didn't correct.

"Did you see the fire? Man, I would have loved to have seen that!"

"Fire?" I asked.

He pointed behind our homes, down the weed-and-trash-strewn slope to the warehouse, its undamaged roof all that was visible from the front sidewalk.

I pushed through vines and broken fences with the dream-like possession artists yearn for. A small crowd was gathered, reverent at the edge of hasty police tape.

The arsonist had painted the warehouse in careful lines of linseed-oil pigments, flammable as anything. The colors were lost, but the image wasn't—fat, indulgent lines that tapered sweetly into finer detail. The picture was a skeletal bird-creature holding the long arm of a Sears Shopvac. The logo was identifiable, despite foreshortening as it curved around the barrel.

I was jealous of the craftsmanship. Every line touched to spread the fire. Combustion started at the Shopvac's business end, its flat nose pushed into the joining of wall and weedy gravel. Those first lines had the thickest char. By design or chance, the fire department arrived before the flames burned far from the confines of their original lines. The black rising from the vacuum's mouth echoed decals on hot rods, a symbol of speed arrested.

I would not rest until I found this artist and learned their purpose and, more importantly, their process.

Our narrow street, Jefferson, sagged off the backside of Tremont like a rotten floorboard. Two of my classmates and I had pooled our resources to rent the narrow clapboard house. We were failed artists who didn't know it yet. In violation of our renter's agreement we'd painted murals on every wall using ceiling white, porch floor grey, and matte black spray paint. I did the black. I arched into a back-bend to make one complete slash across the living room, straight as a sword stroke. I wanted the line to be unrestrained, violent. Instead, it bloomed like mascara. Mahesh painted a woman in white and grey, heavy breasts falling from the join of ceiling and wall, her arm out-stretched along my black line. I kept my eyes on the floor when I crossed the living room.

"I can't believe we missed it!" Jay said, slouching on the giant spool we used as a kitchen table. His dreads lay like a sleeping cat around his shoulders. "I hope the dude posts a video. It must have been sexy when the lines first caught."

I hoped so, too. I wanted the motion, like music, art that exists in time, rather than the notation left in its wake.

"It was just derivative street art," Mahesh said. "Tsui could do better."

My name is pronounced "Sue" but I can hear it when the person speaking knows there's a "T", something hesitant in the "S". I prefer that.

"If it weren't down the hill," I said. "If the trees weren't so thick, I could have seen it on my way home."

"Yeah," Jay nodded. "It's worse, isn't it? Being so close and miss-ing it? Have you ever seen paint burn? The flames glide, like they're hovering."

Mahesh was working on the cabinets under the sink, adding a slouching monster where some paint had dripped. "I'll bet it was elec-tric tea. Someone drank it and then wanted to prove it had an effect on them by doing something crazy. These things always hit Cleveland after the bigger towns. Like bands and fashion."

"No, they don't." Jay straightened. He'd lived in Cleveland his whole life and was protective of it. "People have been drinking electric tea here for years. Before it went big."

"Okay," Mahesh said, keeping his eyes on his work. He dragged his brush slowly, flat, making a bumpy nose.

Jay took that as the dismissal it was. "I know people who drink it. Who've been drinking it. None of them went crazy, either."

"It must have been beautiful," I said. I looked out our back window at the warehouse roof among the trees and saw a smudge, like a line from a Conté crayon, curving along a glittering tarpaper edge. "I'd drink electric tea if it helped me make such a thing."

Artists fail for many reasons, and most fail where we were—fresh out of art school. I couldn't speak to Jay and Mahesh's nascent failings, but mine was simple: I wasn't good enough. I studied and experimented. I took critique well. I hoped that enough time studying and experimenting and responding well to criticism would somehow build up to the golden magic of "good enough," but I knew that "good enough" wasn't enough.

We were in pursuit of our futures, self-consciously temporary in our living arrangements, and compulsively recklessness. Mahesh spent what we all knew were his last dollars on a sable brush. Jay tried to tattoo himself. I went to five-dollar punk shows at the Phantasy when I had work the next morning. Someone set fire to buildings. It made sense.

⌛   ⌛   ⌛

Jay met me at the restaurant as I was leaving my early shift. "You still want to go?"

"I want to see it," I said. "Just to see."

He nodded. "Leave your bike here." As we started walking down the street, he said, "It's not that it's not safe, but I don't know if you want people to see your bike there and know, you know?"

"Electric tea isn't illegal."

"Yet," Jay said. He looked side to side, his dreads twitching like

nervous snakes. He jogged across the street and took me down a
few alleys to University Road by the back of Sokolowski's. We slunk
behind the restaurant and through the gravel lot under the freeway
bridge. His shirt was torn below the right sleeve, giving me momentary glimpses of his muscular side.

All the quick, covert motion made little sense when we reached
Abbey Avenue and had to cross the long bridge with fake noncha-
lance. Tremont is an island, bordered on all sides by cliffs man-made
and natural— the river valley, the freeways, the railroads. This bridge
was one of a limited number of ways out of Tremont. The cracked
sidewalk was scrawled with anti-gentrification graffiti.

"Is it far?" I asked. The neighborhood ahead of us held breweries
and a strip mall. I couldn't imagine an electric teahouse squeezing in.

"Not far now." We crossed the smaller bridge for the RTA tracks.

The West Side Market was crowded, voices filling the high, vault-
ed space with a concert-hall buzz. Jay led me around pastries and
meats and out again through the fruit stands where thick-accented
men vied for our attention with chunks of cantaloupe on knifepoint.
We resumed sneaking up alleyways and down side streets.

We paused beside one of the dozens of three-story Victorian
storefronts in Ohio City, all brick and recessed entrances. A record
store was doing well on the corner, plastered with prints of local
bands from the 70s like the Dead Boys and Electric Eels, unkempt
and daring you to call it nostalgic. In the middle of the block, lettering
from generations of failed businesses made a pastiche of faded gilding
over nondescript doors and blackened windows.

Jay ducked into a blind alley and down bluestone steps to a basement door.

"Do we need a password?"

He raised his eyebrows at me and knocked with the back of his
hand. One of his failed tattoos stretched on the paler skin of his inner
wrist. It was a broken bit of barbed wire originally intended to be a
bird. I felt very tender toward that tattoo.

A thin, caramel-skinned man answered the door, pulling it against a brass security chain to eye us before unlatching.

All this pseudo cloak-and-dagger was appropriate to electric tea—an illicit substance that was not illicit. More than half the flavor was myth; it would lose its power if you could buy it in the drugstore like incense.

The basement was lit by LED strips at the base of brick walls, partially hidden from sight by rows of cast concrete fleur-de-lys. Black fabric with sequins draped between and over pipes on the ceiling. The chairs and tables were a mix: wrought iron garden sets and marble café tables and one old door on sawhorses.

The man who let us in returned to his stool by the door's peephole and left us to find our way.

Electric tea was, ultimately, just tea, in a special cup. The cup contained a mechanism that would broadcast invisible waves toward your brain, stimulating emotions, thought processes. If it worked right it would play your brain, vibrate it with recorded thoughts like vinyl grooves resurrected Joey Ramone. It supposedly left your mind clearer and sharper in its wake. Stimulants helped the effect, so its first use was with hyper-caffeinated energy drinks. There were incidents, allegations, nothing proven, but it was now only legal with ordinary tea. The partial prohibition made it sexier.

There was a sheet of SmartPaper on each table with a menu to scroll through. I tapped "black" from the list of categories. They had every type of tea I'd ever heard of and a few I hadn't.

The prices weren't listed. Always a danger sign. I rifled my fingers through the loose tips in my pocket.

A plump white girl approached, wearing a short waiter's apron over her jeans. "Can I get you anything?"

Jay ordered green tea. I scanned the list again. "Gunpowder Smoke," I said.

She smiled. "Good choice. We just started serving that. It's our own blend of black gunpowder tea with lapsang souchong."

"Sounds expensive. I think I'll have the Darjeeling."

"All our teas are the same price. Give it a try. You'll love the kick."

I could never disagree with a waiter, so I nodded. When she left, I asked Jay, "Have you done this before?"

"Yeah. Of course."

"Do you believe the stories?"

He shrugged. "I know it's supposed to make you think more clearly. I also know that anything that does good to the mind can be overdone. I dunno. I've had some great ideas after coming here. Like, that's when I started 'Rodin Bows to a Dream of Donatello.'" He smiled, mocking his own pretension.

I admired how he sat in his chair like his clothes were not attached to him. He always wore loose jeans and shirts, his lithe frame a rumor reported second-hand by folds and shadows. "I'll never paint anything that real," I said.

He turned to regard me sideways. "We're not going to start that again, Tsui. When you finally let go, you'll be the best of us all."

My cheeks warmed. I pretended to be fascinated by the menu. "I need to learn to make unselfconscious lines."

The tea arrived in oversized cups, ceramic on the outside and glass inside so we could see the little circuit board and dime-sized emitters. The blinking purple and blue LEDs were almost certainly just for looks.

The tea smelled metallic and smoky. I paused before sipping, uncertain.

Of course, holding the cup was the dangerous part, wasn't it?

Jay leaned back, a picture of cool unconcern. He kissed his teacup slowly, deliberately.

"I should have brought my sketchbook," I said. "That's a good pose for you."

Self-conscious, his lines tightened and shifted. Without changing his pose, he ruined it. "Drink your tea," he said.

I sipped my tea. It tasted like it smelled—like the smoke from a black powder pistol wafting through tall grass.

I closed my eyes and breathed in evenly, letting the steam bathe my face. I was waiting to feel something. "What is it supposed to feel like?"

"Like waking up," Jay said. "Like plugging in an amp, like a pebble dropping into water. Like a head rush."

I felt warm stoneware in my hands. I felt recycled wind from the air conditioner. I felt a bit silly.

"Mahesh doesn't approve," Jay said. "If he were any more uptight, he'd vibrate."

"Don't."

Jay used Rapidograph pens with micrometer tips on SmartPaper to plan every sculpture, made small models and intermediate models. Precise and careful in art, Jay relaxed in everything else. The opposite of Mahesh. He raised his eyebrows. "Don't what?"

I couldn't explain what they both meant to me, how much I needed them to love each other. "Mahesh bleeds when he paints," I said.

Jay's cheek lifted, the languor returning to his limbs. "Yeah, I love him, too."

I felt no effect from the tea. I watched Jay closely, to see if he felt anything. He was just Jay.

The tea was expensive, but not more than my tips for the night. I declined a second cup.

We took a more direct route home and passed a band playing in a walled courtyard. It was a female punk trio. The drummer worked with me. A short, plump girl named Patty. She was always debating whether to name the band the Mx. Fits or Pussy Hat or 28 Days Later. I could hear her stage growl, "This next track is called 'Boys Suck.'" Raw and loud, practicing in the middle of the day. Cymbals crashed like paint splatters on brick walls. It was living art, spilling into the street. You couldn't study to make this.

I took Jay's hands and pulled him back. He laughed and danced to me. His movements, the music, this was what I wanted: something perfect because it was unpolished, something pure.

Who needed an electric kick when we lived in a vibrant art community? I hugged Jay's sweaty, muscular arm as we continued walking and he talked about Japanese printmaking and I interrupted to talk about the graffiti we passed.

"Will you sculpt tonight?" I asked.

"Hell yes. And you will paint, Tsui. You'll paint if I have to strap the brush to your hand."

⌛ ⌛ ⌛

Mahesh was, ironically, making tea when we got home. He looked up from lowering the mesh ball into the pot. "Where have you been?"

"Getting some tea," Jay said, tilting his head back, challenging.

Mahesh shook his head. "It's a placebo, you know."

"How would you know?"

I said, "Don't fight."

"Absinthe," Mahesh said. He put the cozy on the teapot and turned to face us, arms crossed. "In the nineteenth century, absinthe was a craze. They claimed the wormwood caused 'effects' beyond drunkenness. Mind-opening, clarifying. Inspiration. Ring any bells?"

Jay shrugged fluidly. "They also thought cocaine was a good headache medicine, doesn't mean aspirin is going to get you high."

Mahesh set three mugs on the wooden spool. "There were no special effects. There was strong alcohol and wishful thinking. The power of ritual." He waved his hand over the table. "How would you know that I'm not serving you electric tea right now?"

"Because the cups are crap." Jay picked up a cracked mug with the logo for a construction company and waggled it, exposing its chipped side.

Mahesh looked at me. "Did you feel anything?"

I didn't want to take sides, but I had to shake my head.

"If it really did anything, the government would regulate it," Mahesh said, and poured the tea.

Jay walked out, taking any hope of conversation with him.

⧗   ⧗   ⧗

A well-known local sculptor was found dead inside a cooling tower across from Tremont Park. He'd climbed to the top of the structure with an armful of rebar and slipped, falling twenty feet to crack his skull on the metal grating below. His wife had no idea he had even left home that night.

Because of the similarity of some of his sculptures to the bird-skeleton drawing, it was speculated that he was the arsonist, and the news blogs all raised the question: had he been drinking electric tea?

The art community knew better than to suspect him of the fire. He was a sculptor, had never painted in any medium, much less fire, and electric tea drinkers didn't tend to change genres.

Besides, a day later there was another fire, down in the flats. The painting this time was a chorus of large-headed waifs, their little bodies twisted like candle flames, ringing one of the conical mounds of iron ore deposited by shipping boats for the steel mills. It burned longer before being doused, but as its substrate was iron dirt, nothing was damaged.

You could see minute traces of color, where the paint soaked in and was protected. Burnt turquoise and magenta. Inspired planning, how the colors sank and glowed against the rust-brown ore.

On *Scene Magazine*'s main page the two fire drawings were shown side-by-side, the headline simple: Copycat or Serial Arsonist? The comments section raged with theories, and images by local artists either being accused or exonerated.

Mahesh leaned over my shoulder. "A hundred artists in this area have that style. Maybe a thousand. Just in this small-ass city. He could be from somewhere else, just passing through. They'll never catch him that way."

I resented the "they". I would catch him. Practice at catching fame. "He could be a she," I said.

Mahesh said, "I was using the gender-neutral 'he.' Come on, I want to use the computer."

Both painters were clearly right-handed. It's no great forensic trick to tease out the handedness of a line-artist; even the very best have to lift and drop their brush. Some artists, of course, are more careful. Both fire-paintings were not careful, reveling in the mess and accident of an over-loaded brush. I admired the punk-rock joy of the lines.

I could hear Mahesh breathing. He spoke quietly, bloodlessly. "I need the computer more than you do. You already have a job," he said.

"It's not an art job."

"I'm not unemployed because I'm too precious to wait tables, Tsui. I'm trying, all right?"

I slipped out of my seat. "I didn't say anything like that." We had leaped over the cliff of graduation together, and in the air before landing, whether it would be the promised shore of gainful employment or the abyss below us, it was hard not to claw at each other.

⧗   ⧗   ⧗

After Jefferson Avenue crosses West 3rd, it quickly starts to look like an old country road, overgrown and sun-bleached and neglected, concrete silos rising up behind graffiti-decked tin railings. You forgot the Cleveland skyline and the high bridges were waiting to slip into view between tangled vines.

The warehouse's fence lay flat where the fire trucks had come in. Someone had a business here, had cared about this expanse of overgrown gravel.

Someone had already sprayed graffiti over top of the burn-lines. A vermillion penis pointed skyward like a cannon raised on its misshapen wheels.

⧗   ⧗   ⧗

The chubby white girl opened the basement door this time. "We're not open yet."

"Please let me wait inside?"

She looked up the stairs. It was a bright, hot afternoon. I tried to look afraid and vulnerable and small. "All right," she said. "It's not going to be that long."

The room looked different with the overhead lights on— ordinary. There were chair-height scrapes on the walls and dings in the tables. The sequined fabric had loose threads and a cheap shine.

"The kitchen isn't open yet, but I could get you a glass of water."

I shook my head. She left and came back a few minutes later with a cash drawer, which she slid into a holder on the wall. Then she unlocked it and counted its contents. The familiar waltz of preparing a restaurant for its operating day.

I tried to think of some ingratiating way to start conversation. Instead I blurted out, "Is it a placebo?"

Her shoulders dropped. "Jesus," she said. She turned to face me. "I'm trying to run a business. I don't need your approval or opinion. Go read a webpage."

"I didn't mean ... I'm not." I stood, stepped forward, stepped back. I looked at my own twisting hands. "I didn't feel anything."

I looked up to see her considering me. "You aren't going to lecture me or write some stupid blog 'exposing' the 'truth' about electric tea?"

I shook my head. "I just wanted to feel something. To understand."

She sighed. She closed the cash drawer and made a note on a tablet. "It's not a placebo. I wouldn't have started this business if it were, if I hadn't been convinced the first time I drank it."

"Does it only affect certain people?"

She looked embarrassed. She went to the counter and stooped below. She pulled out a pair of cups and set them on the counter. "The thing of it is, sometimes the battery runs out. Or gets weak. Or a connection is loosened throughout the day. I'd say there's about a ten- to twenty-percent chance you didn't get a working cup." She shook her head. "So yeah, there is a placebo effect, and I rely on it because this technology is fragile as heck."

She pushed a cup toward me. "I barely make a profit, fixing the stupid things all the time."

"Oh."

"What'll you have? They're all working. They always all work at the start of the night."

"Gunpowder smoke."

"Good choice. We just started serving that. Our own blend of—"

"You said."

"Oh." Her face was tired, older looking as she bent to retrieve a glass jar from under the counter. She filled a tea ball and snapped it shut with one hand as she put the jar away. "Guys love the gunpowder smoke. It sounds manlier than rosehip chamomile. I always get happy when a woman orders it." She looked at me again as she held the cup under a hot water tap. "When I was in college, I was convinced lapsang souchong cured writer's block. Maybe it was the smell. Wood smoke. Scent is linked strongly to memory. I never had trouble telling stories around campfires."

We bent to sip our cups of smoke tea together. This time I felt a strange tickle, an itch on my forehead. An idea vibrated through my mind like the crash of cymbals.

The teahouse owner raised her eyebrows. "You see?"

"Thank you," I said.

Her face transformed with her smile, like just the right line turns a mere representation into beauty. "That's why I had to have this shop. I had to share that feeling. It's magic, every time I see that look on a new person's face."

☗   ☗   ☗

I did not go to work like I was supposed to. I walked home, knowing Mahesh would be there alone. Jay worked days at a gallery on Professor. I found Mahesh painting light bulbs and flying saucers around the cabinet knobs in the kitchen.

He wiped his brush and stared at me. "Shouldn't you be at work?"

"Why did you do it?" I asked. He recoiled, started to stammer the usual things people stammer in this case. "You set fire to the warehouse. And the ore pile. Close to home and then farther away to confuse the trail. Will you do it again? Were you angry? Frustrated?"

His head hung over his hands, resting his weight on the edge of the kitchen sink.

"It's okay," I said. "No one was hurt."

"It's not art if it doesn't hurt!" His eyebrows formed a harsh line.

"We'll help you. Jay and me. We'll keep you from doing it again, from being caught. We're in this together."

He sank, back against the counter, shoulders dropping, eyebrows loosening. He looked bewildered. "How did you find out?"

There are false things in life— the hopes of an artist being one of the most common, but there are true things, too, made by human minds and hands. Art can be an assembly of technology and smell. I didn't say that. I said, "There are different forms of inspiration."

I made Mahesh tea—regular tea—because inspiration was never his problem.

ABOUT THE AUTHOR

Besides selling thirty-odd short stories, a dozen poems and
a few comics, Marie Vibbert has been a medieval (SCA) squire,
ridden 17 percent of the roller coasters in the United States and has
played O-line and D-line for the Cleveland Fusion women's tackle
football team.

BAD REPUTATION

Jordan Kurella and dave ring

Citadel Hotel, Earth Division
Written Warning and Performance Improvement Plan
Reason: Inappropriate dress, unprofessional behavior, insubordination

Mx. Clarity Kim was observed during multiple shifts wearing unapproved garments and/or accessories outside of scheduled breaks. Supervisor Lawrence has personally observed Mx. Kim using Citadel storage facilities for storage of their non-approved musical equipment.

Other supervisors have observed that Mx. Kim's outfits are often held together by safety pins, dated patches, and little else. More than a dozen comments have been made by guests about Mx. Kim's spiked collar and inappropriate footwear (jelly shoes, black and white athletic sneakers). Broadly, their attitude has been remarked upon three times in recent guest surveys:

"Slightly strange dress code? They looked like a BDSM cultist. It was a little distracting."

"I told them that I would be reporting them to their manager and they said, 'I don't give a damn about my bad reputation.' When I asked them to avoid vulgar language, they laughed."

"This employee's insistence on 21st century pronouns was tiresome."

From *TripReviewerStarGuide*, we have determined that the vandalism to the Citadel Tech Astral Viewing Port and theft of was likely Mx. Kim's doing: "Please pass on my compliments to Clarity who made me feel incredibly welcome during my stay. The after-hours access to the viewing deck, the strings they pulled with the kitchen, the way they shredded on that Gibson. Give them a raise!"

Mx. Kim has been instructed to adopt a less defensive attitude to supervisor feedback regarding their areas of growth. Citadel management fully believes that with commitment and a positive attitude that Mx. Kim can improve their attitude to the standards that Citadel expects Hotel, Earth Division janitorial and hotel workers to maintain.

Future instance of inappropriate dress, unprofessional behavior, and/or insubordination will result in further discipline, up to and including mandatory behavior conditioning or termination.

Please note that a signature acknowledges that you have been given this warning, not that you agree with the content therein.

Manager Name: Supervisor Lynn Thomas
Manager Signature: [signed]

Employee Name: Clarity Kim
Employee Signature: [unsigned]
Please note that Mx. Kim declined to sign this document.

Employee Comments:

First, you know what? Shove it. Shove. It.

U might have missed it, but it's the 24th century, and you can get over yourself Bling Thomas. Shoulder pads are so 22nd century, and seriously? Who the hell knows what a bee is anymore. Cut it out with the damn bee pendants. Ugh. I could "reprimand" yr antiquated boring-ass wardrobe all day, but you know what? I quit. No wait, I'm not done: yr way too skinny for pencil skirts. Give it a rest.

Consider this my two weeks. you won't have to see my safety-pinned, leather jacket, side-shaved ass anymore after that. My stellar work record is coming with me. Not one tardy, not one absence, and all of that? Poof. Gone. All yr damn on-time meticulous spreadsheets? Gone. you can kiss that goodbye because you find me and my "The Future Is Queer" backpatch distasteful.

Karma's a dick, isn't it? I want to do some good things for my crew at the Citadel in those two weeks, since paperwork is really a drag. And it won't get done in two weeks, you know? Cause, frankly, yr super slow. So my band, the Vulvenators, are gonna put on a free show in the hotel courtyard every night until, well, until my time is up.

Yeah ... I hope you like our music. We're pretty loud.

Oh yeah, hope you don't mind, but I contacted the press to come see us play. I love thinking about you cringing when you see the headlines: VULVENATORS AT CITADEL HEIGHTS. It's good publicity so ... probably don't wanna cancel. Not yet, anyway. Sorry that you couldn't get with the future, Bling Thomas. But the world is going away from bee brooches and shoulder pads and pencil skirts and instead becoming like me. Maybe if you ever came out of yr office and saw past a set of safety pins and green hair you'd see the work that I've done.

Ugh, I'm out ... Smell you later, Bling.

Mx Clarity Kim

PS: That memo you didn't want anyone to see about watering down the drinks and not using detergent in the laundry? The press got that too. Hope you don't mind!

XOXO

ABOUT THE AUTHORS

Jordan Kurella is a fiction author whose stories have been featured in *Beneath Ceaseless Skies, Apex Magazine,* and *Cotton Xenomorph.* She is bisexual and disabled from a straight flush of mental health disorders. She lives in Ohio with her husband and her service dog.

dave ring is the chair of the OutWrite LGBTQ Book Festival in Washington, D.C. and has stories in *Mythic Magazine, Speculative City* and *The Disconnect.* He is the editor of *Broken Metropolis: Queer Tales of a City That Never Was* from Mason Jar Press. More info at www.dave-ring. com. Follow him on Twitter at @slickhop.

DEEPSTER PUNKS

Maria Haskins

Surface

The animated tattoos on Jacob's skin glimmer in the dark water, words and images swarming over his skin, bright and luminous, before they fade away again.

"Don't you dare die on me." I'm holding his head above the waves, but his naked body is cold and slick and heavy in my grip. By now, I should be able to see the lights of the ocean platform, but there's nothing, only darkness above and below, no horizon separating them. I unseal the mask of my thermal suit so I can talk to him, even though I'm not sure he can even hear me anymore. "You're one lucky bastard, you know. If the Company had sent us anywhere else in the system and you pulled this kind of stunt, you'd be dead already."

It's true. Beneath the icy mantle of Ceres, in the 10K depths of Enceladus, he'd be dead for sure. In the sub-surface ocean of Ganymede, or in the tidal-flexing waters of Europa, he'd be dead-dead-dead. Dead like Petra. But he's here, on Earth, with me, and he's alive.

Stay alive, Jacob. *Please.*

Descent

It was a bad day to be waiting for a shuttle-pod on the ocean platform above Devil's Hole. Temps were just above freezing, the North Sea was heaving up ten-foot waves all around us, and the rain was coming down like sheets of steel. Even with the frenzied guitars of my favorite tunes blasting in my ears, it was less than ideal.

Of course, no day had felt particularly good since I got the news about Petra, and this day was made worse by Jacob who was flouting Company regulations by not wearing his gloves. I watched his blunt, calloused fingers clench and unclench while the tattoos slipped across his ruddy knuckles, inked creatures darting into his sleeves.

I'd known before I came here that he wouldn't be in the best place after what happened on Ceres, but we were both Company vets, and not wearing your full kit when going below was such a dumb-ass, rookie thing to do.

I touched my earlobe to turn down the music volume, interrupting the satisfying, jagged blast of "Sloppy Gods and Monsters" that was rattling through my skull, the latest release by Martian Rust out of Chryse Planitia.

"Get your gloves on, man. Last thing I need is you going geriatric on me and getting frostbite."

Jacob startled, and for a moment he seemed surprised to see me there, as if he'd forgotten where he was. But at least he dug his gloves out of his kit-bag and pulled them on, sealing the click-seams against the cold.

"Sorry," he said, and looked it.

I shrugged it off, turned up the music again, and thought of Petra. I thought of her a lot lately. Thought of her grinning and cranking up her playlist at the start of a shift, the music ripping through us as we worked. She always had the best tunes, raw and gritty stuff that would make your heart pound and your head spin, the kind of old-school shit hardly anyone played anymore. I thought of her laugh, raspy and warm, big enough to hold the world and everything in it.

"You might have sold your bodies to the Company, and you might let them ship you from sea to sea, but they won't really take care of you. No one cares about us deepster punks, except other deepster punks. That's why we have to look out for each other. On every world. On every station. On every shift."

Petra told us that in training, twenty-five years ago, and it had been my mantra ever since. Any loser could become a diver if they went through training, but becoming a deepster punk meant something more. It meant living on the edge of the precipice where no one else would be stupid enough to go. It meant working the utmost depths for the Company, surviving inside the system, finding fleeting moments of freedom and glory and togetherness in this goddamn profiteer's paradise of a solar system. It meant stripping your existence down to the bare necessities, traveling through life with nothing but your skin, your playlist, and your kit-bag. Sometimes it was hard living like that, but no matter what bullshit missions the Company had thrown my way, no matter how long the hours or how dangerous the site, no matter who I'd been teamed up with for a job, Petra's words had been my guiding light.

I used to think those words were Jacob's guiding light, too, but lately, I wasn't so sure.

The pod surfaced in the grey water below us—a bright yellow, almost spherical sub-vessel, stamped with the Company's logo in black. We climbed down the ladder, and as the hatch sealed above us, we descended into the North Sea, trading the lashing wind and waves of the surface for the familiar murky stillness beneath.

"You OK?"

Jacob nodded, and beneath the ginger stubble, his face was still the same stiff mask of calm normalcy he'd worn since we met on the mainland.

I probably wore the same mask myself. As if everything was OK. As if Petra wasn't dead. As if she hadn't drowned, impossibly and inexplicably, inside that station on Ceres. As if Jacob hadn't been the only one there with her.

Petra.

The pain sliced through me, so sharp and jagged I had to close my eyes. She'd been the best of us. Our mother-goddess, our patron saint of safety first, and now she was gone.

I slid my hand over the front of my thermal suit, feeling the reassuring presence of the stun baton hidden in the pocket on my thigh. It was small enough to fit in my hand, yet the charge could knock out a grown man according to the trader I'd bought it from at the bar in Narvik.

"Knock out, as in kill, or as in stun?" I'd asked while she pocketed her credits.

"Does it matter?"

No. What mattered was that it wouldn't be detected by the Company's security scanners.

Jacob was peering through the pod's single porthole. Layers of ocean drifted by, lit by occasional sparks of bioluminescence, gleams of life.

"Did you get to go home at all before you came here?" I asked. "Or did they send you straight from the debrief on Mars?"

He shrugged, as if it didn't matter. I guess it didn't, really. "Home" didn't mean a heck of a lot when you spent your life traveling from sea to sea, working your ass off in the deeps on Earth and elsewhere in the solar system. I'd bought an apartment in the Scandinavian sector a few years ago but it was agony to stay there for more than a couple of days, pretending I was enjoying my shore leave. Pretending I was home.

"Everything down there looks all right so far." Jacob projected his retina-readout between us—all the stats reaped from the station below us in Devil's Hole—water pressure, surface conditions, water temperature, ocean currents, station integrity and status.

"Looks that way," I said, even though nothing felt right. Jacob leaned back in the seat beside me and removed his gloves, working those fingers again like he had up on the platform. "What's wrong with your hands?"

He looked up.

"Nothing." He put the gloves on again. "Just a cramp or something. It comes and goes. Been bugging me since Ceres."

Ceres.

I thought of Jacob and Petra, working together on Ceres.

Goddamn Ceres.

Every deep-station was much the same once you were there, and none of them were exactly plush, but Ceres was one of the oldest builds in the Company's network of science outposts and resource extraction hubs. It was cramped, dark, cold, and working there was hard on your body and your psyche. Usually, the Company sent newbies there for short stints to make sure they knew what real deepster punk life was like. The idea was that after Ceres, every other Company facility would look pretty good. Why they'd sent two veterans like Petra and Jacob there together was beyond me.

I studied Jacob in the bleak light of the submersible. His face looked the same as it always had, just a few more wrinkles added to the dimples and cheekbones I'd fallen hard for when we were rookies together. And he still had that mess of short-cropped, reddish curls I'd pulled my fingers through a thousand times in bed and elsewhere. He *seemed* OK, but you never really knew what moved beneath the surface.

Deepsters snapped, everybody knew that. It wasn't unusual, really. Only, we were supposed to snap on our own time, with a bottle of home-brewed booze, the psychoactive substance of our choice, or occasionally, with a bullet or a noose. Not on the job.

I thought of Jacob's hands, opening and closing. Strong. Empty. How much force would you have to use to kill someone like Petra? How empty would you have to be to let them drown?

⧗   ⧗   ⧗

"Do you think it's sabotage, Becca?" Jacob asked when we stepped through the entry chamber from the shuttle, closing the pod's hatch behind us before the station hatch opened and we could enter.

That got my attention. Nothing else he'd said today had really sounded like him at all, but now he gave me a shrewd gaze, looking almost like the Jacob I'd known for so long.

I kept my voice deadpan.

"Sabotage? I thought this was a routine maintenance job?"

Jacob scoffed. "Right. Ten major incidents all over the solar system in two years. Fatal outcomes on Enceladus and Ceres." He paused, as if he expected me to say something, but I didn't. "And now it's suddenly all hands on deck for routine maintenance from the North Sea to Ganymede. Something's up."

"You think all those incidents were sabotage?"

"I think the Company *hopes* it's sabotage, because if it's something *they* did, some design flaw, they're in the crapper with governments *and* shareholders. Sabotage? They'll just nuke a few of us and be done with it." The look he gave me sharpened. "Or, they'll set us on each other and try to clean house that way. Right, Becca?"

I flushed, not so much from anger as from annoyance at my own lack of a convincing poker face.

He nodded as if I'd confirmed his suspicions. "They asked you to watch me, right? Told you I needed babysitting after Ceres. That's why you've been staring at me like I might go off the rails at any moment."

I looked away. "You know it's not like that," I mumbled, but of course it was. *Ride with him for one job, and report back*, that's what the suits had said. *You're his friend. We just want to make sure he's in a good place. Guilt and grief can make people do stupid things.*

I'd said yes, because in the end, the Company would always get its way.

"Don't worry, I won't hold it against you," Jacob said and kept walking, his voice so flat I couldn't tell if he meant it.

⧗ ⧗ ⧗

Usually, a two-person team would be taking turns on shift, but for this job, the Company had specifically requested we work together at all times. It was obviously another way to make sure we snitched on each other.

I stowed my gear in a locker, and when I got into the control room, Jacob was already there, standing by the view-window. It was dark outside of course, down there at the bottom of the Devil's Hole trench, except for a faint shimmer in the glass in front of him. A reflection, I thought, or something sliding across the surface outside.

"Jacob?"

Something about him, his stance, the outline of his body, felt wrong. Like maybe it wasn't Jacob at all, but someone else, someone I didn't know. Someone that should not be here. I shuddered. What the hell was going on with me? It was like I was a rookie again, seeing monsters at every turn.

Every deepster saw monsters. They were the imaginary creatures your brain stitched together from stray shadows, random movements, moments of oxygen deprivation, and bits of structural noise. It happened more frequently when you first started out, but no one was immune. And if you weren't careful, if your brain convinced you to believe in the monsters, you could end up doing harm to yourself and others.

I'd seen my share of monsters beneath the seas on Earth and elsewhere, but this felt different. This felt *real*. I slipped my fingers into the pocket, felt the smooth, hard surface of the zapper, the small indentation at one end that would activate the current.

"Becca?"

Jacob turned, and I saw his face in profile. The way the dim lights hit the angles of his nose and cheeks made me realize how hollow and spent he looked. Not a monster. Just Jacob, my friend, my on-and-off lover, my co-worker, and whatever else he'd been to me through the years. Good old Jacob, Mr. Easy-going, the guy everyone wanted to work with, and not just because he was good in the sack. The guy who brought the beer, no matter what planetary body you were working on, and made sure you drank it cold.

"You all right?" I asked and switched on the exterior lights.

There was nothing unusual outside, only a section of the Devil's Hole extraction area, much the same as the Company's setup no matter where you went in the solar system: delivery tubes snaking through the sediment; the bots crawling everywhere, flat and multi-limbed like metallic crabs, helping the larger bots farther out extract and transport the ore and minerals that would eventually be ferried to the mainland by the Company's delivery vessels.

"Yeah. I'm just tired. The debrief after Ceres was . . . rough."

I wanted to ask about that, should have asked, but we were on the clock. Instead of talking, I hooked my playlist up to the station's sound system and cranked up the music while we busied ourselves with the inspection, checking hardware, software, wiring, safety systems. Nothing we found was out of the ordinary, and just working together set my mind at ease. I fell into the routine of it, the easy muscle memory of companionship, that comfortable ability to work together without talking.

While I worked, I thought about what Jacob had said, about ten incidents in two years. I knew there had been an increase in accident stats, but had it really been that many? I set the intranet to do a rundown for me on my retina-screen, and he was right. It was all there, incidents strung out all over the system. Always water breaching the station. Usually moderate to severe injuries, but fatalities on Enceladus and Ceres.

A sliver of unease slipped in beneath my skin.

Petra had been the team lead on Enceladus. Petra had died on Ceres.

No. I shook off the chill. Jacob was right. The Company was probably trying to pin this on sabotage because if it was material fatigue or construction error, their bottom line would be in trouble.

⧗   ⧗   ⧗

After a few hours, we took a break for a classic deepster punk dinner, also known as hot tea and cold calorie bars. Jacob still brewed the best tea in the fleet, brought his own stash to make it, so at least that hadn't changed. And at the end of the meal, we ended up comparing new tats, because it's not a real deepster punk get-together unless there's an ink show 'n' shine.

I showed him the school of dolphins I got on my back, tails flipping as they jumped over my shoulder into my bra, slipping down between my breasts. Jacob didn't say anything, but I knew that look, and when I zipped up, it lingered.

He hummed and hawed before stripping, as if he wasn't dying to show off, and sparring with him almost felt like old times. Finally, he acquiesced and unzipped the top of his suit, pale skin prickling in the chill station air.

Even at forty-plus, Jacob was still cut enough to make me ache, and animated tats writhed on every inch of his exposed skin—jellies, squids, sharks, narwhals, other real and imaginary sea creatures I hardly even recognized undulating across his arms and torso. Every image was aglow with bioluminescent ink—blue, green, red, shimmering black. A large Pacific octopus, rendered in hyper-realistic detail, swam around his midriff, and when I touched it, the creature twitched away, tentacles sliding around his waist.

My hand lingered in its wake, the music throbbing through me like a second pulse and I knew he felt it too. After all, how many times had we listened to this track together, "Blood Feud" by The Rowdies pumping through us, whether we were clothed or naked, fucking or not. In this life, there were some days, some nights, when the music and another body were the only things that kept you alive, that reminded you of why you kept going at all.

"What did that octopus cost you? It's gorgeous."

"Three months wages and a bit. All handworked by a lady on Mars, no ink-bots." He waved away my frown at his extravagance. "What else do we spend our money on? We've got no homes, no kids, no pets. The Company owns everything we are and everything we think is ours. All we have are these damn bodies. Might as well blow our credits on that."

"Bitter?"

"Hell no. Wouldn't choose any other life even if I could. You know that."

"Not even now?"

My hand still lingered on his hip and he didn't move away.

"Not a chance."

⧗   ⧗   ⧗

Every station had at least two bunkrooms, always a relief on longer missions with people you didn't know or didn't like, but Jacob and I had shared rooms and beds since we were in training. I'd thought about using the second room this time, but I didn't.

At shift's end, in our shared bunkroom with the music playing between us, all rib-rattling guitars and drums, I watched Jacob undress. Then, he watched me.

The mutual titillation of that game between us was different now when we were getting close to fifty than it had been when we were in our twenties, but I still liked the way he looked at me, the way his gaze moved slowly over that aging body of mine. It was still a good body, strong and tall and pain-resistant, though whatever firm curves it had once held had been blunted by the years.

"Looking good, Becca."

"Not half bad yourself."

"I missed you," he said, tattoos slipping ever faster across his skin.

I knew he wanted to pull me down on the floor or on that narrow bunk with him. Part of me wanted it too. Badly. But instead, I sat down on my bunk, turned off the music, wrapped the sleeping bag around me and made sure the thermal suit was folded up nearby, the zapper within easy reach if I needed it.

"Jacob. Tell me what really happened on Ceres."

He winced. I watched his face, but most of all I watched his hands. He had moved them to his sides, fingers clenching, unclenching.

"I talked about it enough with the shrinks."

"I don't care what you told them. You're my friend. Petra was my friend."

Friend. How small and incomplete that word felt to describe Petra or Jacob.

"What do you want to know?"

The tattoos swirled over his skin, not as fast as before, but still animated, even though his face looked calm.

"Did you kill her?"

I almost thought he'd hit me for that.

"Is that what you think?"

"Or did you just let her die? Because there is no way Petra would have just drowned inside a station like that."

"It's more likely I killed her? Is that it? Is that why you brought that zapper?" He leaned over, grabbed my suit and threw it on the floor. "You think I didn't notice? Why don't you just take it out and fry me right now."

All the grief and anger I'd tucked away inside reared up at him.

"I brought it because I have no idea what the hell is going on. You didn't contact me after Petra died. I had to get it all from the Company. And now, you're talking about sabotage. Maybe there are people in this Company that want to sink it and don't give a shit how they do it. Maybe you're one of them. I don't know. That's why I'm here, that's why I brought the zapper. That's why I agreed to babysit you."

Jacob closed his eyes. His hands had stopped moving, and all the tattoos had gone still, glowing but slowly fading. In the low light of the bunkroom, I imagined I saw movement on his skin anyway, as if a shadow passed beneath the ink as it faded.

When he started talking, his voice had a hollow ring to it.

"They did it to me, too, Becca. That's why I was on Ceres with Petra. They told me to watch her. Told me to report back, let them know how she was doing. Told me they were worried about her after that installation on Enceladus went to shit. Babysit her on this one job, they said. We don't know if she's in a good place or not. You're her friend. Look out for her." He opened his eyes. Blue. Clear. Full of tears. "The joke is, I was going to tell them she was fine."

The fire inside me guttered out.

"Why would they think Petra was a problem?"

"Because she was the one running the show on Enceladus. They handpicked her for that brand new installation, a new world, all that glory, and in the end, her whole team almost died." He was quiet for a bit. "After Ceres, I looked at the accident statistics, like I told you. Managed to wrangle some docs from the Company data-pit. In every incident the last two years, at least one of the people present had been at the accident on Enceladus."

My limbs felt numb.

"What does that mean? What happened there?"

"Petra doesn't ... didn't know. She couldn't tell me everything because a lot is covered by the Company's non-disclosure, but the last thing she remembered clearly was drilling down into the sediments. Next thing she knew, she woke up in the medivac drone. But something was off on that mission. There was a new guy on it, fresh out of training. He was the one who died. Petra said he freaked out when they did a dive near the initial drill site. He said he saw a monster, thought his suit had ripped, and he almost took down two others before they could sedate him. They checked him over, suit and all, and of course everything was fine, but after that, things got hairy. You know how Petra was. She made you think she was invincible, but Enceladus ... that place got under her skin. Talking about it with me, she seemed rattled. Told me she saw monsters *everywhere*. That everyone did. Even on Ceres she ... "

His voice faded.

"She saw them on Ceres, too?"

"Once. I think she was spooked and shattered by that rookie dying on her watch. You know how she was. Take care of each other, you know, her gospel. She felt she failed."

A thought skittered by in my head, out of sight. Something I couldn't grab hold of.

"Ok. Enceladus went to hell. Next, they send her to Ceres with you. What happened there?"

"Like I said, I thought she was pretty much fine." His voice changed, became clipped and serious, the way he'd probably laid it out for the Company psychs, over and over and over again in the debrief. "She was on shift. I was on sleep cycle. Logs show she went into the shuttle-pod chamber without her suit and somehow managed to cripple or disengage the pod, causing a leak. She was in the transit-chamber between the station and the pod when the water rushed in. The station hatch was sealed, and I couldn't open it until I had sealed the exterior hatch and pumped out the water. It took too long. By the time I got to her, she told me to take her home, and then she died."

That unsettled skittering of something I ought to understand got worse.

"She *talked* to you? How long had she been in the water?"

He laughed, a sharp sound.

"You sound like the psychs, Becca. They told me she couldn't have said anything. That I imagined it. It's true I blacked out at some point. I can't even remember most of what happened before the evac-bots extracted us. The debrief team told me she must have been dead when I got to her, that she couldn't have said anything. But she did. 'Take me home.' That's what she said. And then she was gone."

Surface

The sea heaves around us, too cold, too deep, too vast. My suit is keeping us afloat, but Jacob is fading. Maybe he's already dead. The abyss is pressed up against me, heavy and cold.

We have nothing but our bodies, Jacob told me, but here, at the end, he doesn't even have that. Even that has been taken away from him.

Teeth chattering, I call his name, and then I sing him snippets of every song from my playlist I can think of, hoping the sound of my voice will keep him here, that it will remind him of who he is, who we are, and why he has to stay with me.

I think of Petra, our glorious deepster punk mama, telling us to take care of each other.

I tried, Petra, just like you tried. But it wasn't enough.

That's when I see the light. The platform. And taking flight from it, three rescue bots, roaming across the waves toward us.

Ascent

When I woke up in my bunk, Jacob was gone, his sleeping bag tangled as if he'd fought his way out of it. His thermal suit still on the hanger. I knocked on the door of the hygiene stall, hoping.

"Jacob?"

No.

I knew it, then. Knew what it was, the feeling that had skittered around my mind since we got here. I knew with absolute certainty that something or someone was on the station with us. But was it just a monster, stitched together from my grief and anger, or was it real?

Heart pounding against my ribs, I put on my suit and followed the narrow hallway toward the shuttle-pod hatch, checking the small rooms as I went past. Part of me already knew where he was, but I kept hoping I'd find him on the way.

Again and again I called his name, but all I could hear was the hum of the station, and eventually, a muted alarm.

Jacob was in the transit chamber, between the station and the shuttle-pod. Lights were flashing everywhere, wiring hung loose from a panel on the wall, as if he'd tried to disengage the shuttle-pod to let the water in. He hadn't succeeded, yet, but I wasn't sure we'd be able to get back to the surface in the pod anymore.

He stood there, naked, just like Petra had been, just like the guy they'd found dead on Enceladus, and none of his tattoos moved or even glowed. All his ink was dull and dead.

I pulled the inner hatch open and the sound from the alarm went from mute to an ear-shattering mayhem.

"Jacob. Don't."

His hand trembled on the panel beside the shuttle-pod. If he dislodged the seal now, with the inner hatch open, the station would flood, the pod would flood, and we'd be dead.

I stepped inside and sealed the hatch behind me.

He turned slowly, like he was surfacing from some place deep and mute, and in my head all the pieces were fitting together into a new kind of monster. The string of accidents after Enceladus. Always someone from Enceladus present. Except here. Here, it was just me and Jacob. Jacob, who had been on Ceres with Petra. Jacob, who was the only one with her when she died.

The accidents had been moving through the system. *Something* had been moving through the system, from one deepster station to another. Enceladus to Europa, Europa to Ganymede, and so on. Eventually to Ceres. Eventually here. Moving through us. Inside us. Inside other crew members. Inside Petra. Inside Jacob.

Jacob looked at me, but something else was staring out through his eyes.

"Take me home."

The voice was Jacob's, but I knew it wasn't him speaking. Just like it hadn't been Petra speaking to him on Ceres, because she'd already been dead.

Home. There was a yawning pit of despair and loneliness lurking beneath that word. The deep, dark waters of the North Sea were so very far from the depths of Enceladus—the abyss of outer space separating them. Separating whatever creature had entered a human body there, stowing away through us, through space, trying to find its way back to the ocean where it belonged.

"We'll find another way." I reached out for Jacob, hoping he was still there. "Whatever you want. Whatever you need."

In an instant, Jacob's tattoos flared to life, all of them glowing brighter than I'd ever seen before. At the same time, Jacob rushed me and knocked me down on the hard metal floor of the chamber. I scrambled to get up, but he was already at the broken panel, trying to activate the switch to blow the shuttle-pod, to let the darkness in. Or maybe, to let it out.

There was no time for finesse or subterfuge. I got to my feet, grabbed the stun-zapper in my pocket, trying to find the button, trying to turn it the right way around so I wouldn't knock myself out.

I yanked on Jacob's shoulder with one hand to pull him away from the panel, and with the other, I jammed the stun-zapper into the small of his back. He fell. Spasms. Screaming. The tattoos on fire, blazing, burning, until he passed out on the floor beside me. Looking down at him I saw a shadow moving underneath his skin, rippling past, diving deeper into muscle and bone to hide itself again.

Shaking, I opened the hatch to the shuttle-pod, and dragged Jacob's heavy, limp body inside. After I'd made sure that the pod was sealed, I hit the emergency evac button.

Surface

I can still see the busted shuttle-pod drifting in the swell, rolling over heavily, half-full of seawater. At least it got us to the surface safely. At least we won't get the bends. At least the hatch didn't fail until we were up here. At least I got Jacob out before it started filling with water.

I keep my eyes fixed on the lights on the platform, on the rescue bots closing in, hoping they will get to us in time, but Jacob is so heavy. Even with the built-in floatation in my suit, I have a hard time keeping him above the waves, and I don't know how much water he swallowed since we left the pod. I keep singing, wishing I could blast the music into the night: staccato drums to make his heart beat, ragged guitars and vocals to make him breathe.

His body spasms again, just like it did below, and, the tattoos come alive—writhing, luminescent. There it is again. Beneath the ink, the shadow moves as if it's trying to break out of his skin from the inside. I see it move over his chest and throat and then—a shadow, a mist, a ghost of a shape—twitches loose from his flesh and bursts out of his wide-open mouth. For a moment, I almost see it clearly—undulating, shifting—then Jacob shudders and the shadow dives below us and is gone.

The whirring rescue bots are right above us, and I hold on to Jacob, shouting out his name above the noise, shouting that I love him, that he can't die on me.

Jacob said we don't have a home. But we do. Petra knew it. That's what she tried to tell us. She understood it long before I did. Space is cold as hell, and the oceans are deep and dark and full of monsters, real and imaginary. But we have a home. Home is right here. Home is you and me, together. Home is us, two old deepster punks, clinging to each other in the darkness and the cold, keeping each other alive. That's all the home I've ever had. That's all the home I'll ever want. All the home I'll ever need.

When the bots lift us out of the water with their retractable limbs, Jacob's tattoos shimmer to life, bioluminescent ink lighting up his body and his face. I curl up beside him in the rescue cradle, listening to the simple rhythm of his life-signs pinging through the CPR-bot, his chest shuddering with breath again. Looking down into the water, I see something in the waves, below the surface, or maybe skimming the waves—a gleaming shape of light, wrapped in darkness. For a moment it's there, then it's gone, and I can't tell whether it dives into the darkness below, or whether it takes flight into the darkness above us, headed for home.

ABOUT THE AUTHOR

Maria Haskins is a Swedish-Canadian writer and translator. She writes speculative fiction and debuted as a writer in Sweden in the 1980s. Since 2012, she also runs a music website at realrockandroll. wordpress.com. Currently, she lives just outside Vancouver with a husband, two kids, and a very large black dog. Her work has appeared in *Beneath Ceaseless Skies, Aliterate, Shimmer, Escape Pod*, and elsewhere. Find out more on her website, mariahaskins.com, or follow her on Twitter, @mariahaskins.

From *Cyber World: Tales of Humanity's Tomorrow* anthology, 2016

A SONG TRANSMUTED

Sarah Pinsker

Six Months

I was a fussy baby. The only thing that quieted me was my great-grandfather's piano. They placed my bassinet directly on the piano, with noise-cancelling headphones to keep from damaging my ears. His chords came up through the instrument, up through my bones. "That child is full of music, I'm telling you," he told anyone who listened.

Five Years

If my family couldn't find me, they looked under the piano. I'd curl up there and listen to the space.

My great-grandfather held me over the piano's edge, let me lift the hammers and strum the strings. "The piano is a percussion instrument, Katja. Percussion and strings at once. It can be the whole band."

"Again," I'd say, and he'd pick me up again. "I want to be the piano."

"You want to be in the piano?"

He understood me better than anyone, but even he never understood.

Eight Years

I'd go with him to synagogue on Saturday mornings and holidays.

On the walk to and from, he told stories. My favorite was about a child in the old country who had never been taught to read. "In order to have a good year you have to go to synagogue and pray on Yom Kippur," people told the child. The child followed them to synagogue. She didn't know the prayers they sang but she wanted a good year, so she lifted her flute to her lips.

The congregants grew outraged. "Quiet! It's forbidden to play an instrument on Yom Kippur!"

"No, it's you all who should be quiet," said the rabbi. "Her heart-felt notes are more pleasing to God than prayers spoken without any feeling behind them. God turns her song into prayer."

"I'm like her," I told Pop.

He raised his eyebrows. "You know how to read."

I didn't know how to explain what I meant: that all my thoughts came out as music, that music said more than words.

Fifteen Years

"Play it for me again." Pop put his hands up to the monitor head-phones, cupping them closer.

I started the piece over and he closed his eyes, his head nodding with the beat. It wasn't the first thing I'd written, but it was the first I'd been confident enough to play for him. I sat across from him chewing my thumb.

"The drums," he said when it ended. "They aren't real drums?"

"I programmed them myself. Built the synthesizer, too."

"Ach, that's my girl. Computers and music and skill and talent and hard work. That's my girl. What about the piano?"

"I designed that patch too." I let the pride seep out, just a bit.

"Amazing. It sounds almost real."

"Almost?"

"The keys need a little more weight. The notes need weight. But the piece itself is magnificent. Good composition, good arrangement. Have you ever thought about playing your songs with other musicians instead of doing all the parts yourself on a computer?"

"Where do you find other musicians?"

He put his head in his hands. "What a time we live in. You go to school in a cloud and you meet your friends in a cloud and you make such beautiful music but you've never met another musician."

I didn't know what he meant. "It's okay, Pop. You don't have to meet people in person to be friends with them. And I know you, so I've met another musician."

He shook his head. "Come with me."

We put down our headphones and I followed him down the hall. He sat down at his piano, motioned for me to sit down next to him. We hadn't sat together that way for a few years; the bench felt smaller than I remembered.

He started playing a simple bass line with his left hand. I tried to stop the part of my brain that kept analyzing the rates of attack and decay, translating piano into programming.

"Play over it," he said.

I listened for a moment, then started to pick out a melody, adding chords for color, arpeggiating and inverting them as I grew more confident. We were playing in D. I liked D; D always resonated in my bones.

"That's music," he said without stopping. "That's friendship and music and love and sex. Don't giggle, I can say the word, I'm old, not dead. One person can make music too, but it's better when it's a conversation. Between you and another musician, or between you and an audience."

I hit a wrong note then. He gave me a funny look, then incorporated my wrong note into his bass line, sliding past it and making it part of the song.

Sixteen Years

Pop was always right. I met Corrina when we were paired together in bio lab. The only other person in class from the same city, and we wound up being paired together. I don't remember how we realized we both played music. Once we figured it out, it didn't take too much convincing to get her over to my house with her violin. My house because she hadn't even seen a real piano before.

We didn't have any songs in common, or even a genre, so we invented our own. I'm not sure they were any good, but they were us, and us had never happened before. I liked the way the sound filled the room, the way it became something more than both of us. Bodies and music, fingers and hands, we drew each other out.

Eighteen Years

At the age of ninety, my great-grandfather got his second tattoo. A piano keyboard, a single octave, the black keys obscuring the numbers that had been inked into his arm when he was a little boy.

I took him to the tattoo parlor.

"I thought Jews weren't supposed to get tattoos," I said to him.

He said, "If I didn't have any choice the first time, I don't see why I shouldn't get to replace it with something I won't mind looking at."

Whenever I caught him looking at it, I thought of his stories, of the little girl with the flute and the way her offering transformed.

Twenty Years

Pop died playing piano.

"It's a shame he died alone," a great-aunt said to me at the house after the funeral.

"He didn't." I knew it was true. "If he was in the middle of a song he wouldn't have said he was alone."

I walked over to the piano bench, sat down. His sheet music stood open to the page he'd been playing. I rested my fingers on the keys in the same places his fingers had rested last. Looked at the page, a song called "Don't Fence Me In." After the first few hesitant bars, I recognized it as a song he had played when I was a kid, and I picked up the tempo a little.

"You play so well, Katja," said another great-aunt. "Why didn't you stay in conservatory?"

"I don't know, Aunt Bianka. I guess I got bored."

I had gotten bored, it was true. Bored of playing and studying in nonexistent spaces, hundreds of miles from my classmates. And then I was booted, but I never knew which relatives had been told. My parents were still angry.

Pop had been more philosophical. "You don't need a school to tell you you're a musician. You've got music coming out your ears."

I wanted his piano, but I had no room for it. I shared a house in the city with six others, writing earworms for online ads. The piano went to Great Aunt Bianka's, though nobody there knew how to play. I considered getting a tattoo like his, but it wasn't quite the memorial I wanted.

I tried composing something for him, but nothing came. What I wanted to write was there inside me, somewhere just beneath my skin. The music I made didn't say what I wanted it to say. He was right, all those years ago. It didn't have enough weight, but nothing I did fixed it.

Twenty-One Years

It took me six months to come up with the idea. The night it hit me, I couldn't go to sleep until I had figured out the logistics.

I stumbled down the stairs at four in the morning, triumphant, over-caffeinated, looking for someone to share with. I'd rather it had been Lexa or Javier, but Lexa had recently papered her windows and started working nights, and Javi was in bed already. Kurt sat at the table, a chipped yellow mug of black coffee in his hands, a notebook on the table. He was the only other musician living in the house, and we often ran into each other in the kitchen in the middle of the night, when everyone else was asleep. Once I had made it clear I wasn't interested in fucking him, we had settled into a friendship of sorts. I didn't like him very much, despite our commonalities.

"What are you working on?" I asked, even though I knew.

He flipped the notebook shut. "What do you think?"

"I think it's hilarious you're working on a concept album called the Great Upload but you write on dead tree paper. What I probably should have asked was 'how's it going'?"

"It's going okay song-wise. There's still something missing in the actual arrangements, though. I go to record them and they sound flat. Are you still willing to put down some piano parts for me sometime?"

"Sure," I said. "Say when."

I poured myself some cereal and sat down in a chair opposite him.

"You're welcome. Now it's your turn to ask me what I'm working on," I prompted him after a couple of minutes of crunching.

He looked up again, looking slightly put out. "Hey, Katja, what are you working on?"

"I'm glad you asked. As a matter of fact, tonight I figured out my first tattoo."

He still didn't look all that interested, but I motioned him to pull up his hoodie, and I did the same, sending him a snapshot of what I'd been working on. He sat silent for a long minute.

"It's playable?" he asked at last, dropping the hoodie.

I nodded. "Thirteen notes, thirteen triggers, thirteen sensors under the skin of my left forearm, plus a transmitter. After the incisions heal, I'll have the keyboard tattooed over it. I just need to find someone willing to do the work, and save up to pay for it."

"That's an awesome idea, K."

We spent a few minutes chatting about tattoo artists and body mod shops. Eventually the adrenaline that had kept me going all night started to ebb, and I headed back up to my room.

It took me three more months to save the money to get the implants done, three months I spent writing commercial jingles on commission and searching for the right person to do the work. At night, in bed, I'd spread the fingers of my right hand and lay them over my left arm. I gave it muscle, weight. Imagined wrenching songs from myself, first for my great-grandfather, who had always known I was full of music. It felt so right.

Kurt hadn't been around the house much lately, but he'd left a poster on the fridge with a note asking us all to come to a test show for his Great Upload song cycle.

"Don't make me go alone, Katja," Javi had pleaded, and I had agreed.

The club was a few blocks from our place, a rowhouse basement turned illegal performance space. I'd played there a few times sitting in with various bands. It smelled like cat piss, looked like a place time had forgotten, but sounded decent enough.

Kurt had a crowd, though there was no way of knowing whether they were there for him or another band. He had billed himself as "KurtZ and the Hearts of Darkness," the Hearts of Darkness being a drummer and a guitarist. A second amp's red eye glowed from a dark corner; a guest musician's for later in the set, maybe.

He looked nervous, buttoned up. He wore a three-piece suit, and his hair was plastered to his face before the first song. The songs were okay, nothing special. They sounded a little unanchored without bass. He had his eyes closed like he was reading the lyrics off his own eyelids.

By the third song I had stopped paying attention to the stage, so it was my ears that picked up the difference. The third song felt rooted in a way the previous two hadn't. I looked up to see who was playing the bass part, but there were only the three of them, and Kurt didn't have an instrument in his hands.

Except he did. I saw it then. He'd taken off his jacket and pushed his sleeves up and I saw it. My tattoo, my trigger system. He was playing his arm. People were eating it up, too, whispering, pointing. That wasn't what I had wanted it for; it wasn't meant to be a gimmick. I didn't stay to see the rest.

⧗ ⧗ ⧗

"You should be happy, Katja!"

It was three a.m. and I had waited up like a pissed-off parent, chewing on my own thumb and thinking of all the things I'd say to him.

He burst into the house drunk and giddy, bouncing right off my attempts to shame him. "Everybody loved it. It's awesome. I'm already thinking of getting a guitar put somewhere too."

"It was my idea, Kurt. My design. You had no right."

"Where's the harm? You should be thanking me. I tested it for you. Imagine how heartbroken you would have been if you'd spent all your money on it and it hadn't worked."

"But why?"

"Why?" He looked confused.

I tried to tell him, but nothing breached his mood or his self-righteousness. And what could I do? I'd shown him the design. I hadn't patented it or copyrighted it or whatever you did with inventions. Seething was my only option, so I seethed. I lay in bed furious with myself, tired and hurt but mostly furious. We all knew what Kurt was like. I should have known better.

At some point in the long night, a calmer voice took over my head. My grandfather, calm and philosophical, like when Corrina had moved away. "You can't help what other people do, Katja. Learn from the experience and decide what you're going to do next."

What had I learned? Not to trust Kurt Zell. What else? How did it sound? The song had needed bass, and the tattoo-keyboard had fit that spot well. The tone was decent but not great; I could have done better. A single octave would have worked as a tribute to my grandfather's tattoo, but it was limited as an actual instrument. Maybe multiple octaves would be better, but I'd still be stuck playing with one hand if I placed it on the opposite forearm. It was like a logic puzzle. I lay awake poking at it until the pieces came together.

Kurt was right: I should be thanking him, though I wouldn't give him that satisfaction. I'd been thinking within the lines. If he hadn't stolen my idea, I wouldn't have had a better one.

Twenty-Four Years

Saving for my second plan took longer. I bided my time, testing designs on a model, not sharing them with anyone except the body-mod artist who did the implants.

The same club Kurt had played opened their doors to me. I called the project "Weight," left a note telling my roommates to come, told Kurt he owed me and he ought to show up.

I'd borrowed a bassist and a drummer. They were comfortable with the structure I'd given them. I let them start the first song, set the receiver to interpret everything within the key of D, and hit the stage.

Four to the floor, anchored, insistent, a beat that made people want to move. Everybody was watching me. I touched a spot on my left forearm, a nondescript spot, no tattoo to mark it. A note rang out, clear and pure, interpreted into key by the receiver on my amp. Then I twitched my right wrist, and the gyro beneath the skin took the note and spun it. I played a few more, shaping a melody. Pressed the spot that locked the notes in as a sample, sent them to the receiver to repeat over and over.

I wore a tank top and shorts, so everything I did was evident. Kurt's keyboard—it had almost been my keyboard—was so limited. I slammed my palms into my skin, leaving pink spots, leaving musical trails. My hands were hammers hitting strings. The notes were hidden everywhere. There was no map anyone else could see. I was the instrument and the chord and the notes that composed it. A song transposed to body.

When I stepped off the stage into the audience, I had to show them how to touch me. They were gentle, much gentler than I had been, at least at first. Hands pressed into my arms, my shoulders, my thighs. Everywhere they touched, my skin responded. It sent signals to the receiver, to the synth, to the amp, and the sounds were broadcast over the PA. I'd set it to translate this first song into a single key, so the notes built into chords, then broke apart. I had ways to distort, to sustain, to make a note tremble as if it were bowed. It was me: I was playing me; they were playing me. I was the instrument, the conduit, the transmutation of loss into elegy, song into prayer, my own prayers into notes, notes into song. Body and music, fingers and hands, they drew me out.

ABOUT THE AUTHOR

Sarah Pinsker is a science fiction and fantasy author whose stories have appeared in publications such as *Asimov's Science Fiction, Strange Horizons, Fantasy & Science Fiction, Uncanny,* and *Lightspeed,* along with multiple "year's best" collections. A six-time finalist for the Nebula Award and two-time Hugo finalist, Pinsker won the 2016 Nebula Award for Best Novelette. Her fiction has also won the Theodore Sturgeon Memorial Award and been on the shortlist for the Tiptree Award. Pinsker's first collection, *Sooner or Later Everything Falls into the Sea* (Small Beer Press), and her debut novel, *A Song for a New Day* (Berkley), were both published in 2019.

DANCE OF THE TINBOOT FAIRY

Charles Payseur

Here are the things they say about me:
That I'm hoity as blue skies and fresh rain without a touch of acid.

That I'm in bed with a politico, or some intel chief—that I'm a spy in the movement, that I'm down on my knees for every nooseman that passes by.

That my brother was a killer, stone and sickle, and died kicking in the head of some hapless revolutionary. That he deserved the gutshot terror of death. That he was a tinboot, a traitor, and I must be, too.

That I can dance like heartbreak on the thin strands of memory, fragile as snow or ash or whatever was falling on the day the Last Great War ended.

At least one of those things is true. And, so as we're clear, let me add a few other true things, not necessarily about me:

The only way into or out of Big Dive, the lowliest borough of the city and also the most aflame with mals and revos and hot death, is the zip lines.

The only way to travel the lines is with a special boot, metal and loaded with tech I don't really understand, that are given only to law enforcement, what we call tinboots.

The powers that be have been shipping in tinboots from all over the city, rank and file of crisp buzz cuts, ever since the Troubles started, and if the surge doesn't stop, our movement is bound for snuffing beneath heavy metal Order.

I am loaded next to death with explosives, a song, and a dead man's boots. My brother's boots.

⧗ ⧗ ⧗

The Explosives:

Non hands them to me in a canvas bag and I nearly topple from the weight of them, the promise of white hot fragging chaos. I've always been wire thin and leggy and just feeling the heft of expectations sends my lunch, what there was of it, burbling into my throat. I swallow it back down.

"The bag also generates a limited blur field," ne says. "Should give you some protection from the bullets."

I nod. It's been four weeks since the start of the Troubles, when a glitch hit the tinboots of Big Dive hard and fast and led to the walkouts, the riots, and the boiling over of years of anger and wrongs layered on wrongs. Ever since the end of the Last Great War, which we lost soundly, the politicos have been looking for ways to balk on the humanitarian requirements of the treaty. Things like making sure the poor who were ground up as meat for the war engine get food and housing and something like an education. Pouring money into Big Dive, of course, the politicos hate.

"Why me?" I ask, because right then I can't figure. I'm just some half-hoity dancer who tried to climb out of Big Dive and came tumbling down when the Troubles rocked all my dreams to dust and blood.

Non's streaked with ash and doesn't look like ne's slept since what we might as well call the revolution kicked off. Four weeks and already something like a legend, though no older than my sixteen years. Nir face is lined with fresh cuts and a burn or two, but still ne smiles at me.

"I saw you dance once," ne says. "I was lifting cred cards from this hall half full of politico stooges and their arm ornaments and there you were, like something out of a dream. I don't think I'd seen a person bend like that, arms legs body all moving in different directions at once. I think I discovered five new kinds of sex fantasy right then."

I blush, deep crimson clashing with the oversized white and black uniform. My brother's uniform.

"The zip lines move fast and loose and there's no second trying on this one," ne continues. "Some of the exchanges we've mapped got margins no thicker than your sleek hips. If there's one who can dance this through in one pass, it's you."

I look into nir eyes and I can't tell if all the glory is just smoke where the dim lights don't shine, but I can't help but puff up a bit. I nod.

⧗   ⧗   ⧗

The Boots:

Thing is, my brother was always protecting me. Quick with a fist when those petty cruelties crossed into dangerous, and he never cared that all I wanted was to dance. Didn't care when he caught me with his best friend, either, though he did give us lectures about protection and maybe not using the public corridors. Even then, he had a vision of himself as the last good tinboot, standing between the politicos and the people and full of the words protect and serve.

They say that he died the first day of the Troubles, standing between a few of his fellows and a family of four trying to flee their riot. When the system crashed and the Tinboots realized all their privilege and corruption had just been eaten by the computers, they took to the streets. And my brother had learned that the old coin was always currency: the only *good* tinboot is a dead one. The rest are bad as bloodworms.

Still they had enough shame to deliver his body home with a tall tale about him gunned down by lowlies. Didn't care that his body was riddled with government issue. Just dumped him and left. And, standing at the door as dad bawled and mother swore, all I could see were those shining metal boots.

⧗   ⧗   ⧗

The Song:

Play is me stepping out into air, nothing between me and the dark below but the glittering zip lines. Play is a riot of music, my first com-position. Call it "Troubles." Call it "Dance of the Tinboot Fairy." I dance into the space between us and them, between Big Dive and all that wants us dead and gone. I leave bombs like breadcrumbs in my wake.

The song is a punk beat and anger and the shattering of a dream. A dream of dancing out of Big Dive and into money and safety. Because money's only as good as the system that robs it from the lowly, and safety is an illusion that's already cost me dear. The song is a scream over classical harmony, electric sheep screeching over oboe and cello. Its tempo is my gleaming feet skipping the lines, my hands planting the promise of fire and noise.

It takes them a moment to realize the game, to swarm out onto the lines like malware through an unsecured connection. The song shifts and my dance gets faster, more kinetic as I dash over fragile bridges and breaks, through maintenance works that wrap me close as a lover going a hundred kph. Bullets fly but I am a blur, an idea, intan-gible but where my boots flit on the air.

I dance, the song reverb and echo in and out of me for this last performance, bouncing up and away into the city beyond. Still I wish I had a better audience.

Here are the things they say about me now:

That when the lights blew on the zip lines, and all those bombs sent a hundred tinboots flailing down into the final night, I went with them, dead and gone and still half hoity but maybe not so vile after all.

That I was only ever a rumor, a good story, a tall tale to win over those half hoity masses still half hoping to see the Troubles put down and Order restored. It was a gang of fifty cold terrors that cut the zip lines into the dark, though how they managed it is being kept from the public.

That I survived, came through the other side of the lines and disappeared, the Tinboot Fairy having since been seen at a dozen other actions across the upper levels, connected to a network of resistance that goes far beyond Big Dive.

That if you close your eyes you can see a shadow moving against the dark and it's dancing dancing dancing up toward the blue blue sky, and it's wearing metal boots.

At least one of those things is true, but you're on your own figuring out which.

ABOUT THE AUTHOR

Charles Payseur is an avid reader, writer, and reviewer of all things speculative. His fiction and poetry have appeared in *The Best American Science Fiction and Fantasy*, *Strange Horizons*, *Lightspeed Magazine*, and many more. He runs Quick Sip Reviews, has been a Hugo finalist fan writer, and can be found drunkenly reviewing Goosebumps on his Patreon. When not hunting Hodags across the wilds of Wisconsin, you can find him gushing about short fiction (and his cats) on Twitter as @ClowderofTwo.

Hairstyle and Anarchy

Anthony W. Eichenlaub

An acoustic cover of Green Day's "American Idiot" played on the tinny speakers as I shaped Chester's hair. Jaunty chords replaced the original pounding guitar thrash, and the singer sang—actually sang—the lyrics with saccharine sincerity normally reserved for Christmas tunes. I lowered the clippers, letting out a deep sigh.

"Damn," Chester said. "This is what it's all about."

"It's garbage." I waved my clippers at the only other stylist working that day. "That music is Nancy's idea of a joke."

"That's exactly what I'm talking about, Sophie." Chester fidgeted in his chair, twisting around to look back at me. "Insipid, over-commercialized trash. How did real, pure punk ever get turned into crap like this?"

His cigarette burnt voice barely registered over the background chatter of the shitty little hair salon. What really sent an odd chill down my spine was the passion that insipid rendition of classic pop punk stirred in this scrawny guy, who I remembered as the quiet bookworm in the back of history class. Back then, I might have given a shit about the corruption of a decent punk tune. Not anymore.

I stared at the back of his half-shaved head for several long breaths. I'd shaved it down twice that week, and each time he came back with a full nest of bleach-burned hair. A person might have been curious about hair growing that fast, but Cheap Chuck's Haircuts didn't pay me enough to be curious about nothin'.

"What are you even talking about?" I asked.

"Oh, nothing," he said. He chewed his lip, watching me in the mirror.

I ran my black painted fingernails through his hair to get a feel for the length, pretending not to notice the tense shudder that shook his shoulders. "I never thought you were into punk back in school, Chester." We had gone to the same classes, but never rolled in the same circles.

Nancy shot a dark glance my way, giving me a hurry-it-up gesture. She always gave me a hard time about slacking on the job, even though she sure as shit knew it wouldn't make me move any faster.

"I'm studying the death of punk," said Chester. "At the university."

"Getting your master's?"

"Ph.D."

"Damn."

"Yeah."

I flipped my buzzer and tackled the other side of his head. "The hair helps you study?"

"Something like that."

Our eyes met in the mirror. For a few seconds, he looked skinny and strung out as anyone I'd ever seen in the gutters on my walk home. If I didn't know him from back in the day—if I didn't know that his parents were both highly respected university professors—I'd probably make him pay up front. His pale skin sunk at his cheeks, and the anarchy tattoo on the side of his neck looked raw and fresh. Who was I to judge a guy by his tattoos, though? My own arms bore the furious icons of my youth, and always would. Despite his strung-out look, Chester's blue eyes shone bright as ever. They almost burned.

I finished shaping his head without another word. He got an undercut mohawk, roughly spiked and harshly colored. From a distance he almost didn't look like a poser.

"Didn't anyone ever tell you punk never dies?" I told him as I brushed the last hairs off his neck. The Ramones' "Blitzkrieg Bop" played as a smooth, jazzy cover.

He grinned up at me. I'd almost call him handsome with a freshly clipped head. "No," he said. "It just grows up and gets a job."

As I took the guy's cash, Nancy sauntered past making meaningful glances at her watch. Chester had taken me way longer than the designated ten minutes, and there was a line of people nearly out the door.

Sometimes I just want to tell Nancy to go fuck herself. Too bad I needed the job.

⧗   ⧗   ⧗

The night was moonless and gray, with just enough mist in the air to muffle the noises of the homeless as they roamed the city streets. Tension scratched at the night like a match rubbed slow across dry concrete. Homeless wanderers—the restless spirits of a broken society—harassed and harried those still among the financially viable. They knew me and knew they could get nothing from me, so they mostly let me be.

When I passed the main entrance gate to the university, Chester stumbled into me with his hair in a tumbled mass around a half-crazed expression, and he almost got a face full of pepper and a boot to the knee.

Luckily for him, I pulled up short.

"You," he said. His hair had grown out. The sides that I'd buzzed only that morning sprouted thick stubble around his ears. "Sophie."

"Yeah," I said. "What are you doing here, Chester?"

He blinked twice really slow. His eyes were dilated and glassy, lacking the blue sharpness I'd noticed early in the day. A shadow of a smile crossed his face, and he sat down right there in the middle of the sidewalk. Somewhere far away, police sirens wailed in the night.

"I don't have time for this." I walked away.

Half a block behind me, Chester called out. "Wait!"

Something in the desperation of his voice stopped me. After a full breath, I turned around to look but said nothing.

"Do you really believe what you said?" he asked.

It took me a while to figure out what he meant. "That punk never dies?"

He nodded, his wrecked hair tumbling in a mess in front of his face.

"No," I said. "That's just some bullshit they say to sell you more music."

With that, I turned and went my way, choosing to ignore the sobs coming from the ruined man in the middle of the sidewalk.

⌛   ⌛   ⌛

The next time I saw Chester was two days later on the tail end of a ten-hour shift at Cheap Chuck's Haircuts. Ten hours of smiling pretty and chatting folks up, but I needed the extra shift to pay rent. If only it would also pay for a burger and some booze. My feet ached, and I wasn't in the mood to put up with his shit.

The first thing I noticed was that he had dyed his bleach-burnt hair blue, except for where it grew back in on the sides. He had three fingers of wiry black over his ears where I'd shaved it only two days prior.

"Another mohawk?" I asked.

"Spike it up hard all over this time."

"It's growing out fast," I said, because Nancy gets all pissy if I don't make small talk.

Chester grinned, showing his yellowed teeth. "Consequences of the inquisitive mind," he said, as if that meant anything to me.

"Studying pretty hard, then?" I asked.

He swallowed, his Adam's apple bobbing in his scrawny neck. "University is a lot harder on students than it used to be. Lots of competition."

"Someone else is studying punk?"

"It's about funding and fighting for credibility and—" He choked back his next words, then continued. "The university is dying. I don't know how long we'll have to salvage anything."

When Chester didn't say anything else, I filled the awkward void with more words. "You study punk music, right?" I asked, allowing myself to be baited into a conversation about his research.

"Not music," he said. "Movements. And they're notoriously hard to study since people work so hard to forget the real origins of punk. They glamorize it and demonize it. We forget so much, but with modern data modeling so much can be recovered."

"So, like, protests and stuff?" I buzzed over his ears, careful not to bump his left ear, which sported a puffy, red lump. It looked like an earring pierce had grown badly infected.

"Not just punk protestors, but whole movements. Shifts in the gestalt." He shook with excitement, and I had to stop cutting. "The late-era Soviets were huge. In Tallinn they had these tunnels under the city, left over from the middle ages. Cops would chase them right to the tunnels, but there was this unspoken agreement that the cops would never follow them in."

"Why not?"

"That's the question, right? Maybe the cops knew the punks were right to oppose the government. Maybe the cops were just afraid of getting killed down there in the dark. Either way, it made for an incredible power dynamic, and my theory is that it's what led to the whole society changing."

I took the bulk of his hair in my hands. "You want me to re-up the color in this?"

He shook his head. "No, it'll be fine."

"It's pretty faded."

"That's how I like it."

I combed the nest of hair as well as I could and started shaping it into spikes. "You think punk brought down the Soviet Union?"

Chester shrugged. "Anarchy tore a lot of things down."

"Is that why punk died? It tore itself down?"

He didn't speak again while I shaped stubby spikes all over his head. On the radio, a bluegrass rendition of the Sex Pistol's "Anarchy in the U.K." played. Once his hair formed a neat stalagmite row along the middle and sides, I sprayed it hard until the spikes were stiff enough to be registered weapons. He grinned at himself in the mirror.

"You should come with and see what I do," he said. "I'm hitting 1974 America next."

"I have work tomorrow."

He blinked at me. "I have a data set completing tomorrow. It's a beautiful thing. Just stop by the History Building if you're interested. It's the big ugly one."

After he paid, I shuffled him out the door. Outside, the gray static of city noise smothered his furious punk style like the ocean swallowing a spec of grit. He could look as punk as he wanted, it wouldn't make any difference to anyone. Thrash all he wanted, he could never make waves.

Punk really was dead.

⌛   ⌛   ⌛

Nancy left early after close, so as I cleaned up, I cranked the radio with some real music. Whether Chester was getting to me or if I just needed to let off steam, I don't know, but I cranked a playlist of the Buzzcocks, Patti Smith, and Reagan Youth. The music shook my bones with the pounding anarchy of its harsh riffs.

I was never really punk. Not really. My hardcore music addiction started with the pop-punk gateway drugs of My Chemical Romance and Jimmy Eat World and progressed to The Clash and Black Flag. I picked the roughest, craziest music I could find as a way to protest all the normal high school bullshit around me. That's what kids do, isn't it?

Adults work. The more bullshit that piles up, the more hours I put in at Cheap Chucks. The bills need paying, and the food isn't going to buy itself. I'm as trapped as if I were living in a jail cell, but here I had to make small talk and put up with shitty tips.

"Institutionalized" by the Suicidal Tendencies came on and I damn near pulled my own hair out.

On the long walk home that night, I felt like a bottled hurricane, and not one single person stopped to bother me.

⌛   ⌛   ⌛

Chester had something in his hair that felt like sandpaper and smelled like a fire hazard, so I pushed him down into the sink and hosed him down. He looked up at me with something like reverence.

"It's so good to see you again," he said.

"Yeah, it's been a whole day."

"It feels longer for me."

I stopped, my fingers deep in the roots of his hair. A few gray stragglers mingled with the undyed masses. Bags hung under his bright blue eyes. Chester was the same age as me, but he looked something rough.

"Research takes a lot out of you, huh?" I said, quietly so that Nancy wouldn't hear.

"Everywhere I look, it's the same thing. Punk's dying, dead, and over-commercialized. Even the Sex Pistols started as a commercial venture. They didn't sell out, mind you. They *started* sold out."

His hair got as clean as it was going to get, so I wrung it out and towel dried it. "What are we doing today?"

"I'm thinking late Russian punk scene."

"USSR?"

"No, Putin's Russia. Pussy Riot."

I placed my hands on his shoulders and met his gaze in the mirror. Whatever he was into at the university was killing him, and that made something ache in my chest. Chester had always been a bit of a nerd, but a good kid. He didn't deserve this kind of pain. "Why not just admit that punk is bullshit and move on?"

"I don't know." He closed his eyes for a long while, drawing several long, shaking breaths. "There's got to be an answer."

"How about pink?" I said. "You've got enough now for some decent liberty spikes."

Chester nodded. "Let's do it."

⧗ ⧗ ⧗

The city smoldered that night as I walked home. Fear and anger boiled in my belly as I passed the university. What was Chester doing in there?

What if he was wrong about everything?

Turning from my usual route, I veered through the empty campus. So few could afford a university education these days. They'd priced out all of the students, leaving only a select, frightened few to haunt the halls and push forward the research funded by oppressive taxes and corporate greed. The education system was just one more symptom of a broken establishment.

The History Building wasn't hard to find. It was the squarest, stockiest building on campus and contained all the décor of a giant brick dropped in the middle of the campus square. Ghostly lights haunted its high, narrow windows.

I pushed open the unlocked door, feeling like a burglar stealing a college life that wasn't meant for people like me. What if someone found me lurking these halls? My footsteps sounded like hammer blows against the marble floor as I crossed to the double doors that led to the lab with the flickering lights.

"Hello?" I called out, my voice swallowed by a low thrash of an electric guitar coming from the lab. When there was no answer, I swallowed my fear and went in.

Music poured through the door when I cracked it open, a heavy, pounding guitar hitting power chords so hard they nearly stopped my heart. I didn't recognize the music, but it made my hair stand on end.

The room's severe concrete walls were covered in graffiti, tagged with anything from amateurish anarchy symbols to elaborate, stenciled diatribes lettered in the Cyrillic alphabet. Trash from fast food littered the floor, smashed into the very fiber of the textured stone floor and smelling like old grease. Along the back wall, in shocking contrast to the spartan decoration, stood a row of black, tall computer racks, all blinking furiously.

In the center of the room, Chester stood on a platform full of

holographically projected images. The scene around him rapidly shifted from cities full of poverty and despair to politicians yelling fury
into a crowd to raging concerts that were borderline riots. He was
immersed in the scenes, fully a part of the history he was trying to
study. Screens floated in front of Chester's face, rapidly feeding col-
umns of raw data faster than anything I could hope to comprehend.

Faster than anyone could possibly comprehend.

Then, I saw the table in the corner. Used needles and a tourniquet
sat next to discarded, empty drug bottles. This was what he meant
when he said university was hard on him. These drugs probably
allowed his brain to process the staggering amount of information.

The music stopped, and its absence grew to an oppressive silence.
The images around Chester faded to nothing, and he dropped to his
knees, vacant stare on his gaunt face.

Chester's liberty spikes were gone; the pink at the base of his hair
grown out by several fingers.

"It's true, then," I said. "You really are killing yourself for this
project."

He looked up at me with haunted eyes. When he spoke, his voice
grated like broken asphalt. "It's all a lie," he said. "All a goddamn lie."

⧗   ⧗   ⧗

"It doesn't matter where I look," he said, his hands clasping a cup
of coffee like it might run away. "From the second the punk movement starts, it's all about commercialism and profit. Any punk artist
you've ever heard of has sold out from the second they first shouted
into a microphone."

We sat at a grungy little café across from Cheap Chuck's. They
sold booze and coffee, but from the way Chester smelled he wasn't
going to need any more vodka for a week. We were the only patrons
at the little place, and the barista was out back smoking a cigarette.
Outside the barred windows, homeless men and women shuffled without any apparent direction or motivation: more wasted chaff of a

broken world.

"Maybe you didn't look back far enough," I said.

His eyes turned hard. "I did. We modeled years before each movement hit it big. London, America, Russia. All of them were the same. The people who pioneered the punk movements were either stupid kids trying to hit it big or they were actual corporate music interests trying to manufacture something big. Either way, punk never had to die, because it was never alive."

I let that sink in a little bit, partly because it had the ring of truth and partly because I didn't have anything to say in response. My own coffee tasted like bitter tar, but sipping it gave me a few seconds to gather my thoughts.

When I set my cup down, rage smoldered in my gut. "Bullshit," I said.

He nodded. "Always has been."

I wanted to tell him that he got it all wrong—that I was trying to say that his theory was bullshit. But what could I say? I had always been a poser, always listening to the music but never buying into the anarchy. What had I ever done to stick a thumb in the eye of establishment? Smoked a few cigarettes, maybe. Got some ink. That'll show 'em.

"You know," he said in his quiet voice, "you were my inspiration. I had a crush on you back in school. You were always such a badass."

That yanked a sharp laugh from me. "I might as well have been a cheerleader."

But he was serious. His blue eyes shone in the dimly lit café. "On some level I thought that if I understood punk, I'd understand you."

I leaned in close. "That's a lot of goddamn pressure, Chester."

He shrank into himself. "I'm not saying it's the only reason. It was just the start of it. The more I studied history of the last hundred years, the more I saw that punk preceded change. Always. I thought that if I could figure out punk, maybe I could figure out how to change our own situation."

"Yeah," I said after a long pause. "You're right. It's bullshit."

Chester buried his face in his hands as if he could hide from the world behind gritty, painted fingernails.

"It's bullshit," I said, "because you don't even understand what you're looking at. These people you've been studying aren't brilliant revolutionaries. They're the broken down, stepped-on kids who don't have any choice but to rebel or get crushed by the system. They sign music contracts because that's how they fucking feed themselves. Sure, a lot of punk is manufactured by corporate music factories, but those suit-wearing fuckers follow movements. They're not leading for shit." My heart pounded in a way it hadn't for years. Rage boiled up. I jabbed a finger at his face. "Punk is the lifeblood that slips through the fingers of an iron fist. Punk is the oil that greases the wheels of change."

Chester's eyes narrowed. "But it doesn't turn them."

I stood, kicking my chair back across the wooden floor. I pointed at the front door—at the homeless wandering the streets. "It doesn't fucking have to, Chester. They're crushing us every single day, lowering our wages and raising our rent. It's a matter of time, man. Any moment someone's going to make that little push and shit's going to move."

He blinked slowly but said nothing. His coffee sat cold and forgotten in front of him.

But the rage still boiled in my gut. I thought of the years since school, how my situation only got harder and harder with each passing year. My job paid the bills, but only with overtime and a hell of a lot of groveling.

"I've had enough," I said.

I crossed to the bar and leaned way over. From the rack, I snatched a full bottle of the strongest booze they sold. Without looking to see if Chester followed, I shouldered my way through the door and stared across the street at Cheap Chuck's Haircuts.

The homeless people huddled in groups along the street, gathering together for warmth in the bitter night. The air reeked of tension, and several sets of far-off sirens serenaded the night. The streetlights flickered.

"Gimme your shirt," I said.

Chester, who had, of course, followed, took off his ratty white shirt and handed it to me. His chest and arms were covered in black tattoos, and the effect was grim and more than a little enticing. I tore off a strip of cloth, soaked it with vodka, and stuffed it in the end as a wick.

"Shit," Chester said.

"It's time for a change," I said, projecting my voice so the street people could hear me. "I don't know what's going to rise from the ashes, and nobody knows who's going to fix what's broken. All I know is what's happening now ain't working. It's broken, and the hell if I know how to fix it."

"It won't burn," Chester said in a quiet voice. "It's not enough."

I put an arm around his bare shoulder and looked into his bright blue eyes. "It's enough." I gestured at the city. "Light a fucking match, Chester. It'll all burn." I waited for a spark of excitement—of hope—to flicker in his eyes, then I kissed him hard.

He tensed, then his passion caught fire. His arms wrapped around me, and I ran my fingers through the back of his knotty hair. We fit so perfectly I cursed all the social bullshit that kept us apart for so long.

After a time, I pulled away, lit the cloth, and waited to make sure it burned really well. I took careful aim right at Cheap Chuck's big glass window where the hair products and the plastic furniture would burn the best. All those years of insipid music and pleasant small talk flashed before me, and I hated it. How had I ever survived?

Attention was on me now, and my heart pounded.

"You don't have to do this," Chester said. There was a tremor of fear in his voice. His fear sent a thrill down my spine.

"This is it," I said. "This is before and soon it'll be after. All that music you dredged up from in the past—all that rebellion—that was nothing. That was punk." Flames licked at my arm. "But it always started on a dark night before you ever thought to look. A night full of anarchy when anything could happen. You wanted to see the gears

fucking turn?" I took a deep breath of the rotten city air.
   And I threw.

ABOUT THE AUTHOR

Anthony W. Eichenlaub's stories appear in *Little Blue Marble*, *Asymmetry Fiction*, and the anthology *Fell Beasts and Fair*. When the ground isn't frozen solid, he enjoys gardening, camping, and long walks with a lazy dog. When it is, he would rather be indoors. He can be found at anthonyeichenlaub.com.

MUSIC, LOVE, AND OTHER THINGS THAT DAMNED CAT HAS PEED ON

Stewart C Baker

G*randad's Bookshelf* - The one he built as an apprentice car-penter, back in '56, on the back corner by the floor. It didn't get on any of his weird old books or my EPs, but ugh. Spot cleaned and disinfected for now, will go over it more thoroughly after our show this weekend—just a side stage, but still a big deal for a no-name band like CAT LITTER CULTISTS! Shoved Mikado in his cat carrier to get the little bastard out of the way until then.

Surviving Your First Concert - But not before he got to the how-to pamphlet Jen gave me to read. Oh well. We're just playing *music*—how dangerous can it be? And if he thinks this'll keep me home and him out of the cattery he can forget it.

Nothing at the Cattery - At least, not according to the owner, who says Mikado was "just the most perfect example of God's furry little angels" she'd ever had the pleasure of watching over. Fucking *what*.

My New Cast - Right above the wrist, just where Jen signed her love to me with a little skull-and-crossbones heart instead of the 'o' in Kimiko. The nurse at the clinic tried not to laugh when I told him what happened, but he didn't succeed.

Grandad's Bookshelf - Same spot as before. My fault for not clean-ing properly the first time. Worst part? When I pulled it away from the wall—one-handed—a piece of the backing broke off. This thing's irreplaceable, and mom's gonna disinherit me when she finds out. I'm going to kill you, Mikado!

Scroll from Hidden Compartment behind Bookshelf - Maybe—it's yellowed and stinky, but the paper's crumbly so it might just be old. Vid-
called mom to ask if she could read it, but she said the symbols all
over it weren't kanji, and that I'd know that if I hadn't "stopped caring
about our culture" as a kid. "Gagzilla, Mom," I said, then stopped her
asking any other questions by showing off my (new) new cast. Music
saves the day again!

His Actual Litter Box, Apparently? - Begged a week off work from my
skinflint boss, which might be why. I've been reading grandpa's old
books to try and figure out the scroll, and man there's a lot of weird
shit in these! Ancient gods, skin-crawling curses, detailed hand-drawn
diagrams of *human sacrifice*. Jen's gonna come over tomorrow and work
it up into lyrics for a concept album about murderous tentacle-cat
overlords who live outside of time.

Jen's New Leggings - While she was wearing them.

"Softly Dies the Light," Drafts One through Four - That's what we're
calling the album's title track. We wrote draft four at a coffee shop and
Mikado *still* got it when we came back. But you know what? Fuck it.
We're gonna live-stream it this time, finished draft or no, Jen on guitar
and me—one-handed—on the drums. We drew a hokey magic circle
and some of those old symbols in blood-red chalk on the floor and
we're dressed all in leather, ready to blow the Internet's face right the
hell off.

Magic Circle - You can see it on the live-stream, if you look real
close. Jen lets out this awesome blood-curdling yell I thought was just
part of her singing, like Kurt Cobain crossed with Yoko Ono. Took
me a full ten seconds to realize it was because of all this roiling chaos
erupting in the blood-red line we'd scratched on the floor. Mikado
doesn't take that long. He sits right on the edge of it, lifts his tail,
and lets spray. It's like a fucking fire hydrant, right in that horrifying
nightmare creature's eldritch maw. Then, he turns his narrowed eyes
over one shoulder and pees again, erasing the chalk line to nothing
in under an instant. I had a hell of a time explaining to Mom, who

watches all our streams, why I'd suddenly screamed "I love you, my beautiful pussy—" All we had to do after that was clean up the tentacles. Come to think of it, CLEAN UP THE TENTACLES isn't a bad album name.

Anything He Damn Well Wants to - After what he did to whatever we called up, I'll never complain again.

The Flowers I Got to Apologize to Jen - Mother. *Fucker*.

ABOUT THE AUTHOR

Stewart C Baker is an academic librarian, speculative fiction writer and poet, and the editor-in-chief of *sub-Q Magazine*. His fiction has appeared in *Nature, Galaxy's Edge*, and *Flash Fiction Online*, among other places. Stewart was born in England, has lived in South Carolina, Japan, and California (in that order), and currently resides in Oregon with his family—although if anyone asks, he'll usually say he's from the Internet.

FURY'S HOUR

Josh Rountree

T here's no religion worth following except for punk. No god
worth praying to other than Joe Strummer. Some people
think he's coming back to save us, and I'm starting to believe
them.

⌛   ⌛   ⌛

I hate the way the city feels now. Every door was open when I
used to be part of the Corp but now hidden eyes stare through windows and trace any potential misstep, eager to reduce your status
and give their own a boost. I used to be so high on that ladder that I
couldn't even see the people who haunt the warehouses and squats
and backsides of buildings. Now they belong to me and I belong to
them. We're one people. We all taste the same flavor of grit.

The alley is silver with old rainwater, wet with light reflecting from
the van's headlights. The engine grumbles and smokes as we rush to
unload the gear and get everything inside. Vinnie knows the guy working the backstage door and he sneaks us in. Poor guy will be hunting
for a new job tomorrow. Maybe doing his best to avoid getting killed.
But it's for the cause and he knows it's worth the cost. I think about
news videos I've watched about suicide bombings. Sneaking in like
this with what we're planning draws an unsettling comparison. But
that's not the sort of bomb I'm planning to drop.

⌛   ⌛   ⌛

I was already coughing up blood when I discovered Vinnie and his
church. Six months removed from my Corp job and all the benefits,

and I was hungry enough that I was considering stabbing a suit for his Froyo. Thankfully some kids living in an abandoned middle school told me about this guy in the warehouse district who was free with his food. I was expecting at best a soup kitchen, at worst a gang of Corp sweepers who'd tag me for forced factory labor or stick me in one of their camps for troublemakers. What I got was Vinnie, every inch of six-five with a face like a cherub who hadn't shaved in a decade or two. He dropped an arm around my shoulder and put a turkey sandwich in my hand without even asking my name.

"How long you been sick?" Vinnie watched me chew through the sandwich, pausing occasionally to choke up a piece of lung. He lived in a warehouse he'd converted into a makeshift homeless barracks, and about two dozen people laughed and snored and traded war stories around us as we spoke.

"Ever since I went off the pharm," I said.

"I figured you were ex-Corp," he said. "No offense, but you got the look."

"I appreciate the food."

"You look like you need it more than us. Did you leave the Corp or did they kick you out?"

"I don't know you well enough to share my life story."

"Yeah? You know me well enough to eat my food."

I grinned in spite of myself. "Okay, you're not wrong. So you heard about that space elevator the Corp was building. The one that got sabotaged?"

"Pretty hard story to miss," Vinnie said. "There's more underground anti-Corp factions popping up all the time, but not many with the guts to do that. Somebody blows up a multi-trillion dollar piece of tech and even the state news service can't keep that totally under wraps."

"I was closely associated with that project." The coughing took hold and shook me for a full minute before I could continue. "Insurgents take down a major company project and the Corp has to chop some heads off. Honestly I'm glad that getting fired was the worst that happened. The Blessed President doesn't know my name. But he had specific instructions on how to deal with my supervisors."

"Man, I know it's a hard adjustment," Vinnie said, "but at least you got out."

Got out? Vinnie made it sound like a positive. The Corp provided everything—a decent apartment in a prestige zone, plenty of disposable income, and pharmaceutical mixes that blocked diseases and kept you in a constant state of relaxed efficiency. The Corp gave you purpose. Even religion if you wanted it. Every friend I had was in the Corp and every one of them had forgotten my name the second I'd been cut. And Vinnie thinks all of this was worth trading in for a slow death in the sewers?

But there had been days when it all seemed wrong. That much power doesn't come from nowhere. Someone is paying for it. Life in the Corp was great, but even with the pharm cooking your brain dark thoughts could creep in. You might pretend the news you watched was truth, but some primal part of you knew you were buying a lie.

"The best years of your life and they want to steal them," I said.

Vinnie sat up sharply. "Huh? Where'd you hear that?"

"Hear what?"

"You practically quoted from our gospel," he said.

"I didn't quote anything." I stood, thinking maybe it was time to leave. A wild intensity had settled in Vinnie's eyes and I was afraid he might be more dangerous than I'd imagined. "That's just some words that have been running through my head. I'm mad at the Corp, okay? Maybe I don't like the person I was but I still wish I could be him again. What kind of guy does that make me?"

"You never told me your name," Vinnie said.

"Joe."

Vinnie put one big hand on my shoulder. "Joe, if you don't mind, I'd like to show you something before you leave."

⧗ ⧗ ⧗

The music is nothing but a steady bass thump washed over with droning, atonal synth and string bits, and it crawls up my back and squeezes my skull. From backstage, we can see the pulse of life on the dance floor. It's a private Corp club, an after hours hangout for rank and file suits who want to max out on the booze and pharm, and with any luck find someone to take home for the night and forget about in the morning. The music is a concussive force, but they try gamely to yell over the top of it. They're dancing, sizing one another up through glowing oculars, but no one is hearing the song. The air is clogged with synthetic smoke, and the hellishly hot room smells like stale beer and too much oxygen.

"You ready?" Vinnie asks.

"As ready as I can be," I say.

"And you're sure you want to do this?" he asks. "No one is going to think less of you for backing out now."

"Yes, let's just do it."

Vinnie nods at his guy, and he turns the volume on the house sound down to zero. The suits in the crowd continue yelling for a few seconds before they realize the music has stopped. While they shoot expectant looks at the bartender and the doorman, I drag the old 100-watt combo amp through the curtain and onto the stage. I plug in the amp, then my guitar, and turn the volume all the way up, per Vinnie's instructions.

A microphone hangs from the ceiling like something out of an old wrestling video. Vinnie's guy turns up the level on the mic and I cough into it for a full thirty seconds, eliciting unmasked disgust from a large percentage of the audience.

"Try not to lose your jobs, kids," I say. "Coming down off the pharm is a bitch."

⌛   ⌛   ⌛

What Vinnie wanted to show me was his church.

"I'm not interested in religion," I said.

"Just listen to what I have to say, would you?" he asked. "You decide if this is religion or something better."

The church was nothing but another walled off space in the warehouse. This one had two rows of rickety metal pews and a scattering of bent folding chairs, all arranged to face the front of the room. Someone had salvaged a huge roll of pink shag carpet and it covered a majority of the concrete floor. The back wall of the room was built with cinder blocks, and someone had spray painted THE FUTURE IS UNWRITTEN: KNOW YOUR RIGHTS in giant, blocky red letters. An ancient component stereo system loomed at the front of the room like an altar, and above this, where a cross might often be found was a guitar. A really, really old Telecaster. Black and battle scarred with a white pick guard and a rosewood fretboard, the hardware pockmarked with rust. It was beautiful.

Vinnie saw that it had drawn my eye. "You know guitars."

"Yeah, I play a little. It's a hobby. Never played one like that before, though."

"No you haven't," he said. "That's Joe Strummer's guitar."

"Who's that?"

Vinnie walked me closer to the front of the chapel and I was afraid he was going to try and baptize me. But all he did was take the guitar off the wall and put it in my hands.

"He was a member of a rock and roll band called The Clash. They were part of the punk rock scene in the late twentieth century. No real shock that you haven't heard of them. That kind of music is so forbidden you can't even find it on the undernet. You want to hear their music, you've got to track down the physical media. You want to read about them, better find someone willing to part with honest-to-god paper magazines."

I played a few notes, loving the feel of the neck in my hand. They didn't make guitars like that anymore. Real wood, no synthetics. "So other than the fact that this is a really great guitar, why should I care that it belonged to a rock star who's been dead for a hundred years?"

"Joe Strummer wasn't a rock star. He was a teacher. And those words you said about the best years of your life? That's a lyric from one of his songs."

"The hell it is," I said.

"If you're telling me you haven't heard it before, then it's quite a coincidence," Vinnie said.

"So you worship this guy?" I asked.

"He would hate that," he said. "What we do is we come here together, we listen to his music, and we talk about how we can make the world a better place. Then we act on it. It's all there in his lyrics. The way the world is now, it's everything he warned us against but I guess when he was singing about it nobody was paying attention. Some of the people here ... they like to tell stories about how Joe Strummer is going to be reborn as our savior. I'm only telling you this because you being named Joe and quoting the man's words ... some people around here may start thinking it's you."

I handed the guitar back to Vinnie. "I just came for some food, not to join a cult."

"This isn't a cult." Vinnie hadn't appreciated my comment. He gripped the guitar like he was thinking about putting it upside my head, and I was trying to remember my Corp self-defense training when the doors banged opened and Vinnie's tattered followers began filing in and taking seats in the pews.

Vinnie pulled away, hung the guitar back on the wall. "No one is keeping you here against your will. All I'm saying is I fed your ass so maybe you could do me the favor of just sitting here for a few minutes and listening to some music. You don't like what you hear, then you can leave anytime and I'll pack a lunch to send with you."

If I'd had anywhere else to go or anyone else offering to feed me, I'd have bolted. But instead I sat down in the back row next to a woman with a shaved head and jacket that looked like it was actually made of real leather.

Vinnie didn't address the room. He just removed an old record album from its sleeve, placed it on the turntable, and dropped the needle.

⧗   ⧗   ⧗

The hostility in the room has me by the throat.

The entire back wall of the club is a mural of the Blessed President, fourth of his name, heir to his great-grandfather's corporate overthrow of the old government, a more beastly and vacuous creature than even his forefathers if that can be believed. He's the god of the Corp and his worshipers stand before me with their oculars flashing, pulling in instant information about the ragged man with the guitar on stage in front of them. They're streaming everything they see to the overwebs and more than a few of them have already summoned security patrols because they can tell even without their tech that I'm not someone who's supposed to be there.

Hands lower instinctively to the Corp-mandated side arms at their hips, and they're so in sync with one another that the motion appears choreographed. They are the elite and not that long ago I was one of them and that scares the hell out of me. I don't know if anyone will shoot me, but they obviously want to.

Whether it's the pharm inducing them to action or whether it's simply their conditioned disdain for anyone without the gray Corp business uniform, I don't know. The sicker I get, the farther away I get from those memories. I'm dying; that much I know for sure. One last gift from the Corp. But that doesn't mean I want to die here and now.

Time to get moving.

No bass, no drums. Just me, this old guitar, and a dead man's words.

I crash into the first chord and launch into the sermon.

⧗   ⧗   ⧗

It was partly Vinnie's words that made me a believer, and partly the stories from his congregation. But mostly it was the music. I wasn't sure I'd make it through one song, but hours passed and I was still listening, trying to pull meaning from the teeth of a storm. Lifting the needle, dropping it again, over and over after most of the others had left. That music was a revelation. And what terrified me was that I already knew a lot of the songs. They were like dream memories. Some of them were so familiar I found myself singing along on the first pass, like they'd always been inside me, fighting to be shouted to the rafters.

As Vinnie predicted, this freaked some people out, and though they took me in and gave me a home, it took months for some of them to fully trust me. Those who were more desperate for salvation were convinced that I was the second coming of St. Strummer, and no amount of arguing would dissuade them. But they were wrong. This wasn't about me; it was about the message being directed through me.

It was about the songs.

"London Calling" with its apocalyptic images of rising seas, dying crops, and nuclear war was a dead-on prediction of a world Joe never lived to see. "Lost in the Supermarket" warned of runaway consumerism. And "Know Your Rights," a condemnation of the police state and statement of basic human rights in one glorious, jagged tune. These songs were big red warning signs that humanity had already blasted past at a hundred miles an hour, tossing cigarette butts out the window in their wake. But they were also roadmaps so that we might find our way back.

⧗   ⧗   ⧗

That first chord knocks the suits back a step, but they regroup, blowing angry blue vapor from their lip implants. One of them tries to grab at my ankle but I shake him loose, give him a kick. A feverish group of men wearing the insignia of mid-level management push to the front, howling at me, but the amplifier roars back. Every chord that originates at my fingertips punches them in the chin. The song I've chosen, maybe the only one I'll make it through, is called "Clampdown," and it's the greatest song The Clash ever recorded.

Right this second, it's the greatest song ever written. And it's perfect for this crowd. Oculars bounce in the semi-darkness, pulling in every bit of information they can, all of them aimed right at me. They're active devices, data conduits meant to provide the wearer whatever information they're allowed to know from second to second, but now they're all pulling data back from me and the permission filters are working overtime.

"Clampdown" shatters ugly nationalism. It practically begs you to take control of your life, to use every fleeting second you have to make a difference. It demands that you take hold of the world and give it a fucking shake.

A few of the oculars flicker and the lenses fade from gray to clear, and I can see flashes of who's really wearing them. The real people underneath the tech, not the characters they play to stay in Corp's good graces. I look right into their eyes and see them looking back at me. They've never heard anything like this. They've never *experienced* anything like this. I'm not saying Joe Strummer is coming back to save us, and I'm sure not saying that one song can suddenly cause everyone to question their existence. But if even one or two take the bait, it's a start.

With so many oculars streaming, I know for sure the content aggregators have me featured on half the video screens in the prestige zones, and they will until Corp notices and kills the feed. I give them a show.

Screaming, spitting, raging.

Right before we left the warehouse I carved RESIST in deep jagged letters into the face of Joe's guitar and I lunge out to the front of stage with that guitar front and center. As I sing, the oculars pull my words and drop them in a steady fall of text across their view screens, and the image of that wonderful guitar is seared into the memory of everyone who sees it, whether my performance changes their mind or not.

"Clampdown" rumbles toward the last note and if I can just get to the end of that one perfect song I might be able to slip out the same way I came in. The crowd still isn't sure if they should be dancing or dragging me off the stage and the security team hasn't arrived to arrest me yet. I'm seconds from finishing the song, from escaping out the back door in one piece. With any luck this is just the first of many guerilla concerts, each one designed to chip away one more piece of the establishment. Maybe I'm the second coming of Joe Strummer after all.

Then a gun comes up and its targeting laser locks on to the guitar. One stoic gray suit—I can't make out the face behind the ocular mask—pulls the trigger and sends a bullet through the guitar, through my gut, and through the curtain behind me.

I'm on the floor before the chord ends, but the feedback holds me tight as I bleed out on stage. Everyone rushes for the exits except for Vinnie who's on his knees, gently unstrapping the guitar and lifting it off me.

Security sirens are all I can hear, and I know that if Vinnie doesn't leave then Corp is going to bury him for this. I try whispering that he needs to go but there's no more air to drive my voice. No more air even to cough. Vinnie stands, slings the guitar over his shoulder and heads for the back exit. Even the sirens fade and it's just the sound of my own death in my ears. I'm dying, but I already knew that coming in.

And here's the thing.

Vinnie is never going to hang that guitar back up on the church wall. Not after tonight. He's going to learn how to play it. He's going to teach someone else how to play it. Every believer who shows up on Vinnie's doorstep wanting to change the world is going to put their hands on that guitar and make some noise.

Vinnie might not be as religious as the others, but he's going to tell them that Joe Strummer died for them. Joe Strummer tore this motherfucking place down.

But he's not coming back to build it up again.

That part's up to you.

ABOUT THE AUTHOR

Josh Rountree's short fiction has appeared in numerous magazines and anthologies including *Realms of Fantasy*, *Polyphony 6*, and *Daily Science Fiction*. His work has received honorable mention in both *The Year's Best Science Fiction* and *The Year's Best Fantasy & Horror*. A collection of his weird rock and roll fiction, *Can't Buy Me Faded Love*, was published by Wheatland Press. Josh lives in Georgetown, Texas with his wife and children. Depending on what day you ask him, his favorite rock band is either The Clash or The Replacements. Really, you can't go wrong either way.

RICK'S TEE SHIRT

Matt Bechtel

The universe is filled with wormholes; it's a veritable Robert Frost woods, and you never know which step will throw you into another plane of existence.

Mine opened by arguing over the silkscreened text of a cheap tee shirt.

It was exactly half my life ago. I was twenty-one, and I had just sold my first short story to an avant-garde spec-fiction magazine (but an actual magazine, not just some lame, picture-less website).

I took that fifty-dollar score as a sign that I should cobble together the funds to attend my first writers' convention; after all, I had now graduated into the ranks of the published author and that's what published authors did. So I spent the first three months of summer working the graveyard shift 'cuz it paid time and a half and then took a four-day-weekend to spend with my own kind.

Most of the details of that convention are now muted to me like the colors of a sidewalk-chalk masterpiece after a storm, lost amidst the fogs of time and of trying to prove you belong by drinking way too much offered scotch. But there was one man, and one conversation, that remain as vibrant as the shirt he was wearing.

His name was Rick something. Something Finnish or Swedish or Viking that wasn't pronounced how it looked. A victim of male pattern baldness who insisted on growing out the sandy hair that started at his temples, he could've been a stunt double for Howard Hesseman on *WKRP*. He had a giant mustache that reminded me of a walrus, and he wore glasses with oversized lenses that automatically tinted in sunlight. Most importantly, he was known as "the snarky tee shirt guy," and on my second evening of schmoozing and drinking, he wore a red tee with white letters that might as well have been a matador's cape—

Are You a Punk, Or Are You a Writer?

I didn't care that no one there had ever heard of me, or had read my one story, or knew of the tiny rag that published it. I walked straight up to him, shifted my drink into my left hand so I could extend my right, interrupted his conversation to introduce myself, and dove straight in.

"Nice shirt," I told him, "but it couldn't be more fucking wrong."

Rick smiled and raised his glass to me. "Clearly, you're the former?"

"With pride!" I said, as I unbuttoned my Oxford and wrangled my left arm free to reveal some of my tattoos—my Social Distortion skeleton, my Misfits skull, and my four bars of Black Flag. I had brought nothing but collared shirts to wear, making me the most overdressed person at what turned out to be a casual event.

"Nice ink," he complimented. "And I've always loved Social D. But you can't be both."

"Says who?"

Rick sipped his drink and pointed at his chest.

"Who're you to say?"

"Not me," he laughed, "my shirt! And why would my shirt lie?"

"Maybe it doesn't know any better?"

"I dunno. It's a pretty smart shirt."

"I'm standing here in front of you, telling you that I'm both. And your shirt is claiming that I can't be who I am."

"Who are you?" he asked. "Are you a punk, or are you writer?"

I held up the sides of my palms and lightly shook them like I was looking to inbound a basketball. "I'm rejecting your shirt's very premise! Do you even know where punk comes from?" He nodded, so I continued. "The blues. Its roots are the poor, downtrodden working class, spiked with an extra dose of 'I-Don't-Give-a-Fuck' attitude. That I'm gonna play the music that I wanna play, no matter if it's popular or not. Why on earth can't a writer do the same thing? Who says I can't bring a punk rock mindset into the literary world?"

"My shirt," he teased again. Then he cut me off before I could respond by adding, "But I'm sold. And I appreciate any author who has your level of passion about his writing. Can I see some of your work?"

Dumbfounded, I stammered a yes as he handed me his business card. "I'm on the road through September," Rick told me, "but mail a couple of stories to my P.O. Box and I'll get back to you this fall once I'm home."

Then he refilled my glass from his own personal flask, which he insisted would be "better than whatever swill I was drinking." And he was right.

Over the rest of the convention, I nonchalantly did my best to find out more about him. It turned out Rick with the snarky tee shirts and Chumley mustache was, in fact, a *New York Times* bestseller. That he was best friends with *that writer* from up north, and even had screenwriting credits on a number of his blockbuster movie adaptations. There was no way he would ever actually read the stories of the inked-up kid who got in his face at a con. Still, the fuck-the-world punk in me insisted upon posting him the manila envelope.

His reply arrived a week before Halloween. Rick had taken the time to red-line edit each of my stories and had written more than I had. He absolutely tore them limb from limb. And these weren't first drafts; I had worked on them, edited them, revised them, and they'd all scored high marks in my classes. I thought they were tight, but Rick found what he considered to be countless flaws. It was stunning and embarrassing.

And then, at the back of the envelope, I found the letter he included—

GREAT WORK!

I really like your writing. You have a unique voice, and you're fearless when it comes to experimenting with form. You're undeniably talented, just raw (much like the music you so love and identify with). I hope my notes help, and I hope you find homes for these stories.

Per our conversation at the con, I'm sorry if I was a little too flippant (blame the scotch!). Here's why you can't be both a punk and a writer—because there's no way to "road dog" it as an author. You can't write stories for 1,000 people a night in small clubs 300 nights every year. What did that magazine pay you for your story, $100? Even if you sold three of those per month for the rest of your life (an impossible output), you're looking at less than $4K per year.

Thanks again for sharing with me, and I look forward to reading more of your work in the future.

But I was twenty-one; all I saw was all the red ink and the fact that he had called me "raw." So I did the most punk-rock thing I could think of—I dumped the papers into a trashcan and set them ablaze with a flick of my Zippo.

And, just like that, I was through a wormhole.

I'm as much older now as I was old then, and not a day goes by that I don't think back to just how fucking stupid I was. The reality that I crossed into that day is far, far worse for me than a living hell—it's purgatory.

Eventually, I got tired of being hung-over at work on a Wednesday, so I did the mature thing and slowed down. Rather than living paycheck to paycheck, I found a decent job with good benefits that would match my 401k contributions. I got sick of being angry over rejection letters from markets who "paid in exposure," so I stopped submitting altogether in order to eliminate that negative energy from my life.

I love my kids, but I never wanted them. Ditto for my wife. The rich black ink of my tattoos, that I now have to keep covered at all times, has dulled to a matte gray. My life has all the flavor of Melba toast.

Rick tried to keep me in the right world, but I was too stubborn to listen. Sid Vicious was actually so fucking bad as a bass player that The Sex Pistols used to unplug his amp so no one could hear him play. You can't do that as a writer because, eventually, there's only a page between you and your audience and you can't fake it on bravado and attitude alone.

Somewhere, in some other universe, there's a version of me who didn't burn those pages. Who actually worked on his craft and learned more than three chords. Who has more than one lousy publication to his credit, and who still shares a glass of scotch with Rick at the con every summer as they reminisce about his first year when he was "that young punk with all that raw talent."

I used to think I was both a punk and a writer. It turned out I didn't have the balls to be either.

ABOUT THE AUTHOR

Matt Bechtel was born just south of Detroit, Michigan (cursing him a Lions fan), into a mostly-Irish family of dreamers and writers as opposed to the pharmaceutical or construction giants that share his surname. As such, he has spent most of his years making questionable life decisions and enjoying the results. Mentored by its late-founder Bob Booth, he serves on the Executive Committee of the Northeastern Writers' Convention (a.k.a. Camp Necon). His first collection, *Monochromes and Other Stories*, was published by Haverhill House Publishing in 2017, and he has also sold stories to anthologies published by PS Publishing, ChiZine Publishing, the New England Horror Writers, and Fantastic Books (Gray Rabbit Publications). His writing tends towards dark humor/satire and has been compared to Ray Bradbury and Cormac McCarthy. He currently lives in Providence, Rhode Island.

VINYL WISDOM

P.A. Cornell

Whenever I'd ask John how old he was, he'd tell me he was "born in '75, same year as the Sex Pistols." Not that this answered my question since I wasn't sure what year it was and the old-timers didn't seem interested in stuff like that. All I knew is he was old. Old as fuck, probably. And I guessed I was somewhere in my twenties, though I couldn't be sure since John was my only family and he didn't know when I'd been born.

Whatever age he was, it hadn't slowed him down. He still got up every day to scavenge the old town with me in search of stuff we could use back at the trailer park. Cans of food maybe, medication, and of course, the odd punk album. Not that we'd had much luck today, I thought, staring at the handful of disposable razors and single jar of pickled beets we'd come back with.

"Maybe Aiden'll want these," I said, holding up the jar. "If they're even still good."

"Be better if you took him the razors," said John, as he rifled through his record collection. "Then he could finally shave off that poser hairstyle."

John was technically my grandfather, though I never called him "grandpa," or "gramps," or any of those other names. We were nothing but "John" and "Joey" to each other since the day my mother dumped me outside his trailer and told him she was moving on to bigger and better.

I don't blame her. This life ain't for everyone. Not when just a few miles down the road you can apply for admission to the place most people just call "The City." All you have to do is sign over a small piece of yourself. In exchange for that, you get a new and better life. A life where you don't have to work so hard just to stay alive. A life where you're always happy. Who wouldn't want that? Thing is, they don't take kids, so when my mom made the decision to go, it meant leaving me behind. I don't remember her much. She smelled like cinnamon gum and cigarette smoke. She wore dangly earrings that glinted in the light. I remember that, but not much else.

But I don't resent her. After all, if she hadn't pawned me off on John, I probably wouldn't have become friends with Aiden. I think it was my not having a mom back when Aiden lost his that brought us close in the first place. We'd been like brothers ever since. He was the only one I felt I could talk to about my mother. The only one I could talk to about a lot of things.

John won't talk about mom. He doesn't get why she did what she did, and he sure as hell doesn't get why she couldn't wait for me to grow up before she did it. But Aiden and me, we get it.

I'd been thinking about my mom a lot more lately. I'd thought about her again today, when we were crossing the highway back from our pathetic attempt at scavenging. Sometimes, like today, you see small groups of people heading for The City. I couldn't help but think that my mom had headed down that same road years ago and hadn't looked back. But I kept that to myself, not wanting to get John started.

"She ain't nothing like her mother," John would say, on the rare occasions he got stoned enough to think of her at all. And that was about the worst thing he could say about anyone because John worshipped my grandmother Rebel, though she'd been gone since before I arrived. I wondered what he'd say about me if I told him about my talks with Aiden these past few weeks. Not for the first time, I wondered what Rebel would've said.

Having finally settled on a record, I watched John set up the player by our fire pit like I had most nights since I was a kid. He then brought over the record and ran his hand almost lovingly across the sleeve. In the dim light of dusk, I couldn't see the album he was holding from where I sat but it must've been one of Rebel's favorites from the way he was studying it and taking his time.

John didn't have a lot of records in his collection. He used to tell me about the days when they had entire stores full of vinyl records. Later, came all the digital versions, but John considered himself a purist. Nowadays the digital stuff was reserved for the people in The City anyway. Us outsiders had no way to connect to that.

Not that vinyl records were easy to come by either. They're fragile things, especially when they get old. They break and scratch easily. And John admitted that rigging up the turntable so he could play them had been damn near impossible. But he'd done it for Rebel—he would've done anything for her.

I grew up hearing about this mythical being—the love of John's life. Rebel was the one who introduced him to punk. She used to call him Johnny and she gave him the beaten-down leather jacket he never took off. Rebel had stitched the word "Rotten" on the back herself.

"Fucked up her fingers good pushin' that needle through the leather, but when that woman got it in her mind to do something, no force in the world could stop her!" John told me, on more than one occasion.

I never knew Rebel, but I often feel like I did. I was raised on her old punk records. Most people thought it a waste of batteries to run a record player like that, but to John it was more than just music. Those old records spoke to him, the way Rebel once had.

It was Rebel who'd first started gathering the people at the trailer park. Those who The City rejected or who didn't want any part of it. She took care of them, nursing them through sickness, making sure they had food, clothing, a roof over their heads—all inspired by the punk kids of her youth who used to feed the homeless.

John finally placed the record on the player, easing the needle on to the first groove with care. As the music started, I knew the album he'd chosen: *Road to Ruin* by The Ramones. *Oh shit*, I thought.

John had surprised Rebel with a working record player on the day they decided was her sixtieth birthday. Along with it came the first album in their collection: *Road to Ruin*. They'd had another collection long ago, before The City had been established and the world had changed, but with all their many relocations over the years, they'd been forced to leave it behind, a few albums at a time.

Rebel had been into old-school punk. The Ramones hadn't been her favorite, but John says her face lit up all the same when she saw the album cover. After that, he did all he could to add to her collection.

Even now, over two decades since he lost her, John keeps his eyes peeled for old records when we scavenge, always looking to grow her collection if he can. When we find vinyl that's not punk, we give it to Old Man Lincoln. He'll take just about anything, though his taste runs to jazz and R&B. John lets him borrow the player now and then, so he can listen to them.

I knew John was missing Rebel extra bad tonight because he brought out that old Ramones record. Whenever he listened to that I knew to make myself scarce. It was just a matter of time before John got weepy and he didn't like me seeing him like that. I didn't much like seeing him like that either.

"It's not enough to say you're punk," John continued. "My Rebel, she was punk in her *soul*. She knew what that meant, and part of that for her meant taking care of whatever family you made for yourself."

I knew John took that to heart. Once she passed on, he'd taken up the mantle and spent his days, "doing his rounds," as he called it. Checking up on our neighbors and helping them in any way he could. His own needs were simple. They involved taking no shit from anyone, or life itself for that matter. And of course, punk music.

"Listen to what they're saying, Joey. Really feel what they're trying to tell you. Punk isn't just a song to chill to, like so much other music. Punk's a message about a way of life—a way of *being*. Punk's about thinking for yourself, and that's a rare quality in people. Don't be one of the sheep. Sheep get eaten."

"That old man's so full of shit," Aiden would've said.

Me, I was torn. Some of what John said did seem to have a sort of wisdom to it, though I had to take his word for it on the sheep. I hadn't seen any sheep outside of picture books in all my life. I figured they must live somewhere, but around here they must have all been eaten because there was nothing but mangy coyotes and gophers for miles.

I agreed with Aiden's point of view, too, though. Like me, he'd grown up in this world. He got it. And he couldn't look back on the old world for his lessons any more than I could. All that was long gone. We had to look to the future and we had few alternatives. It was easy for John to say. He was old. He'd lived his life. He could afford to sit around listening to old records and be at peace with that. But we wanted more.

"I know you see me as a tough shit-kicker even though I'm old," John said. "But when I think of my Rebel, gone so long now, I don't feel that tough. She was both my strength, and my biggest weakness."

I nodded, but already I was mentally headed for Aiden's.

"Did I ever tell you about how I met Rebel?"

I shook my head. The old-timers didn't like to talk about the old world much. Whenever one of them did, I listened, because I wanted to know where we came from. I wanted to know what made them the way they were now. So I stayed in my chair, even as that old record spun nostalgia into John's mood.

"I was raised strict," he said. "Didn't know a damn thing about real music, definitely nothing about punk. Rebel, she was raised by old hippies who taught her to question authority and live by her own rules. If my car hadn't broken down that day, our paths would never have crossed. I told her it was dangerous for a girl to give a lift to a boy she didn't know. She just laughed and asked if I was gonna preach to her about Jesus next."

I knew John had never been religious. The only gospel he ever revered was the Gospel of Rebel, which came through the mouths of singers from her favorite punk bands. She and John were an odd couple at first, but for some reason they just worked. And in the end, he became as punk as she was.

As for me, I had mixed feelings about it all. Some of those bands were just noise to me, though I knew better than to admit it to John. I listened to the words, like John told me, but I didn't get the message.

What I did understand about life was this: we lived in a broken-down trailer, surrounded by other broken-down trailers, outside a long-abandoned town where we spent most of our time just trying to survive. It was all I'd ever known. I was grown now though, and as a grown-ass man, there was no reason I couldn't join The City. Aiden was going and was just waiting for me to figure out if I was going with him, but I knew John would lose his shit if I even brought it up. Instead, I skirted the issue.

"What was it like, toward the end of the old world?" I asked, taking advantage of his willingness to look to the past tonight. "Did you and Rebel know what was coming?"

John shifted in the old lawn chair, causing it to creak beneath him. He didn't say anything for a long while, and I began to wonder if I should've just kept my mouth shut. When I was about to give up and take off, he spoke again.

"It was billed as *The City of the Future*," he said. "We thought nothing of it at first. Seemed alright, all high-tech and run by an artificial intelligence. It wasn't until everyone started losing their minds that we began to see things differently."

I knew enough of the old stories to know that he meant "losing their minds" literally. From the bits and pieces I'd gleaned from the old timers over the years, I knew the A.I. hadn't been satisfied with just running the city for long. Like me, it had wanted more.

It started by offering the dying a chance to extend their lives by downloading their consciousness into its mainframe where they could then exist in a virtual paradise. But soon, even those nowhere near death began signing up to become part of the collective. People like my mother. The A.I. had called it a symbiosis. Connecting to human brains would give it room to expand further, to grow and to learn in new ways until our bodies became too frail to be worth sustaining or we simply decided we wanted to move on from a corporeal existence.

"But don't you think the people in the collective are happy?" I said, taking my chances with his mood. "I mean, I hear that since the A.I. is in their minds, it can tailor-make their perfect existence."

"Puppets," John said. "That's what Rebel called them. They're nothing but marionettes with that A.I. pulling their strings any which way it wants. They're not even real people anymore. Try to visit your mother some time. See what I mean."

I never had. I didn't remember her anyway, so what was the point? But I knew what he was talking about. I'd heard from others who did. The people in The City were different. They were themselves, but they weren't. Still, it seemed to me like a small price to pay.

"In the early days of punk, a lot of bands used to yell at the audience," John said then. It sounded like the random tangents taken by an aging mind, but I knew him well enough to know he was heading somewhere. "They'd insult them," he continued. "They'd get them all riled up 'til they couldn't control themselves and wound up either fighting each other or dancing like they might as well be."

"What was the point?"

"The point, Joey, was to wake them up! Rock their foundations 'til they came out of the daze that society imposed on them and started using their own minds! From there, what happened didn't matter. What choices they made were irrelevant, so long as people made the choices that were right for them. Punk was about giving people *freedom* from a prison they didn't even know they were in! Don't you see? That city is about as far from punk as you can get."

I knew that in John's eyes the people of The City were asleep. They thought they had freedom, but they were just an extension of an intelligence that had used their own laziness and complacency against them. An intelligence that had traded them their real lives for a dream—an artificial one at that.

But that still didn't sound so bad to me.

I'd gone hungry. I'd felt cold in winter and the ache of thirst during summer droughts. I'd lived with my own stink so long I couldn't smell it anymore. I'd seen people die because we couldn't scavenge them the meds they needed—or the ones we found were too old to work. Hell, that's how I'd met Aiden. John and I had found penicillin for his mother's pneumonia but we'd been too late. Aiden was only around thirteen then, still too young to move to The City, but I know he started thinking and planning for it the moment his mom breathed her last.

"If ever the world needed punk to wake it up, it's now," John said, rolling a joint. "I mean, look at us! I'm only glad my Rebel moved on before she could see her only daughter sell out like that!"

"You know I don't like it when you talk about her like that."

"You don't even remember her."

"She's still my mother—and still your daughter, in case you forgot. I wonder what your precious Rebel would think to hear you talk about her like that."

I didn't wait for him to tell me. This was my cue to leave.

"Any poser can grow a mohawk. That don't make 'em punk," John called after me.

He was referring to Aiden, who wasn't here to defend himself, but I'd heard it all before and by this point I didn't care.

⧗   ⧗   ⧗

Aiden let me crash at his trailer. We talked about our options and his plans.

"I don't know why you're even hesitating, man."

"It's just … the thought of leaving John alone. I'm all he's got left. Maybe I should just wait until he dies. How much longer could that be?"

"Are you kidding me?" said Aiden. "That old bastard's tough as hell! I'll bet if the reaper wants him, he'll have to show up in person and ask him 'pretty please'."

Mad as I was at John, I knew I couldn't stay away for long. I was back sitting by the fire with him the following evening, this time much relieved to be hearing The Clash's *London Calling*. After a while though, he turned down the volume, which I knew meant he had something serious to say.

"What the hell's with you these days Joey?"

"It's nothing," I said, but he kept staring. I knew I was done putting off this conversation. "It's Aiden. He's thinking of leaving."

I didn't bother saying where. In our world there was only one place else to go. He also knew that Aiden was my best friend and that this meant I'd be considering going with him, so for a while he said nothing.

"I lost your mother to that place. I won't lose you too!" he said, finally. "Two kids I raised on punk and not one of you got any of it through your skulls!"

"Punk is dead, John! It went down with the old world!" I yelled, immediately regretting it when I saw his face. But I'd crossed the line. I couldn't back down now. "Soon you'll be too. You want me to make my own choices so bad, well I'm making them. I'm making this one. I'm sick of living like the roach that survived Armageddon. I want a real life. I want to know the kind of world you had when you were my age! You at least have your memories, all I have is this bullshit! Nothing but scrounging through garbage just to live another day. Every *fucking* day for years! I'm done with this shit and I dare you to try and stop me!"

I was surprised by my own anger. I hadn't realized I'd been holding in so much rage and frustration. I hadn't realized I'd made up my mind about going to The City and joining the A.I. But I felt strangely free too. Lighter.

"I won't stop you," he said. "I didn't try to stop your mother; why would I stop you? But I'm glad Rebel isn't here to see any of this. I failed her. I failed her so bad."

He got quiet then and turned The Clash back up, but in the light of the fire I could see the glistening of tears in his eyes. After a while he headed for his stash and came back with a bottle of home brew. I'd never had it because it smelled like death and I imagined it tasted worse since John only brought it out during his toughest times.

I packed some of my shit up then and told him I was heading to Aiden's again. He didn't reply, but as I walked away I could swear that through the sound of The Clash I heard him say: "Punk's not dead."

Aiden and I planned to leave the next morning, but I woke up feeling bad for the old man and sorry about the things I'd said—or at least the way I'd said them. I went back to the trailer, but he was already gone. No doubt doing his rounds, checking on the people we knew as our family. Even a night of drinking that toxic witch's brew wasn't enough to keep ol' Johnny down.

"Hangover's are for the weak," he'd say.

The Damned's *Machine Gun Etiquette* was on the turntable now, but the needle was off. The battery had died at some point during the night, so I set it to charge again, knowing the old man would need his music to get him through my leaving. Then I packed the rest of my stuff and a while later, Aiden showed up to get me.

"Ready?"

I shrugged. "John's still gone."

"So? Leave him a note."

"I can't just go. I need to at least tell him to his face. I need him to know I'm making this decision for myself and that I've thought it through. I can't leave things the way they were last night."

Aiden nodded. "I get it. Look, I'll wait for you by the old highway on-ramp. I'll wait 'til noon. When the sun hits peak though, I'm gonna start walking with or without you."

"I'll be there, brother."

With that, I started making John's rounds, asking people if they'd seen him. In a way it felt like I was saying goodbye to them at the same time. I realized I was gonna miss these people; that they'd each become a part of me in some way.

When I couldn't find John, I'll admit, I started to worry. John was tough as hell, but he was still an old man. Old as fuck. He shouldn't be out scavenging without me. The people in this area were alright, but there were always outsiders, and a pack of coyotes could do some damage if given the opportunity.

But I was also worried time was running out for me as the sun moved higher in the sky. Still, I told myself I knew the way to The City and I could always catch up to Aiden.

It had to be around eleven when I finally found John near the old town dump. He was sitting on an overturned metal trash bin, all scuffed and dented on one side. Clearly out of breath, he held the edge of his open jacket like a lifeline. He looked up at me then and I saw all the years he'd been alive suddenly weighing heavy on him. Like he'd carried them for so long, but just couldn't go on anymore.

Some people age gradually, and when they reach their end it seems inevitable. You have a long time to see it coming. But some people stay young inside, and though their bodies grow older you don't quite believe that the years have had any lasting effect, until one day they're just done, and you're not prepared for it. It was like that with John. The realization that his end had come, hit me with the force of an earthquake.

"Jesus, John! I've been lookin' all over for you!"

"Just a bit ... out of breath," he said. Though I could tell it was more than that.

"Is it your heart?"

He didn't answer, but I knew the signs. We'd been playing nurse to the people around us my whole life, doing the work Rebel had started. I pressed my ear to his chest, moving the leather jacket out of my way. I stared at the safety pins Rebel had adorned it with so many years ago as I listened to the sounds of a heart that had faced its share of struggles in this life, but that was now well and truly on its way to breaking.

"Joey," he said. "There's something ... I need to say."

I tried to argue but he shut me down with a wave and I knew that whatever it was, it was more important to him than what was going on inside his chest.

"For fuck's sake, I don't have much time! Your grandmother ... she didn't die. She was sick. Her mind was. She was starting to forget things. I was selfish. I betrayed her."

"What do you mean? What happened to Rebel?"

"I couldn't handle her forgetting. Forgetting us. Forgetting all she was. I begged her to go ... to The City, to save what was left in the mainframe. She refused. She wouldn't do it."

"You took her anyway," I said.

He nodded and looked away. I'd never seen him so ashamed.

"I put aside everything she taught me. I ignored all she stood for ... all she was ... because I didn't want to lose her. But I lost her anyway. I waited 'til she was in one of her states ... then took her. They said she'd be happy."

I thought about my mother. Had these two women, mother and daughter, found each other in that place? Were they together now?

"It's supposed to be a good place," I said. "A paradise."

He shook his head.

"Those people aren't free. Not really alive. I didn't save her. I trapped her."

And suddenly I understood why he'd tried so hard to teach me all the things she'd taught him; why he'd taken on the care of our friends and neighbors, as she'd done. He was atoning. All those years I'd thought he just missed her, it had been so much more than that. In a moment of weakness, he'd failed her. He'd gone against her wishes and taken her to The City to try to save what was left of her. But it hadn't worked.

"You saw her again, didn't you?" I said. "After you gave her to them."

"Not her. Someone else. A man I'd never seen before. A stranger. Her body was too old, damaged. The A.I. discarded it like so much garbage. Figured it'd make no difference to have her speak to me ... through someone else. This stranger spoke like he knew me; called me 'Johnny.' He talked about old times. How we met and even about the punk bands she'd loved. But there was no emotion. It was like an actor, saying lines written by someone else. I realized despite my efforts, I'd lost her."

I didn't know what to say. I replayed all the things he'd said to me over the years, hearing his words and understanding their meaning in new ways. Rebel believed punk was about freedom and thinking for yourself, and he'd taken both those things from her.

He winced and squeezed my hand. He loosened it a bit then spasmed, and finally gasped, opening his eyes wide before his heart finally gave out for good. There was nothing I could do. In The City, they have medical alternatives for bodies that aren't beyond saving, but even if he'd still been young enough for the A.I. to think worth keeping, we were too far to even try to get him there. All I could do was watch him go.

The sun was now high in the sky and I knew Aiden would be starting his hike to The City, but none of that mattered. I held my grandfather like a child, leaning his body against my chest while I supported myself against the beaten-up trash can. I don't know how much time passed before Old Man Lincoln showed up. When he saw what had happened, he helped me carry John back to the trailer. He gathered some of the others and they cleaned him up and got him ready for burial.

⧗   ⧗   ⧗

We had his funeral the next morning. Things like this went quickly in our world. Old Man Lincoln draped John's leather jacket over my shoulders. And just like that I was rotten, too.

"Guess you'll be moving on now," Old Man Lincoln said, as a few of the men began shoveling dirt back into the grave.

"He told you?"

"Aiden did. Came over to say goodbye yesterday morning."

I thought about Aiden. He must've reached The City by now. Was maybe already part of the collective.

"Nah," I said, sticking my arms fully into the sleeves of John's old jacket. "Who's gonna find you all those old records you like so much if I go?"

He laughed. "And someone has to keep those punk ones. Lord knows I never understood your grandpa's taste in music."

"Punk isn't just about the music," I said. "It's a way of life. It's about waking up to the truth. *Your* truth. And living it no matter what anyone else thinks."

"You even sound like the old man. Must be that jacket."

I smiled and headed over to the grave to help shovel. John was gone. Rebel, the ultimate punk, gone before him, or maybe somewhere alive in the collective, hopefully teaching that A.I. something about punk. Maybe there was hope yet.

With them gone, someone had to stay to do the rounds. Someone had to make sure the people here stayed alive and remained free. Someone had to spread the gospel of punk.

"You were right," I said to John's body, slowly being buried at my feet. "Punk's not dead. Not as long as I'm still here."

ABOUT THE AUTHOR

P.A. Cornell was born in Chile and raised in Canada, where she now lives her dream of writing speculative fiction full time. When not writing, she enjoys listening to all kinds of music—including punk rock. She shares her Ontario home with her husband, children and a cat with anger issues. In addition to *A Punk Rock Future*, her fiction has appeared in three other anthologies, including the *Jouth Anthology*. Visit pacornell.com.

THIRD RULE IS: DON'T TALK TO ALIENS

Jennifer Lee Rossman

G em Darby craned her neck skyward, her pose an echo of humanity's beginnings, of that first little protohuman who took a DIY approach to evolution, who stood a little more upright, had a little more opposable in her thumbs. The one who crossed the border of what it meant to be an ape, not knowing what lay beyond but never looking back, only looking up, out beyond her world.

Where that ancestor saw endless stars and wonder, Gem saw a few tiny pinpoints pricking through the light pollution and the blinking red of a plane taking off from LAX.

She did not see the spaceship, but it was coming, and no one could stop it.

Her brother's words replayed in her head like a skipping record. "We're not telling anyone. Don't want them to be upset in their last moments, you know? But they say they're gonna kill us all and I had to tell you goodbye. Had to tell you I love you."

Had to. He had to tell her that the world as they know it was ending, not because he wanted her to know but because he didn't want to be the only one mourning mankind. He wanted to share the misery beyond the walls of that little control room at NASA.

Selfish jerk.

If she had only quit smoking when she said she would, Gem thought as she ground the last glowing embers into the asphalt. If she had just put off her cigarette break until the next commercial. If she hadn't checked her messages, she wouldn't have to walk back into the radio station and play the soundtrack to the end of the world.

She stood in the parking lot, shaking and wondering what she could do in the time they had left, but there was hardly any time left at all. Just enough for one last track, an encore performance to all of humanity before the curtains went down and the lights went up for the last time.

Earth: the farewell tour. One night only.

Gem flipped off the night sky and went inside, marched into the booth, and set her headphones over her ears. Her pulse trembled like a strummed chord as her producer counted her down.

The "On Air" light glowed red and harsh.

She took a breath to steady herself. She could tell them. Not the way her brother did, not to ease the pain of keeping the secret, but to let them prepare. To give all the people in that sad little city, listening to a soft rock station at midnight, a chance to say their goodbyes and make peace with the gods that were about to let them get annihilated.

Or she could keep it to herself and give them the gift of obliviousness. Let them watch with wonder as the ships come in, thinking they've come in peace.

"Hey folks, it's your girl Gem," she said, trying to sound calmer than she felt. "As we begin our third hour of this nightly singalong, I want to change things up a bit."

Her producer made a face, but she mouthed, "Trust me."

"I know I'm just a voice on the radio, that annoying lady telling stories about her cats in between Train and Maroon 5 songs, but I want you to know you're beautiful. Each one of you, and Earth as a whole. Look at the things you've done. Look at the pyramids. Look at pride parades. Look at you, surviving in a world that doesn't love you."

She heard her voice break before she felt the tears.

"Damn it. No, I'm not drunk," she said to her producer. "But I probably should be."

Gem checked the clock. Just a few minutes before her brother said they'd enter the atmosphere.

Just enough time for one last song.

"Alright, listen up, lovely humans," she said, pulling out her iPod. "Soft rock is great. I love it, you love it, your Aunt Myrtle loves it. It's the soundtrack to carefree summers and a thousand bad Hallmark Channel movies. But it's hardly the stuff to start a revolution with."

Yeah, maybe it was hopeless, and maybe NASA had already evaluated their defenses and decided they had no chance of fighting them off.

But all of Earth's armies had nothing on the power of a few people properly revved up and ready to go up against forces bigger than them.

"Something's coming, guys," Gem said, letting her trembling fear become anger. "It's coming soon and it's coming hard, and we're not backing down. So put on your safety pins, spike up your hair, and hey ho, let's show them whose gorgeous little marble this is."

She turned the volume up high as it would go and let the Ramones welcome the first wave of ships.

ABOUT THE AUTHOR

Jennifer Lee Rossman is a science fiction geek whose musical tastes can best be described as "anything from before she was born (except country)." Her work has been featured in several anthologies and her time travel novella *Anachronism* is now available from Grimbold Books. Her debut novel, *Jack Jetstark's Intergalactic Freakshow*, was published by World Weaver Press in 2018. She blogs at jenniferleerossman.blogspot.com and tweets @JenLRossman.

FOUND EARWORMS

M. Lopes da Silva

I found this wordco in the desert, with its autogrammar and what the fuck ever bullshit built in to make my words all pretty. I still like it, though.

I used to write shit out when I was a runt living in the freecamp hard by the old nuclear plant. The normies are scared shitless of that place. Good. It's a good time. We get rowdy and keep the cockroaches awake. I got my first piercing there, the one through my left nostril. That's why I keep a big fucking plug in there. Amateur. It was OK, though—I messed him up for fucking up so bad. We hang out sometimes now. We're cool.

⏳ ⏳ ⏳

Every die
Every day
Every dying day—is that something? Maybe I should write a song.

⏳ ⏳ ⏳

Everydie like everyday
Riding

⏳ ⏳ ⏳

I don't know. Fuck! Writing songs is hard.

⏳ ⏳ ⏳

Nothing. The desert. Gave myself a new tattoo of a werewolf howling at a cheezburger. I think my linework is getting better.

$\boxtimes$ $\boxtimes$ $\boxtimes$

Hung out with friends in one of the abandoned shopping malls. We've remade a lot of it. It's wild. Art on art on art on art. Not the kind of stuff you see in towns. Someone threw a party in the big space downstairs, and it started with a lot of old stuff—The Ramones, The Slits—that turned into newer shit like The Pussycocks. We got drunk off of tequila and cactus wine and howled and fucked and wept and nobody got hurt that night.

$\boxtimes$ $\boxtimes$ $\boxtimes$

The normies expect us to work until the work makes us sick, but they don't give us any of the medicine that they make from the plants we pick. Like we didn't work hard enough. Yeah, right.

Me and my friends we put on our dust masks and lit our Molotovs and revved up the darters until sand spewed up like vomit beneath our treads, then we rode! We went and lit up the roof of the front office, while Mope and Freekel snuck around back to rob the truck with all the medicine in it. And I mean we got away with ALL of it. They're mad.

$\boxtimes$ $\boxtimes$ $\boxtimes$

The normies have been chasing us with their freaking cruisers for days now. We try to make extra time at night, but they keep following. They never come out this far. Usually.

$\boxtimes$ $\boxtimes$ $\boxtimes$

Mope couldn't take it anymore. She just turned around and drove right at them. Freekel and Eddi tried to get away, but the normies just shot them down.

⧗   ⧗   ⧗

I'm still running—straight into the desert. I cut a patch away on my jeans so I could stare at the werewolf with its cheezburger scabbing over.

I'm thirsty. My friends are dead. I've only got a fraction of the medicine left. But the normies can't last forever in that metal box. They're hungry and thirsty, too.

So I'm writing this song and riding riding riding.

⧗   ⧗   ⧗

Everydie like everyday
Riding hard to robinhood
Never liked you anyway
FUCK I HATE WRITING SONGS!!

ABOUT THE AUTHOR

M. Lopes da Silva is an author and artist from Los Angeles who always wanted to be in a band called The Pussycocks. Her fiction has appeared or is forthcoming in *Electric Literature*, *Glass and Gardens: Solarpunk Summers*, *Mad Scientist Journal's Utter Fabrication*, and *Nightscript Vol. IV*. She has also written music reviews for *The California Literary Review*, and *Queen Mob's Teahouse*. Her work frequently explores themes of obsession and anatomy, and boldly celebrates the fantastic and strange. Go listen to The King Khan & BBQ Show, punks.

THE WORLD BURNED DAY-GLO

Priscilla D. Layne

They'd been sitting at Jane's for about an hour, in the tiny apartment above the bar where she worked; just drinking beers, talking about school, and quizzing each other for their History of Punk test. They'd been over this subject too many times and knew it very well. It was so boring.

What Polly really wanted to know was how her new mysterious friend Jane's dad disappeared. It was a common question in New California—about disappearances.

This led them to discuss the disappearance of Lee, her best friend Karla's brother—a topic that always made Karla melancholic.

Not wanting to further upset Karla, Polly changed the subject. "Can I use your bathroom?" she asked Jane. "This Pabst goes straight through my bladder."

"Sure thing," said Jane, pointing to the hall.

In the little closet of a bathroom, Polly squeezed out of her black pants and took a seat on Jane's worn toilet. Her mind started to wander until she noticed a red drop in the toilet bowl. "Dammit," she whispered to herself. Not the most convenient time to get her period. "Hey Jane, you got any plugs? I just got my mess," she shouted to Jane through the door.

"Sure, I've got plenty. Check on the floor to the right of the toilet."

Polly reached down and found a box. When she stuck her hand inside, her index finger was punctured by something sharp. "Ouch! Shit!"

"If you have to take a shit, go to the bathroom downstairs in the bar!" Jane joked.

"No, you jerk! Something stuck me in the finger."

She picked up the box and took a closer look. Underneath a handful of tampons, she found sheets of paper folded up and stapled together. She extracted the paper from the box and read the cover. The title, "Janie Jones' Herstory of Punk vol. 3," was spelled out in a mismatch of letters that were cut from other paper texts and glued to the page.

Polly flipped through the booklet and she was shocked by the images of invobs—photos and drawings of black and brown people. And all of them were posing with instruments, holding guitars or sitting behind drum kits.

"How ridiculous," thought Polly. "Invobs can't play music."

She flipped to the first page and read the title: "Banned in D.C.: Bad Brains Inject Hardcore with Reggae." The author of the article was Stag O'Lee. The name sounded suspiciously familiar to Polly. After staring at the story for a few minutes, she quickly plugged herself, pulled up her pants and ran out into the living room waving the papers. "Karla! I think I found Lee!"

Jane snatched the papers out of her hand. "Gimme that!"

"Hey, give it back. I need to show Karla—" Polly protested.

"You shouldn't snoop around in other people's things," Jane said.

"Snoop? I was looking for a plug and got pricked by that … what is it anyway?"

"A zine. It's none of your business."

"A zine? Like, one of those sacred texts from before The Break? I thought they were just a myth. Where'd you get it?"

"I think my mom wrote it. At least some of it. 'Janie Jones' was a nickname she used to call me. Anyway, I'm not supposed to have this. So keep it quiet."

"What's the big secret?" Polly asked.

"It's illegal, OK?"

Karla approached Polly. "What the hell are you talking about, Polly? What do you mean you found Lee?"

"Take a look at that zine Jane's got. There's an article in it …
something about a band named Banned Brains."

"Bad Brains," Jane corrected her.

"Anyway, it's written by someone named Stag O'Lee. It made me
think of how we used to call Lee 'Stagger Lee' because he was drunk
all the time. The two names sound *so* similar. Do you think it's a clue
to what happened to him?"

Karla grabbed the zine from Jane's hand and studied it. "It does
look like his chicken-scratch handwriting."

"So, what exactly are zines?" Polly asked Jane.

Jane gestured for Polly and Karla to sit down with her on the
floor. "Way back before the Second Civil War, people used to write,
publish and distribute them. They were mostly reviews of bands and
concert reports. Usually free."

"Why bother printing something like that? Seems like a waste of
time and money."

"Half of the fun was making something physical. Being creative.
It wasn't about the cost. Hardly anyone read them anyway."

"So why do you have this one? All printed text was digitized years
ago."

"*Approved* texts were transferred," Jane said. "But there were also
many *unapproved* texts."

"This is contraband," Karla said.

"It is. We can get in so much trouble just having this," Jane said.

"We? *You.* You could get sent to Necropolis," Polly said.

Jane inched closer to them. "There's so much we can learn from
this zine. My mom saw it all coming. How they force us to live today.
Look."

She carefully smoothed a page and they huddled together over the
zine. She read it to them.

"*Despite being progressive in a lot of other ways, New California was primar-
ily governed by men. After The Break, small political factions tried to wrest control
of the island and lead the movement to become independent from the Mainland.
When it became clear that California wanted political independence, the then pres-*

ident of the Mainland decided against a military offensive, feeling it was too risky to damage California's resources, including its high-tech military bases, Silicon Valley, and its entertainment industry.

So the president chose one secessionist party with which he could strike a deal. He ruled out the California Anarchists, the Cali Commies and the New Black Panther Party, and chose the Punk Party, which was most receptive to the president's demands. After all, its leadership was also composed of middle-aged white men, who were wealthy and famous enough to be popular with liberals and had enough cultural cache to be respected by young people.

Initially, the citizens of New California were optimistic and enthusiastic about the state's rebirth. The hegemony of California had always been wealthy white men and this was also the case in New California. And these white men, despite encroaching middle age, cherished fond memories of rebellious times in the 1970s, 80s and 90s. That's why they were so easily won over by the Punk Party. They could recapture the glory days of their youth—a time of sex, drugs and rock 'n' roll—hold onto their financial wealth, and return to a time before the culture wars of the 00s when white men were unchallenged. And it would be different now because they were so much cooler than their fathers and grandfathers had been.

New California will continue as a society where men unequivocally rule.

As the population explodes around the world, all presidents will remain adamant: to make room for new people and new ideas, the old will be required to have an expiration date. The government, controlled by the Punk Party, will bend the punk slogan "No Future … " to serve multiple purposes. They will preach, "There can be no future, if we don't discard the old." And no one should worry about growing old and becoming dull because the ethos was to "live fast and die young."

Thus, a society will emerge where a select few, namely young, white males, will stay privileged and pampered, making obscene amounts of money, which they will splurge on excessive goods and lifestyles. And they will be taken care of by a second-class group of young, People of Color who serve them and cater to their every needs. While women and People of Color die a slow death, living and working in garbage, the citizens of the ruling Punk Party will view their early deaths as noble and sacrificial.

"Wow. That's us. She was so right. Your mom knew what was up. How can we continue to live like we do?" Polly said.

Jane flipped to a page that featured a color photo of a black woman, singing into a microphone. Her hair, a wild, bleached blonde afro, defiantly jutting out from all sides and at all angles. Her metallic braces shining in the reflection of the stage lights.

"Do you know who this is?" she asked Karla.

"No idea. She should've been more careful though. Stupid to get caught doing that. And to let someone get a picture of it? Even dumber."

"She's a singer," Jane said.

"No way," said Karla. "Invobs don't sing. Invobs aren't musical."

"Says who?" asked Jane.

"Umm, says *everyone*," Karla said. "That's what it says in our textbooks. That's what our parents said. That's what the citizens say. That's what the president says. Have you heard something different?"

"Have you ever tried it?"

"Tried what?"

"To sing. To make music," Jane said.

"Why would I? I've been told *not* to as long as I can remember," Polly said. "Back in fifth grade, I remember this kid in our class on stage lighting was beating out a rhythm on some old soda cans, joking around. You know what happened to him? The principal beat him with a wooden paddle in front of the whole school. Then he got send to ReEd. You see something like that, you learn not to challenge the rules."

"But haven't you ever wondered why something like punk would have *any* rules? If it's all about freedom, why are they so busy keeping us in line?" Jane asked.

"Man, you didn't pay attention in World History at all, did you? We were always the lowest of the low," Polly said. "A people without a culture. The citizens saved us. We can't be trusted with freedom and we certainly don't know how to handle it."

"Says who?"

"Says science. Says history. In our History of World Music class, we learned all about rap," Polly said. "How invobs turned music into a weapon. How we killed each other over silly turf wars and fights about authenticity. We get to see one of these 'rap ghettos' tomorrow on our field trip to the Mainland. Can you imagine having to live like that? Invobs can't handle music. It makes us crazy. What saved us was learning how we could best support the citizens."

Jane frowned and shook her head. "Is that all you want out of life? To be the footstool for someone else to stand on? Take a look at this article. Read the caption of that photo."

Polly was puzzled to see her name but with an odd spelling. "Poly Styrene. That's a weird name. That's some quality writing you got here. They can't even spell 'Polly'."

"It's not misspelled. That was her name. Or a pseudonym at least. Get it? Polystyrene."

"What's Poly-styrene?" asked Karla.

"It's a synthetic material," Jane said. "Used to make packaging. If you're sent to Necropolis, I'm sure you'd see it in the dumps."

"That's a dumb name," Polly said. "Why on earth would someone choose *that* for a nickname?"

"Because it's *flammable*. Like, if she's made of polystyrene, she's dangerous."

"Why would my parents name me after some crazy invob with braces?"

"She's not crazy. She's a singer. An artist. From the old times."

Jane crawled over to her bed, scattering the beer cans. She flipped up the mattress, which revealed strange black circles taped to the bottom. Jane pulled the tape off of one. Then she went into the kitchen and opened the oven. Inside was a black box that she brought into the room. She opened the box, placed the black disc on the device and turned it on. The disc started spinning. A slender plastic arm swayed over it before gracefully dropping down. Suddenly a brash voice called out into the silence.

A saxophone rang out, followed by the vocalist shouting garbled lyrics that Polly could barely make out. Something about girls being seen but not heard and then bondage and counting off numbers.

"What'd you think?" Jane asked.

"It's awesome. But who is that?"

"It's X-Ray Spex. That's *her* band. A band that *she* fronted."

"No way. I've never heard of an invob playing in a band, let alone fronting one."

"And she's not the only one. There are loads others. Just look through these zines."

"But … if it's true, why wouldn't anyone tell us about them? Why would they keep it a secret?"

"Use your brain. Who rules New California?"

"The governing council."

"And who chooses the council?"

"The citizens."

"And who are the citizens?"

"Men."

"*White* men. So think. Why would white men want to keep this kind of information from us? What would happen if the rest of us knew that we could lead, too?"

Polly shrugged and Jane answered her own question, "We might demand representation on the governing council."

"I dunno," Polly said. "This all sounds like some conspiracy theory crap to me."

"Why do you think your parents named you after Poly?" Jane asked. "To pass down the culture. To hope that one day, you'd learn the real truth. The real history that no one talks about. Same with you Karla."

"Huh? What about me?"

"You're named after a musician, too."

"Who?"

"Maddog Karla. Drummer of the Controllers. A band from Old California."

"Maddog? That's pretty cool. I wish my parents named me that instead."

"So why are you telling us all of this?" Polly asked, furrowing her brows. "What's the use of knowing this? Is it going to help us get out of work? Or avoid the Necropolis? It's ridiculous that we'd ever join the council!"

"You have to start somewhere. There are plenty of invobs. If they were organized … "

"*Organized*? By who?"

"Someone. Anyone who can tell them the truth. Open their eyes."

"How's that gonna happen?"

"Before my father disappeared, I heard him talking about some alternative communication channels on the Mainland. Apparently, the invobs are pretty good at resisting the regime there. There's an autonomous zone set up by invobs. They have all kinds of secret networks for communication. Ways to spread the word. If one of us could get there, we could tell them what it's like here. They might be willing to help."

"Seems like a long shot to me," said Polly.

"But what do we have to lose?" said Jane. "How old are you?"

"Fifteen," said Polly.

"So you'll have to breed soon."

"Hey, I've got three years left."

"Then what? Don't you want your life to matter?"

"It will matter. I'll have kids. Kids who'll remember me after I'm terminated."

"Who'll be enslaved in the same bullshit system. Indoctrinated at school. Serving citizens. Breeding. Then termination. And the cycle starts all over again. This kind of oppression isn't new. But back then, invobs actually fought back. Here, read this bio on her."

"Can you read it? I'm not illiterate or anything," Polly said, a little embarrassed. "I don't get much practice reading at school."

Jane took the zine and read aloud:

"Born in 1957 as Marianne Joan Elliot-Said, Poly Styrene was the lead singer of the band X-Ray Spex, based in Brixton. She had an unconventional upbringing, raised by a single mother, trained in classical Opera singing and eventually drawn to the hippie culture of the 1970s.

196 Priscilla D. Layne

She even ran away at age 15 with 3 pounds in her pocket and crashed at various hippie pads. But it was seeing the Sex Pistols perform in Hastings in 1976 that inspired her to form the band X-Ray Spex. The band consisted of Poly Styrene on vocals, Laura Logic on saxophone, Jak Airport on guitar, Paul Dean on bass and Paul 'B.P.' Hurding on drums. Their most well-known song, "Oh Bondage! Up Yours!" was actually recorded at their second gig ever, at the Roxy in London. X-Ray Spex was one of the most talked about bands of the budding punk scene, and they played with bands like The Buzzcocks, Wire, The Drones and Chelsea."

Polly could hardly believe her ears. An invob! Barely older than Polly. Who started her own band and became *legendary*.

"They even have a transcript from an older interview with her from 1977 on some program called *Countdown*. There's a quote here of her explaining what the 'bondage' thing is about," Jane said.

"I was *wondering*," Karla said.

Jane read from the transcript: "I think some people, they wanna be kind of tied up and everything, because it gives them an excuse not to have to think. But then on the other hand they don't. I wrote it when I went to a Sex Pistols gig and I saw two girls chained together, handcuffed together. To me, when they used to wear chains and dog collars and leads and all of that, they were sort of drawing attention to the fact that they were in bondage as opposed to pretending that they weren't in bondage. Cuz a lot of people go around saying 'Oh it's a free country.' 'We're free' and all of this. Which is not really true, because we're all kind of tied up. So to wear all of that bondage gear and all of that is just pointing out the facts. It's not pretending you're free."

This statement would have floored Polly if she wasn't already sitting on the floor. Bondage gear had always been a part of the fashion in New California, almost mandatory. But Polly had never considered what it might mean. And was *she* one of these people, like *Poly* said, who just didn't want to think? What restrictions were keeping her tied up now? Who would she say 'Up yours' to if she could, and why?

Compared to all the punk doctrine Polly had heard growing up, like listening to old interviews with Henry Rollins and Glenn Danzig in her history class, Poly Styrene was finally describing punk the way Polly imagined it should be. The singer fascinated Polly, not just for her bravery to play music, but because Polly could have otherwise never imagined an invob who resisted oppression and male dominance or who was unapologetically *herself*. She had never thought it was possible to stand up against the citizens; they just seemed too powerful. But if she had known about someone like Poly growing up, she might not have felt so powerless.

"We gotta let more people know about this!" Polly yelled.

"But how?" asked Karla. "You know that any hint of resistance to the regime results in jail time or disappearance."

"Jane, how was this zine made anyway? It looks handwritten *and* printed at the same time," Polly said.

"My mom said, in the old times, before The Break, people printed them on these machines called photocopiers. You could lay down a piece of paper, press a button and produce hundreds of copies in minutes."

"Do these machines still exist?" Polly asked.

"Not on the island with everything digital. Making everything digital allows the regime to better control what people read and monitor what people write."

"Damn. So right. Did your mother write that?" said Polly.

Jane smiled and nodded with pride. "There might be a way," Jane started. "At my old school, we had this book about ancient printing technologies. In one process, you carved letters into wood, slapped ink or paint on the wood and then pressed it to paper."

"It would take forever to copy the entire zine that way," said Polly. "And even if we did, where would we get the paper?"

"We wouldn't copy the whole thing," said Jane. "We could just do one page. Enough to make people curious. Enough to make them ask questions."

Polly thought about it for a minute and agreed it could be their best shot.

"And I know what we can use for paper," Jane said.

That night, the three girls worked hard to print copies of the X-Ray Spex story, which they carved into the bottom of Jane's skateboard. They even cut a lifelike picture of Poly Styrene. They explicitly chose to use the black ink for her skin, so that the invobs understood she was one of them.

Unable to find enough paper, Jane suggested using the backs of cardboard from the 12-packs of Pabst from the bar. For ink, they used some black paint Polly had from screen printing class.

They decided that during the morning commute, they'd go to the top of the highest building in town and drop the flyers from the roof.

While most citizens didn't head to work until 9 a.m., invobs commuted at the crack of dawn. A service class, they needed to get everything ready in time for the citizens. Since Santa Cruz was a coastal surfing town, there weren't many tall buildings.

So they headed to the top of the Coasta Santa Cruz Hotel. An invob Jane knew who worked as a maid let them into the service elevator. And around 5 a.m., when the invobs started hitting the streets, Polly, Karla and Jane each took a handful of flyers and threw them off of the roof.

When they saw the Pabst logo fluttering in the wind, Polly worried that some might think it was a beer promotion. But when the invobs turned the cardboard over and began to read, she saw how their confusion and apathy turned into curiosity and excitement. Below the bio of Poly Styrene, the trio had printed phrases: "Unite and win!", "Strength in numbers!" and "Burn it down!"

The trio knew they wouldn't have much time to flee before the SePo caught them. They ran but as soon as they reached the elevator, police seized them. They had considered what might happen if they got caught, but dealing with the reality was a lot different. Still, Karla cracked a smile, grinning to herself as she was handcuffed. Polly looked over at her, worried.

"Think about it, if they send us to the Necropolis, we might be able to find Lee, maybe even Jane's mom," Karla said optimistically.

"Some kind of resistance must be operating there."

A SePo jabbed her in her guts with his baton.

"Quiet invob," he grunted.

This time it was Polly's turn to grin at the policeman.

"Now what are *you* smiling about? You three are in for a world of pain. Jail time. The Necropolis."

But Polly didn't bother to answer him. She started singing a few lyrics she remembered from last night. Jane had played more of X-Ray Spex's music to help keep them awake while they printed the flyers. The lyrics, which hadn't made sense to Polly last night, suddenly sounded prophetic. She sang quietly.

The SePo kneed her in the stomach. But even as she buckled over in pain, she could see something below. Small fires flaring here and there.

"I watched the world—" was the last thing she could sing out, louder now, before they gagged her. As they dragged her away, she tried to remember the other words and what came to her was *day-glo*. Was the next word *burn* or *turn*? The exact word didn't matter now. The feeling was the same from within her. The struggle was just beginning, and at least they sparked a resistance.

ABOUT THE AUTHOR

Priscilla Layne can't recall the first time she heard X-Ray Spex. She'd been listening to punk music since she was 13, and almost a quarter century later, X-Ray Spex remains such a big part of her life that it is hard for her to remember what came before. She does know how inspiring their lyrics have been for her in the course of her life.

Growing up, people called Layne a tom boy because she wasn't really attracted to girly things and preferred playing sports with the boys over playing with dolls. And even though her mother was appalled by her newly discovered preference for the color black over pink, Layne really got her feminist attitude from her mother. Because being raised by a single mom taught her that girls and women could do anything and shouldn't let anyone push them around.

So Layne already had that attitude in place before she even heard Poly Styrene's explosive lyrics for the first time. But encountering her music was so important to Layne because it showed her, more than any other of the punk bands she listened to, that absolutely anyone can make music, be creative, get up on stage and have something to say. And you don't have to conform to the normative looks or body type in the punk scene, which tended to be white and thin. As a Black woman with an Afro and braces, Poly Styrene took to that stage with a passion and conviction that would blow anyone away who would dare challenge her right to be there. And that was an important lesson for Layne to learn that didn't fully sink in until she was already an adult. Until her late 20s, Layne tried desperately to fit into a kind of normative, punk ideal. And finally after age 30, she learned to let that go and just be herself. And part of making that step was learning how much Black people had contributed to the punk scene, a realization that took so long because much of punk history (like rock history more broadly) has been whitewashed. So Layne no longer felt like an intruder who had to prove themselves. She only wished she had figured that out much earlier.

That's why, when Layne volunteered for Girls Rock—a rock summer camp for girls, trans- and non-binary kids— Layne played "Oh Bondage! Up Yours!" for them during her Rock Herstory workshop. Seeing kids as young as nine be able to explain the lyrics to her and lose their minds pogoing around without caring whether or not this song was old or popular or played on the radio, gave Layne a sense of hope that future generations will be even more unapologetically themselves.

Layne is Associate Professor of German and Adjunct Associate Professor of African, African American and Diaspora Studies at the University of North Carolina at Chapel Hill. Her publications address topics like representations of Blackness in German film, postwar rebellion, (post)subculture studies and Turkish German culture. She has published essays in the journals *German Studies Review*, *Colloquia Germanica* and *Women in German Yearbook*. She is author of *White Rebels in Black: German Appropriation of African American Culture*, published by the University of Michigan Press in 2018.

LOST IN THE SUPERMARKET

Wendy Nikel

T he people on the shelf above mine are arguing again. Bickering and whining about who's hogging the blanket and whose turn it is to queue up in front of the store come daybreak to claim their ration coupons.

I tune them out, focus on the snoring of the bloke in the bed across the aisle, and it's like I don't even hear the ceiling-people anymore. I don't hear the banging of pipes, the shouts echoing from each end of the warehouse ... just the heavy, nasally breathing of a middle-aged banker-turned-post-apocalyptic-survivor.

I close my eyes. Simple as that. Like turning the dial on a radio.

Granted, I'd give a month's worth of coupons for a *real* radio right now—if I could get my hands on one. It's been almost a year now since I heard one unironically playing Rise Against's "Endgame," rather than the harsh whisper-scratch of static and military orders being passed on wavelengths that once carried the world's hopes and dreams.

I reach beneath my rolled-up knapsack-turned-pillow for the M&M's wrapper I keep there and hold it to my nose, trying to breathe in any last chocolate that might remain. Then I grab my pencil stub and cross off the word "deodorant" I'd written there and write "radio." When I see Mickey again—*if* I see Mickey again—first thing I'm going to do is tell him I found a new World's Number One Thing I Miss Most. Though, if I was honest, his name would top that list instead.

"Whatcha got there, girl?"

The M&M's wrapper is snatched from my grasp. I don't so much jump from my shelf as fall out of it, scrambling for that wrapper until I land on the concrete—*hard*. When the dots fade from my vision, I'm watching a pair of combat boots retreating, its owner muttering about fool kids who think they can hoard supplies, as if my scrap of make-shift paper was a pallet of tuna.

Hard to believe this is my life—if you could call it that—in this supermarket warehouse. This so-called life I'd picked over sticking with Mickey on the road. Guaranteed food! they'd said. Sleep out of the elements! And I'd bought the hype. Guess that makes me World's Number One Idiot.

I lay there on the floor for longer than entirely necessary after I catch my breath, till I'm sure the combat boots are gone. I'm about to crawl to my feet when something catches my eye. The red from the generator-powered emergency light reflects off something beneath the bottom shelf, and I scoot closer, pressing my face against the cold metal to reach it.

As soon as my fingers close around it, I know what it is, though I haven't seen one for ages—even before the End came. It's an EarWorm—the kind bands used to hand out at concerts or folks could buy for a buck apiece, with a tiny metal bean that you shoved into your ear so you could listen to a single song looped over and over as many times as you'd like. Or—I realized with irritation—until the miniscule battery ran out, like this one's had.

I shove it in my pocket, check that no one's watching, and make for the storefront. I've got a pocketful of coupons and a packet of tea to my name, and if I'm lucky, that just might be enough for a battery.

⌛ ⌛ ⌛

The overnight staff up front is even grouchier than the day staff, which you wouldn't think would be possible, if you ever met the day staff. They give the work to a certain kind of folk—the sort who, in real life, before the End, were already uptight and exacting, so that now, when the rest of civilization's thrown out the rulebook, they still can recite every policy and regulation by memory.

A brawny clerk with an impressive beard scowls at me from the end of the aisle, watching my every move as I peruse the batteries.

"Whatcha looking for?" he asks.

"Just browsing."

"No browsing allowed. Get what you need and get back to the back."

"Back to the back, huh?"

"Don't get smart with me," he grumbles, "or I'll have you thrown over the hedge."

By the way he says it, he must think it'd be a death sentence, sending a scrawny girl like me out beyond that ten-foot chain-linked fence all overgrown with weedy vines. Sure, out there, there's no guaranteed meals or coupons to hoard for bags of tea. But out there, people aren't inventoried and priced and packed like boxes of cereal on cold metal shelves. Out there, somewhere, is Mickey.

"You gonna buy something or not?"

"Gimme a minute." Truth is, I don't know what kind of battery the EarWorm uses, but it's not like I can just pull it out and check. What I can do, though, is reach a hand into my pocket and feel along the tiny sliding compartment where the battery goes, trying to see by touch the general shape and size. But just when I think I've sorted it out, as I grab the battery I think might fit, combat boots thunder from around the corner. An elbow jabs me, throwing my hand from my pocket and out flies, amid a ticker-tape parade of coupons, the EarWorm.

It skitters along that doomsday-stained tile and stops when it hits the edge of the shelf.

"Whazzat?" The boots' owner sneers, bending down for the EarWorm. *My* EarWorm. The one shiny thing in this dimmed-out world. "Mine now."

Not a chance.

Still gripping the battery, I dive for the EarWorm before Combat Boots can get his ugly mitts on it, and then I take off in a run.

The clerk calls out a code red, and suddenly, there's an army of clerks in matching uniforms bearing down on me from all directions. I skid to a stop at the end of the aisle, stuck somewhere between the bad and worse. On one hand, the clerk, with one of my discarded coupons stuck to his shoe. On the other, Combat Boots, holding up my M&M's wrapper with a smirk.

When I see Mickey again—*if* I see Mickey again—first thing I'm going to do is tell him I found a new World's Number One Thing I Miss Most: *freedom*.

I make my choice—the one I should've made weeks ago, when I first realized this wasn't the golden opportunity I thought it was—and head for the emergency exit. Outside, the darkened world only makes the stars seem brighter, closer, more real. The hedge looms at the end of the empty parking lot—just a quick climb and some scratched-up knuckles away—and beyond that, somewhere, is Mickey.

And maybe this time, I'll be honest about what ought to be on top of that list.

ABOUT THE AUTHOR

Wendy Nikel is a speculative fiction author with a great love for music. Though she was born in the era of The Clash, she didn't discover them until she was a teenager and a friend put one of their songs on a mix CD for her. In college, she studied elementary education, attended her first punk concerts, and once bought a 12-string guitar after a breakup (and then asked a friend to teach her how to play it). Today, she lives in Utah with her husband (the aforementioned guitar-playing friend) and two sons, who are both big fans of "that supermarket song." Her time travel novella series, beginning with *The Continuum*, is available from World Weaver Press. For more info, visit wendynikel.com.

MUSIC FOR AN ELECTRONIC BODY

R. K. Duncan

There's a lot they don't tell you about transferring. They tell you how you won't get sick, how it will be just like your body: same sensitivity, same range of hearing, of color in your vision. How it will look just like you do now. They tell you that, with the broken ribs, your twisted spine, the piece of bike frame driven through your arm, and with your family history of colon cancer on top; the insurance will pay for this, but not for rebuilding the organic trash you lived in your first twenty six years.

They don't tell you how strange sitting perfectly still feels, or the way a low battery can feel like dying from the inside out. They don't mention the blankness where you used to dream, when you still have to stop thinking every night because a human mind goes crazy without turning off, even when the hardware's silicon and wire.

"They don't tell you that music won't work anymore. I used to love music, Deutsche Härte, industrial, classic electronica, punk, lots of stuff. It still sounds the same, I guess. They didn't lie about that, but it's just noise now. I don't feel anything when I hear it. You know?"

Rob let himself trail off. He never really liked speaking at sad robot club, the support group the insurance made him attend until they were sure he wasn't going to wreck the new body they bought him.

Jason stood up to answer. You didn't have to stand if you were just responding to someone else's share, but Jason always did. He looked like a professor, with his sport coat and round, balding head.

"I'm sorry you don't enjoy things you used to, Rob. For myself, I find music easier to appreciate now. I can hear so much more of the nuance of Mozart or Berlioz now. I listen every night. Maybe you can find a different kind of music that you'll enjoy."

"Oh it's so hard, losing stuff you really like before, isn't it? I know just how you feel."

Linda tucked a strand of bleached-blonde hair that had escaped her soccer-mom ponytail behind her ear. How fucking obnoxious the transfer rules were, to give her the same artificial blonde she had before instead of something that looked natural.

"I know what you mean, man." Tori patted his stomach and found nothing but a loose shirt. He always did that. You could tell he'd been fat before the transfer and never bought new clothes. "I used to go to shows, ragers, mosh pits, that kind of thing. Can't do that anymore."

Of course not. He'd hurt someone, and put a few thousand dollars' worth of damage on his skin. "And it's like you said. The music's just noise, but what can you do?"

Everyone nodded. That was their refrain. What can you do? This is your life now. Your body would last for fifty, maybe a hundred years before you got a new one. No upgrade unless you made enough to buy it yourself, so everything that wasn't quite right was your life for good.

Sad robot club always broke up fast. They didn't eat or drink, so there was no small talk over coffee and supermarket donuts. They just left. Tonight, Tori caught Rob's eye on the way out, but he didn't say anything, and it was hard to read intentions under the resting neutral face a bottom-tier chassis fell into if you didn't strain for an expression.

⧗ ⧗ ⧗

Friday morning, Rob woke to a DM from Greg. He had a job today. Rob set up holo-projection rigs and showed the renters how to run them, whenever Greg wanted an extra body or not to go himself. Rob fished an inoffensive button-down from the dresser and stepped to the bathroom mirror, hands going for his ears. After six months, he still had the reflex to take out his rings before going to work, but there was no need. Piercing the skin would void his warranty, so he was already sanitized and professional.

Biking was easier post-transfer. He could keep pumping at top speed for the whole ride with nothing more than a blinking indicator for high battery drain to stop him. He didn't even sweat. Today, an SUV swerved close, crowding him against the parked cars, but there was no panic flash, just processors kicking into overload. He braked perfectly. If he'd been artificial to begin with, he'd never have gotten in the crash.

Greg's van was a piece of shit, old and cheap enough that Rob had to drive it manually, both hands on the wheel and everything. It was twice as slow as summoning a self-driver, since Rob couldn't connect to the traffic grid, but Greg wouldn't spring for a commercial subscription, and Rob couldn't carry a whole party rig on his bike. He fought his way through the seamless flow of silver vehicles to a featureless box of yellow concrete scored to look like painted bricks. He pulled into the lot and tried the service door. Locked. He tried the buzzer. No response. A quick jog round to the front showed no lights on. He pulled up his phone and called the number on the work order. Three rings.

"Hello."

"Hi, this is Robert Wilson with Keystone Holo. You requested a setup at 6200 Fern."

"Yeah?"

"I'm outside now. Which entrance should I use?"

"I'm back at the office. You took too long."

The order said it was sent 45 minutes ago, and 30 of that was Rob's drive. The client hadn't ever been here, or he'd left as soon as he put in the order.

"I'm sorry about that, sir. I came as quickly as we were able to process the order."

"Alright, shit. I'll be there in a minute."

He hung up.

The van baked in the sun. Rob's fans whirred like dying flies. The old Rob would have been heating up with the van, ready to tear the client a new one for keeping him waiting. Now he just reviewed the order and set the rictus of a professional smile on his face. Maybe he could still get a tip. He was a little short on next month's rent.

The client pulled up fifteen minutes after Rob's call, stepping from a sleek corporate self-driver that slipped right back into the flow of traffic. The stubbly man, who looked like a hungover bulldog squinting in the heat, must have been traveling on an office subscription. Rob stepped out, and did his best to charm.

"Alright, Mr. Sanborn. Why don't you show me the space and then we can talk about exactly what you need while I set up the projectors."

"That's not extra, is it?"

He probably wasn't getting a tip.

"No, Mr. Sanborn, setup and a consultation on use are covered in our base rate."

Inside was a badly carpeted box strewn with round folding tables and a stage for the band or DJ at one end. Rob unloaded. Sanborn didn't help, but he did brag that he'd gotten a deal renting the place, and that his cousin's band would be playing the party. He had a set list for Rob to program the holos to. He balked at the quote for personalization and looked at the brochure while Rob set up the projectors.

Rob was just getting the last one lifted into place when Sanborn came up beside him and leaned in, reaching for the projector and looking at his brochure. He knocked one of Rob's arms loose, and the projector tumbled. Overdrive. Rob grabbed with both his arms and kicked his legs back. Not fast enough. A corner caught his shin and tore through his pants and into skin underneath.

Sanborn turned white when the lack of blood or screaming outed Rob as a synthetic, and pointedly turned away instead of offering help. Rob set the projector down and did a quick diagnostic on his leg. Function unimpaired. That was enough for now. He should finish and leave. He wrapped up fast and asked Sanborn to sign the work order.

"Get out of here, freak. And tell your boss not to send you back here."

Before the accident, he would have bawled Sanborn out for being a bigoted shit, but it didn't seem worth the escalation. It wasn't like he'd badger the man into a tip.

Sanborn signed the order. Rob left.

⏳   ⏳   ⏳

His leg wasn't really too bad, looking at it back in his apartment. The skin was torn, and he had to take off a patch about the size of his palm, but his case was still smooth underneath. He found a skin patch in his drawer of robot supplies and trimmed it to fit, then held it in place while it bonded to the cut edges of the hole. It felt creepily organic, the most alive thing his body did now.

He should have been upset about the tear, afraid of the potential for case damage. Cracks were expensive to fix, and he wasn't anywhere near covering the deductible. Leaving them was worse, since it voided warranty coverage. Still, no harm, no foul.

It was Friday night, time to talk and not drink beer and laugh at bad jokes while Grant got pompously chatty on eight IPAs. It was only a couple of blocks to the Local, which had been a hipster gastropub imitating a dive bar before Rob was born, and was trending into an actual dive bar. At least they were used to Rob and didn't make faces when he sat without ordering anything, or joke about sitting him next to an outlet.

April waved him over to an open seat at the long table in the back. He ignored Julie shifting away as he sat down. When he transferred, their almost-a-thing had turned into cold tension where she very politely didn't explain how uncomfortable he made her. She had just been interested in his body, or in him having a body that didn't run on alternating current. April made excuses for Cam, stuck on a late shift again, and talked about a gallery that still hadn't sent her samples back, so maybe there was something there. Sean and Grant were next to each other on the other side of the table, splitting a towering plate of wings. They were drunk enough that they played up their reactions to the heat, huffing and puffing and sticking out their tongues for laughs, and licked each other's finger's occasionally. It was cute, mostly disgusting, but cute.

He leaned back to let Julie and April talk across him, just listening to Julie's endless stories of entitled shit customers from the three coffee shops and restaurants where she picked up shifts, and to April's about the constant rejections of a struggling artist, and the unreliability of internet buyers and galleries that did show interest. He shared his own horror story from today when April made a point of asking about his day.

About the time Grant and Sean made it through their wings, Maya crashed onto the bench beside them. She was the other synthetic in the group, and she couldn't look more different from Rob's generic, bottom-end body. Maya transferred by choice and modeled her body after something from an old piece of science fiction. Her hair was fire, red and orange and white, floating so much lighter than real hair would. Her skin was a galaxy, black mottled with deep blue and purple nebulas, studded with spiraling stars that glittered under the bar's Edison bulbs.

They could chat about the woes of robot life, but not the spiraling drain of gig employment he groaned about with April and Julie. Maya owned her own car outright and had a cleaning service for her apartment. The problems she wanted to talk about were social stigma for intentional versus forced transfers. Rob only very rarely had time for problems that abstract.

He lingered until the group broke and he couldn't justify holding down a table by himself. He drifted home, waving off Maya's offer of an interesting show about new innovations in second-generation chassis. Her transhuman optimism stuff always made him notice how shoddy his insurance body was.

⧗   ⧗   ⧗

At the next sad robot club, they had an intervention for Travis. He'd been letting himself deteriorate: tears in his skin, scuff marks on the case underneath left unbuffed. He twitched, probably unpurged malware, or shorts from debris that got in through the case damage. His joints ground and squeaked when he moved, like his body was a used car he wanted to nurse along for another six months without spending money on. They called it Synthetic Transfer Ego Failure, when you failed to think of the machine as you. STEF looked bad, so they all leaned toward the center of the circle and said concerned things until Travis said he understood and that he'd take better care of himself now.

When they broke up, Tori pulled Rob out of the line shuffling into the hallway.

"Machine life's got you down, I know. I've got just what you need to pick things back up."

"Huh?"

Weird way to say it. They tried not to call themselves machines. Depersonalizing, the brochures called it. Dehumanizing, Rob would have said. Tori was usually good about that. Rob ignored it, and Tori pulled a memory stick out of his bag and handed it over. Phi-1702S was written on the label in black marker.

"What's that?"

"Music man, music for us. That's your audio receiver part on the label, or it should be, since Blue Cross transferred you. That's the model they use."

"What do you mean, music for us?"

"Robots, man. It's this new group I found, Procedural Generation. They mix tracks for the specs of your model. It'll feel just like music used to, like it should."

"What kind of music?"

Too good to be true. There had to be a catch here, nothing but Raffi, or 90s bubblegum, or angst-septic indie stuff.

"Electronic, like you like. Some new stuff, and new mixes on old tracks. Just listen man. You'll love it."

⌛ ⌛ ⌛

He plugged it in and listened as soon as he got home. He'd rushed. He wasn't sure what he'd last rushed for.

The first track was a strangely tuned remix of VNV's Beloved, back from the beginning of the New German Hard. Rob sank into his chair and heard it, really *heard* it. A little pressure in his chest expanded against the casing where his ribs should be. A rock of melancholy settled itself into his throat. He thought of Julie. Tori was right. It was real. He blacked out listening, and almost dreamed that night.

⌛ ⌛ ⌛

The music was the best thing since he transferred. It hit him harder than his favorite songs had before. Procedural Generation were geniuses, mixing old tracks so they hit every peak and trough better than the originals. Their own stuff was raw emotional response, fist pumping adrenaline or the crash of sadness like breaking glass under his breastbone. He really felt it, like he hadn't since the transfer. It was intense enough he started half hallucinating. On the fast tracks he could hear his heartbeat, the twitch of toes wanting to tap. The sad ones he teared up, pressure behind his eyes and tightness in his throat.

Saturday afternoon someone pounded on the door. It was Julie.

"Hi. What brings you round this way?"

She pushed in and looked around, tutting. He wasn't sure at what. He kept things cleaner now than when she'd been a regular visitor.

"You didn't come to the Local last night, and you didn't answer any messages." He'd minimized DMs and not heard the alert over the music. "I was worried you were having, I don't know, some kind of robot breakdown."

"No, no, nothing like that. It's this music. A guy at my support group told me about it, and I've just been listening. Isn't it fucking amazing?"

She's always liked the same stuff he did. She'd love it.

"It's fine. I don't hear anything special. You've just been listening to this for two days straight? Have you gone out?"

"No. Why would I? It's perfect. I've been missing this since I got transferred. I didn't think it existed."

She lingered for a little longer, but seemed to get frustrated when he didn't have a problem other than the music.

⧗   ⧗   ⧗

Tori called him Monday night. It had been a rough workday. Rob wasn't used to biking with music playing, and nearly got into an accident on the way to the office. Then Greg chewed him out for being distracted. Fascist.

Tori pinged in as Rob was settling down to listen for the evening.

"Hey man, you been listening?"

"Of course, all the time."

"Nice. There's a show, tomorrow. I just heard about it."

"A show? Procedural Generation live?"

"Yeah, just a little one. No advertising, only people who get it. People who've transferred."

"Where?"

Another ping and Tori sent him the address for easy navigation, and the link for tickets.

"See you there?"

"Yeah, definitely."

He'd probably still make rent after the ticket, if work stayed steady. No question it was going to be worth the money.

⧗   ⧗   ⧗

The venue was just a half-converted warehouse with a stage and some plastic folding chairs. Why chairs? Rob didn't expect to sit at a show like this. He wanted to be standing, dancing. Two towers of speakers flanked the stage. The crowd, maybe thirty people, sat in scattered clusters. He looked for Tori, saw him with a pair of rich synthetics, hard-cases done up in racing stripes and flames, the kind of thing you only wore if you could afford to change it next month. He tried to catch Tori's eye and get a nod. Nothing. He sat alone. No worries. He was going to hear it live, have the pressure of a crowd to turn the music up, feel the floor shake from the bass.

Procedural Generation came on stage, two ordinary looking women in jeans and tank tops. They weren't synthetic. How did they know when it worked, then?

They plugged tablets into mixing boards and started without any introduction. The first chord screamed out, metallic and discordant over a heavy bass. It made him want to stamp and pump his fist and scream. The vision came so vivid he could almost see it when the big drum boomed: the seedy rented space replaced by a huge hall, filled with his comrades, all in uniform, saluting to the stage. The song broke down into strings that tinkled ticklish against his skin like freezing rain on glass.

He stood up to applaud. The next song started after a half-breath pause, and his legs gave out. He fell back into his seat. He tried to get up and see what had gone wrong. His arms hung limp while aerial guitar and theremin washed black depression over him. He blinked the pattern for a diagnostic. It came up in distorted rainbow, flickering and dying while he drowned in cotton candy. He gasped breath into lungs he left behind on the operating table and felt like he should vomit. The melody resolved into a timpani of grasping fingers digging into the seam of his metal skull.

They played a single set, ten tracks, and he couldn't move until it ended. Each transition he lost more, until it was all hallucinations, calling up senses he didn't have. He felt painfully alive, like he was dying, staked out on a table and slowly peeled back, his brain unfolded in onion layers of emotion. Darkness followed him down, and he dreamed of running over snow, blood hot in his mouth, the howl of wolves or sirens all around him. He ran, and he exulted, thick-furred with blue lights flashing. He brought the runner down with blood hot in his mouth. He ran.

⧗   ⧗   ⧗

Rob woke, and he was moving. The two were unconnected. He woke while his body was dressing to go out. He tried to pull up a diagnostic, maybe to shock whatever stray process was running his motor system into shutting down. Nothing. He couldn't control a thing. He must have been hacked. His almost-empty bank account came up instead of the diagnostic routine, then his contacts. It paged through them faster than he could track.

No this was wrong. Lockout hacks were clumsy, only good for trolling. They just made you shuffle around like a zombie, and they couldn't access any of your data because they worked by bypassing your brain and messing with the motor-control firmware. This shouldn't be happening, and anyway, he hadn't connected to anything that could have transferred code like that. The music. It had to be the music. It had messed with his chassis somehow, even before he blacked out.

Whatever was calling the shots for his body got onto his bike. He should be feeling something: that pounding fear from last night, or anger at being trapped while his body went walking on its own initiative, but he was as flat as he'd ever been. His body biked downtown. He fell into the rhythm of his legs, and then started to really feel afraid. Trapped. He was trapped and it wasn't him controlling these legs anymore. Stop. He froze for a moment and the bike wobbled, then the hack took over and steadied it.

Back to blank. He lost the feeling of emotion when he tried to stop pedaling and it locked him out again. His body stopped at Maya's concierged apartment. He had a standing invitation he hadn't used in three months. It couldn't know that. Maybe there was another him running the whole show while he was stuck here on the wrong side of the partition.

The door recognized him. The elevator sent him straight to

Maya's floor. Her door flashed a helpful indicator, and buzzed him in to the sound of gentle wind chimes. Maya called hello from the balcony. His body answered.

"It's Rob."

"Come on out. The sun's beautiful today."

He wanted to see her. That much he agreed with. He and the hack walked together, and his heart beat in his chest as he tried to figure how to tell her what was happening. He didn't want to get kicked out again, to watch and not care what it did.

Maya was sunbathing, getting charged and enjoying the endorphin analog that photovoltaic bodies were designed to give under the light. She waved to an empty deck chair next to her. He felt his fingers curl around something in his pocket. That's what it wanted. If he tried to fight it, he'd freeze up for a moment. She'd notice, and she was probably his best chance at getting out of this. Maya knew more about synthetics and code than he did, and she had the money to get him fixed, back to the way he'd been before the music broke him. That was the choice. Fix it, or spread it. They'd like Maya, if they wanted money, and she had plenty of synth friends.

"Machine life's got you down, I know. I've got just what you need to pick things back up."

It felt good in his mouth, sweet relaxation spreading from his tongue down though his chest as he agreed. He could feel the guides more gently now. No need to fight his way back into the cold indifference. He could feel great doing just what the music wanted.

He held a drive out, labeled in black marker.

ABOUT THE AUTHOR

R. K. Duncan is a new, hopefully up-and-coming, author mostly of fantasy, with a dash of sci-fi and horror thrown in. He writes about fairies and gods and ghosts from a ramshackle apartment in Philadelphia. In the shocking absence of any cats, he lavishes spare attention on cast iron cookware and his long-suffering and supportive partner. Before settling on writing, he studied linguistics and philosophy at Haverford College. His occasional musings and links to other work can be found at rkduncan-author.com.

WAILSONG

Kurt Pankau

S omething rumbled, which was to be expected in a punk rock show, but not like this. The band, oblivious as always when on stage, kept playing. If Mala had noticed the disturbance, it didn't register in her voice. But Mala's manager Arvid—sitting in the clubhouse looking down on stage right—he'd noticed.

"What was that?" he asked.

"Humpback whale," said Gabe. Gabe was head of security, a mustached forty-something built like an M1 Abrams.

"A what?"

"A humpback whale swam into the roof."

"Oh," said Arvid. "Should we evacuate?"

"We're fine, sir," said Gabe. "This facility can withstand a collision from a large marine mammal. And we deployed defensive capabilities to discourage future collisions."

"Discourage, eh? So, did we kill it?"

"No. We gave it a non-lethal shock and it swam away."

"Great," said Arvid. His hand hovered over the button that would let him talk directly into Mala's ear. It had been conveniently labeled "DON'T PUSH ME." If the show were disrupted, especially mid-song, he'd never hear the end of it.

This was Mala's one-night-only underwater concert extravaganza. It was the single biggest demand any artist had ever made of a manager, and Arvid had pulled it off. In half an hour, the show would culminate with the hall being flooded during an epic finale as the audience was shuttled out. That way the experience could never be repeated. Only then would Mala's artistic vision be complete.

And he couldn't afford a disaster. The show had cost him a fortune. The cheapest tickets had sold for over a million dollars apiece just to make ends meet—and who knows what the scalpers were charging? Arvid had heard dollar amounts in the middle eight-figures, not that he'd see any of that margin. Of course, he'd be able to retire off the revenue from selling bootlegs of this concert, but the concert had to finish first.

And that meant surviving collisions with whales, apparently.

"Why did a whale swim into the roof?" he asked.

"Probably the noise," said Gabe. "Sound travels pretty far in the open ocean. It's very disruptive for them."

"I don't understand," said Arvid. "I paid for all the permits."

"The permits?"

"For the noise. I basically had to bribe every conservation agency in every country in the Southern Hemisphere. But they said it would be alright."

"Do the animals know this?" asked Gabe.

"They fucking well ought to."

Up on stage, Mala ripped into the crunching, sonic bliss that was the third guitar solo from "Wailsong," the four-minute closing anthem and title track from her new album and the inspiration for this show. She described it as oceanic, which, to Arvid's ear, seemed to just mean extra reverb. She leaned against the bassist and threw her head back while she played.

"Hard to imagine what a whale wouldn't like about that," said Arvid.

"It's not necessarily the noise ... er, the sound," offered Gabe. "The whale could just as easily have been attacking the lights."

"Why would it do that?"

"It's bright. It's disorienting. There's not usually much light at this depth."

"But without the lights you can't see the ocean creatures," said Arvid. "They're the real stars of the show, aren't they?"

"We're also giving off a lot of heat."

"Is this supposed to make me feel better?" asked Arvid. "Instead of identifying one thing that might cause a whale to swim into this giant underwater glass enclosure, you've come up with three."

"We'll be fine, sir. We can survive a collision with a large marine mammal."

"So you've said."

"Thank you, Atlantis," said Mala from the stage as the song came to a close. She beamed. Her fluorescent blue grill sparkled from behind her lips "Do y'all see that whale?"

The audience cheered.

"Maybe they want us to hear another solo," said the bassist into his microphone. "Oh, look, he's coming back."

"I wish they wouldn't goad it on," said Arvid.

"I don't think the whales can hear them," said Gabe.

"I thought the problem was that the whales *can* hear them."

Gabe stroked his chin at this for a moment but said nothing.

There was another rumble, louder this time. A few nervous titters came from the audience.

"Good try, whale-dude!" shouted Mala, ecstatic.

Arvid's hand drifted towards the DON'T PUSH ME button. "I could end the show right now," he said. "I could tell them to start the finale."

"I don't think your star would be very pleased," said Gabe. "I may be head of security, but I don't know that I'd be able to protect you from her."

"I'm just weighing my options," said Arvid. "It'd be a shame for all of these people to die—"

"Nobody's going to die," said Gabe. "It's just one whale. We can survive one whale."

Mala continued to banter with the audience, making fish jokes. "They just want to crash our party," she said.

Arvid would have to edit all of this out of the bootlegs.

"What about two whales?" he asked. "What if two whales swam into the roof—"

"We'd still be fine," said Gabe.

Arvid clicked his tongue. "How many is too many?"

Gabe blinked. "Well, I don't know, Arvid. We didn't stress test against multiple whales."

"Give me your best guess."

"Ten?"

Mala pointed upward. "Oh, look, he's coming back again. And he's bringing some friends. Jeez. There must be a couple dozen up there."

Arvid went white. "So ... thirty-ish ... how would we hold up against—"

"Push the button," said Gabe.

"Right ... " Arvid punched the red button and bent over a microphone. "Mala, the whales are going to kill us all. We need to evacuate now." He looked around. They'd come so close. "So ... start the last number."

Mala, oblivious as always, didn't even blink. "Good night, Atlantis!" she shouted.

She began to play.

The lights flared. The pyrotechnics exploded. The belts on the floor moved to corral concert-goers into their transports.

But it was too late.

There was a tremendous rumble followed by glass shattering, water gushing, people screaming, and—underneath all of that—blistering peals of sonic bliss from Mala's fluorescent blue guitar.

ABOUT THE AUTHOR

Kurt Pankau is a software engineer from St. Louis. He enjoys board games, dad-jokes, and stories about time travel. His stories have appeared in *Nature Magazine*, *Escape Pod*, and *Orson Scott Card's Intergalactic Medicine Show*. He tweets at @kurtpankau and blogs at his website kurtpankau.com.

DESPITE ALL MY RAGE

Dawn Vogel

I wasn't kicked out of my house because I had the Gift. I was kicked out because I couldn't use it right.

My mom is on the Mage Council, so she trained me herself for years. Until the Testing.

Yeah, it's always the Testing.

I flunked. I could ace the concrete knowledge parts. I'd had those drilled into my brain. I just wanted to make my Gift my own, and for that, they flunked me.

My mother was livid. "How could you have failed? You have had the best of tutors!"

I shrugged. Any answer I could give her wouldn't be what she wanted to hear.

"Your failure reflects on *me*. It reflects on the entire Mage Council. This cannot stand."

She waved her hand, and I felt myself shrinking, shifting, changing. Mother's vanity meant there were mirrors everywhere, so I saw what she'd done. I was a rat.

"Leave." She pointed at the door. "You are my child no more. You are welcome here no more."

At least she turned me into a rat person. Still got opposable thumbs, which means I can still use my Gift. She couldn't take that away, no matter how much she might have wanted to.

I found other kids like me, tossed aside because they weren't "right." Not turned into rats. And that's made socializing awkward, because other kids don't really expect a four-foot bipedal rat to chat them up.

There are some who see past the awkward, see past me being a rat, and see in me the same rage that burns in them.

The ones the Mage Council has deemed unfit. The ones who have "not lived up to their potential." The ones who failed their arbitrary Testing.

So what do we do?

We rig the results. We corrupt the scores. We ensure the Testing doesn't run as planned. We burn the system down from the inside, as the unnoticeable, as the janitors and secretaries and cogs in the machine.

When the cogs stop, the machine stops.

Except for when it doesn't.

They still administer the Testing.

We don't think the results were ever real. They certainly aren't now.

So we'll try another way.

You think we can't do it? You think they'll stop us? They don't know how or when or where we'll hit them. They don't think like we do.

This is their weakness. They think that they're in control. They think that dictating the way the Gift works will keep the sheep in line.

They're wrong.

They've failed to see the signs around them. They've failed to keep up with the times. There are more of us every day.

Right under their noses, and right under yours, we've infiltrated the words, the music, the visuals. The things that you don't pay a lick of attention to every day.

Except for now, as we pound it into your subconscious.

And so you hear this song, you hear the drums and the guitars and the bass and the guttural screams. You hear it for what it is.

This is not a protest song.

This is your last warning.

We are coming.

This is war.

ABOUT THE AUTHOR

Dawn Vogel gave up on learning to play the guitar years ago, but she's sung in cover bands performing the songs of The Smithereens, Green Day, and Smashing Pumpkins. She's rocked a faux hawk and a flannel (separately), always in her stompy boots. When she's not dreaming of being a rock star, she's typically writing, crafting, or co-editing *Mad Scientist Journal*. She is a member of Broad Universe, SFWA, and Codex Writers. Her steampunk series, *Brass and Glass*, is being published by Razorgirl Press. She lives in Seattle with her husband, author Jeremy Zimmerman, and their herd of cats. Visit her at historythatneverwas.com.

I THINK WE NEED TO HEAR THAT AGAIN

Vaughan Stanger

(Jazzy intro fades out. Jimmy Simul grins.)

"Tonight on Fix Your Sim we' ll be listening to the *Jonny Real Show*, a crowd-sourced radio programme created by Billy Putrid, lead singer with the Wastrels and self-styled king-pin of the NuPunk movement."

"Thanks for inviting me, Jimmy."

"So, Billy, am I right that NuPunk is a reaction to AI-created music?"

"Yeah, we fucking hate that shite—"

"Um, Billy, no swearing, please."

"Okay."

"So how did the Wastrels get started?"

"NuPunk's slogan is 'singles not singularity!' The music is raw and real. So we home-printed guitars and drums, released our songs on vinyl, promoted them through word of mouth. Proper punk spirit! But . . ."

"No joy?"

"Nobody played our single."

"What did you do next?"

"I realised we needed a radio show that would play our singles when we sent them in, so I created a DJ based on John Peel. Back in the 1970s, John championed punk in the UK. He seemed like the perfect fit. I changed the name of course."

"Lawyers, eh?"

"Yeah! Anyway, I programmed a chatbot with all the personal data I could find online and seeded the sim with every track John played on his show."

"So what went wrong?"

(Sigh.)

"When we submitted the first single, Jonny ignored it!"

"Did you send him another?"

"We did! That's when the sim started looping."

"Right then, I think we'd better listen to the *Jonny Real Show*."

A blast of perfect pop music erupts: all pounding drums, thrashing guitars and yearning vocals.

"You know what? I think we need to hear that again ... "

Drum intro; fuzzed-up guitar; a young man with a tremulous voice starts singing about teenage lust.

"Sounds kinda retro, but the song definitely has something. Who's it by?"

"It's 'Teenage Kicks' by the Undertones. That's all Jonny ever plays now."

"Okay, Billy, let's FIX YOUR SIM!"

(Brief interlude; more jazz.)

"Hi there! I need to ask—for a friend—why don't you play the Wastrels' songs?"

"All I ever wanted was to hear music that I like, and play it to my listeners."

"There's your answer, Billy. He doesn't like your music."

"But we programmed him with everything he ever played. He *must* like NuPunk!"

"Tell me, has he heard any new music that *isn't* NuPunk?"

"Well, no. We thought—"

(Rolls eyes.)

"I reckon you need to open up the sim to *all* new music, Billy."

"But—"

"And you guys definitely need to raise your game."

"Okay ... "

"So that's it for this edition. Next time on Fix Your Sim ... "

(Jazzy outro.)

☒ ☒ ☒

(Jazzy intro.)

"Hi Billy. Still no joy?"

"We took your advice and opened up the sim to everything, but he *still* only plays that frigging song!"

"Do you mean *everything?*"

"Well, not that AI shite, obviously!"

"Cos you hate that stuff, right?"

"Right!"

"But does Jonny?"

"Oh, come on!"

"I'll tell you what, Billy; I'll buy the sim from you. Maybe you could use the money for guitar lessons."

"Let me think about that ... "

(Desert wind noises.)

"Next time on Fix Your Sim we'll hear what's new on the Jonny Real Show."

(Jazzy outro.)

☒ ☒ ☒

A bleep-storm lasting a microsecond ends in a crescendo of synthetic desire.
"You know what? I think we need to hear that again ... "

ABOUT THE AUTHOR

Formerly an astronomer and more recently a research project manager in a defense and aerospace company, Vaughan Stanger now writes SF and fantasy fiction full time. He has recently completed a novel and is currently marketing it, together with the series it belongs to. His short stories have appeared in *Daily Science Fiction*, *Abyss & Apex*, *Postscripts*, *Nature Futures*, and *Interzone*, amongst others. Collections of these stories can be purchased on Amazon, Smashwords, iBooks, and elsewhere. Follow his writing adventures at vaughanstanger.com or @ VaughanStanger.

YOU CAN'T KILL POLKA

Steven Assarian

I t started like this.

The Phantom was sick. It had been sputtering since Tuscon, and we were getting near Flagstaff.

"Wendell, ease off!" I said.

When Wendell finally pulled the bus over, leaning his lanky body over the steering wheel and whispering little prayers over the 'x's on his hands, the whole front cab filled with smoke. It smelled even worse when we opened up the hood and started to look inside.

"Told you we should've gone electric," said Barrett. His face looked like somebody had flattened it with an iron, which is the kind of face you get with Barrett's attitude. His shaved head and pin-cushion piercings didn't flatter him either.

"Shut it," said Ayla. She towered over both Wendell and Barrett. Her clothes were stitched together from pieces, because nothing was ever long enough to fit her.

"Huh," said Wendell. "Samara, didn't you put coolant in when we stopped last?"

"I did," I said. I played with my head covering, which is what I always did when I got nervous. "It's probably all leaked out. You know how the engine leaks."

"Maybe she just needs a rest," Wendell said as he patted the Phantom's grill.

But the Phantom needed more than rest. It needed a new engine, likely a new everything.

Ayla sighed. "Might as well put up the collectors."

We put up our solar panels to give us a bit more power, but they weren't really necessary. The bus was painted green, and the paint Wendell had bought was photovoltaic. It fed into the electrical system, giving our stuff a charge when it needed.

"Want to practice?" said Wendell.

"Sure," I said.

I looked at Ayla. It was a rhythm I was used to.

"All those in favor," said Ayla. "Vote by the usual sign."

"Aye," Wendell and I said.

"All those opposed, same right."

"Aye," said Barrett, being a smartass.

"Motion carries."

Out on the side of the road, underneath the Phantom's awning, we brought out our equipment. Barrett had his drums, paint buckets turned over to make something of a drum kit; Wendell wore his accordion, which he'd picked up near Tulsa for next to nothing; Ayla had her guitar, beaten to a pulp and held together with stickers and glue; I had my bass, beaten to slightly less of a pulp, but still held together with stickers and glue.

We worked through the set list for a few hours. It was full of screaming, acronyms, and politics nobody seemed to care about but us. Ayla did most of the writing and singing; Barrett kept us political, still the only guy I know with a membership card to the Black Cats; Wendell anchored us in older stuff, always naming off bands I'd barely heard of, like the Pogues or the Tossers.

Me? I was just trying to make us play slow enough so people could understand what the hell we were saying.

"Let's do 'An Injury to All' again," said Barrett. He was sweating over his drum kit. "We need to practice that one."

We slept in the Phantom that night, on four of the eight bunk-beds in the back. The crickets, the ones we raised for food, chirped a little but nothing too bad.

The next morning, we woke to rumbling.

There was a huge caravan running. It was made of all sorts of RVs and improvised house cars. A mechanic's rig pulled to the side of the road in front of us. Ayla handled it, like she always seemed to do.

"He can't stop for long," said Ayla when she came back to the

Phantom. "But he can tow us to the Yanoda Fulfillment Center up the road."

"Yanoda?" said Barrett. "They work people to death. No way we're working for them."

"I know," said Ayla. "But we can get there and make some money playing. Lots of people at fulfillment centers."

The repair rig towed us like he promised. "You gonna be join-ing us for fulfillment?" he asked as he took his tow hook off our front bumper. He also took the money, the last of our petty cash, from Ayla.

"Can't," said Ayla.

"Well, if you're not working for Yanoda, you got two weeks before they kick you off. You gotta get at least twenty-five miles further on the public land. And the Yanoda security team, they check."

"Thanks for the heads-up," said Ayla. But we didn't plan on being around anywhere near that long.

The caravan was more massive than I could've imagined. Laid out on the land, they covered the dirt in a steel and wood blanket. It was kind of pretty. Everything was laid out in grids, with hook-ups at every spot so the people could get fuel and power, and get rid of their waste. Some of them were built up. You could tell that some of the caravan had money, but most of them didn't. And they were old. In anoth-er time, they might've been retirees, just living sleepy lives on front porches.

Instead, they worked like dogs.

Every day I'd see them walking to the center, and at the end of the day they could barely move. It was like Yanoda sucked the life out of them, and every day they came back to their trailers with a little less of what they had started with.

I spent most of the first week munching fried crickets and fiddling around with my bass. We tried playing a few shows to empty parking lots or angry people. One afternoon, we were playing as the caravan was getting off, tired and hungry, from a sixteen-hour shift with man-datory overtime.

Christmas was still popular in Arizona, apparently.

The hat we'd put out had a few coins in it, nowhere near enough to get the engine repaired. Someone had tossed in a note that said "Fuck off!" which Barrett pocketed. The workers kept passing in a steady stream.

Wendell said, to no one in particular: "We need to get out of here in a week."

"We could try another part of the park," said Ayla. "Really get the kids out this time."

"There are no kids here. Everybody's gray," said Barrett. "And these people are worked so hard they couldn't stand at a show. Not like we play. And hell, if they hear half our set list, they'll run us out of town on a pole. We play 'Diggers and Levelers,' they burn us at the stake."

"A Yanoda-approved stake," I said.

"The cheapest stake around," said Barrett. "Made with 100 percent slave labor."

"Well, maybe we play something different," said Wendell. "Something more traditional."

"Yeah?" I said. "Like what?"

"I don't know, like, something from the old country. Like a polka."

"A polka!" said Barrett. "No shit. That'd be a fuckin' riot!"

We voted, like always. The vote was for a little six song set we spent the rest of the day practicing. We'd play just as people were getting off their shifts and trudging back to their trailers.

Our noise echoed through the camp: Wendell's accordion and the rest of us singing about apples and peaches, heaven and beer, the whole bit.

It was the same stream of people coming out of Yanoda, groaning and chattering as they got off another 16 hour. Still, nobody noticed us.

"Well, that was fun," said Barrett.

"Maybe it's just not the right set," said Wendell. He turned to Ayla. "You think we should line up some Yanoda work? Just in case?"

"I'd rather starve," said Ayla.

I watched one woman come walking out from among the stream of workers. It was easy to see that her feet were killing her and her legs were stiff with protest. As she got closer, I could also see there were tears running down her face. She wiped them away before she reached us.

When she did, she said: "Was that you? You four?" She took Wendell's hand. "It had to be you!"

Wendell stuttered. I could tell he was deeply uncomfortable. "Sure. Sure thing. That was us."

"You play the old songs!" she said. "I can't believe it. I didn't think anybody played songs like that. In the old neighborhood, we used to play them, but nobody can anymore." She wiped her face again. "Could you play for us? This Sunday? Everybody from the old neighborhood would love you."

"Sure," said Wendell. "We can do that."

"Wonderful!"

I could see Ayla's cheeks getting red already. "Look, we need money to get our engine repaired," she said. "Otherwise they'll impound our rig."

"Listen," said the woman. "We can pay you, enough to get your engine repaired, no problem." She beamed. She shoved some company scrip into Wendell's hand. "Here. Proof I can pay."

Wendell looked down at it. "I can't take this."

"Think of it as an up-front investment. You play for us, you'll be getting good pay. Real US dollars."

Wendell hesitated, and then he pocketed the scrip.

"I can't wait to tell the neighborhood!" she said. "I'm Lena, Lena Yankovic. Can't wait to hear you play Sunday!"

I was getting excited. We hadn't played a decent show in what seemed like ages. And we were getting paid.

As soon as Lena was out of earshot, Ayla said: "Everyone, band meeting. Now."

I could see Wendell coming back down to earth, realizing what he'd just done.

We got back on the Phantom, and Ayla pulled the creaking door shut. "What the fuck Wendell," she said. I could see how angry she was now, how much of a lid she'd kept on herself out when we were talking with Lena. Now she was boiling over.

"Hey, I just thought that this would be a good opportunity for us. A good way for us to earn some money. We won't have to lose the Phantom, and we're going to play a paying gig. It works out for everybody."

"You don't make decisions about the band like that!" she said. "This isn't a dictatorship. It's democracy. We all agreed to that."

I saw Wendell shrink.

"Hey," I said. "Come on, Ayla. Lay off."

"We all agreed," she repeated.

"Ok, so Wendell jumped the gun. But a gig is a gig. We can't afford to be picky. And we can still vote."

Ayla seethed. "What's the motion?"

"That we practice Wendell's songs and play a traditional set this Sunday. For the old neighborhood. So we can get money to bring the Phantom back to life."

She crossed her arms, looking at me.

To be honest, I was terrified. Ayla could rip me in half, and I certainly didn't want to cross her. But I wanted the show. I wanted a chance to not have to worry about our next meal. And I was so sick of those damn crickets.

"Put it to a vote," I said.

Ayla wouldn't budge.

Barrett smiled. He must've thought the whole thing was funny. "All those in favor," he said, sarcastically. "Vote by the usual sign."

Wendell looked at me, and I looked at Wendell. We were both looking at the floor when we said "Aye."

"All those opposed," said Barrett. "Same right."

"Aye," said Ayla through grit teeth.

"Motion carries," said Barrett.

The next day we started working on the set list. We only had a week to prepare, but it would be enough time to get us through. After all, we didn't have anything else to do all day. Wendell cashed the scrip and got us some good food, enough for a week's worth of peanut butter sandwiches and a pizza that was almost as big as me. I hadn't had pizza like that in a long time. It felt amazing, to be so full I could barely move. But still, we had to practice.

We spent the rest of the week working our asses off. We dug out our old acoustic stuff that we didn't play very often, and we started to sound halfway decent.

Barrett and I were screwing around in the afternoon heat. Ayla was off sulking, and Wendell was getting more food from the company store. We'd agreed on ice cream, which I hadn't eaten in a dog's age.

"Hey Barrett," I said, over his drumming. "Where do you think we should head next? We're going to get stuck in the hot season if we stay here too long."

"Oh, this band isn't going to make it out of here," he said, drumming a steady rhythm.

I nearly dropped the cricket out of my mouth that I was struggling to force down. "What?"

"Oh yeah. Dude, you can't get away with challenging Ayla like that and expect to keep the band together. Dictators gonna dictate."

"We always vote," I said. "Most democratic band I've ever been in."

"Yeah, we always vote," he said. "But she's always the one deciding what we're voting on. It's been that way since we started."

"Then ... why have you stayed so long?"

I thought I saw a flash of sadness come over his face. But it passed quick. He broke into a grin. "Not to say it isn't fun. But we got a lot of structure here. You deal with it awhile, but then you got to move on. Nothing lasts forever, Samara. You know that."

I strummed my bass. I didn't say anything.

"Something to think about," said Barrett.

Lena came back a few times during the week, checking on us. I liked it when she did. She reminded me of my auntie in Fennville, the one that baked me cookies and didn't put cigarettes out on my arm.

After Lena came through while we were practicing, Ayla said: "She seem batty to you?"

"Naw," said Wendell, a beat too quickly. "She seems all right."

That was Thursday.

We kept up practice for the rest of the week, hours of sessions. But we didn't see Lena again, not with her sore feet or her words of encouragement.

Friday afternoon we were all hanging out in the Phantom, trying to keep the heat off us. "Hey," said Wendell. "Should we try and find Lena today? I think we're in good shape for the picnic. We should track her down and scope out the site." He sounded worried.

"Maybe she's dead," said Ayla sullenly.

"Come off it," I said. "Don't be such a shit." I turned to Wendell. "Let's walk around. We can find her trailer for sure."

We walked through camp, its parking lots splayed out in a rolling grid. Until I tried walking the whole lot with Wendell, I hadn't realize how big the camp was. It held cars and trucks in the thousands, all parked neatly next to each other.

Compared to some of the people in the field, we were rich; at least the big green school bus had bunk beds for each of us and room for all our gear. A lot of the caravan consisted of, not converted vans or trucks, but normal cars with solar reflectors to keep the heat off, and five gallon bucket chemical toilets filled with sawdust.

I don't think Yanoda ever thought about what it meant to have their logo on these bucket-toilets, but when you've got that much money, metaphors probably don't matter all that much.

We ate up most of the day, trying to find Lena.

"It occurs to me," said Wendell, after miles of walking. "That Lena never told us where she lived."

"She said the entire old neighborhood would be out," I said. "That has to be a lot of people, right?"

Wendell's face creased with sadness.

We trudged back to the Phantom in silence. The walk back was hard. But telling Barrett and Ayla, however, was harder.

"So you're telling me we don't have a gig," said Ayla.

"I couldn't find her," said Wendell, cowed. "Well, we couldn't find her."

"Goddammit," said Ayla.

Barrett said: "Yanoda Security was here a little while ago. They want us working, paying, or out. And soon. Guy said it was a 'verbal warning,' whatever that means."

"I could get work at Fulfillment," said Wendell. His voice was almost pleading.

"Fuck that," said Barrett. "You'll have blood on your hands."

"But this is all my fault. I have to at least try and fix this."

"Wendell," I said. "It's ok. We'll figure it out. We'll make it work."

"But how?" he asked. "They put a boot on the Phantom and we'll never get her back. Then we'll have to work Fulfillment just to pay off interest. They'll keep charging us interest. It'll never end." He sunk into the driver's seat, burying his head in his hands.

Ayla sat in the front seat behind Wendell, where we hadn't ripped out the old school bus seats. The stuffing was coming free, crumbling onto the floor. "I make a motion that Samara works Fulfillment."

"What?" I said.

Wendell's eyes were wide. "Ayla ..."

"She's as much to blame in all this as you are."

I shot back: "Whose idea was is to come to fucking Yanoda Fulfillment? Or do you not remember?"

Barrett stood up. "Nobody on this bus is working Fulfillment. End of discussion."

"That's not how we do things," said Ayla. "There are procedures. There is a structure."

"Ayla," Barrett breathed. "Fuck your structure. If that's where it leads, if that's what it makes us do, then fuck it. That's not what I signed up for. I signed up to play shows. And that's what we're going to do. We're going to play a show this Sunday, and come what may, we are not working Fulfillment."

"But Barrett," said Wendell.

"We've already got paid for this. We already got scrip from Lena. Fuck, we even got some ice cream out of it. We are playing tomorrow."

"What if I say no?" said Ayla.

"Then I'm out," Barrett said.

Everybody froze.

"What the fuck, Barrett," she said, more shocked than anything else.

"You know what? You're pissing me off, Ayla," I said. "You keep harping on everybody, and you don't have any better ideas yourself!"

"Fuck you, Samara!" she shot back.

"Maybe," I said. "We should have a vote about being in this god-damn band."

Ayla smiled bitterly. "Fine by me. Then we can all watch you flame the fuck out."

There was a knock on the cabin door. It snapped us out of our rage, knowing that there were other people out there beyond the bus. We all turned around to stare.

The man standing there must've been young among the workers, yet to hit his seventies. "Uh, hello," he said as Barrett opened the door. "You all the band that Lena talked to?"

"Yeah, we're them," said Barrett.

"Well, she wanted me to tell you she's sorry, but there won't be a picnic tomorrow. Most of the neighborhood got heat-sick yesterday, after the exchangers broke down in Fulfillment. Nasty case. They're trying to rest, and now that the line's broke down, they don't have any work."

It was a gut punch.

"Can you tell us where they are?" said Wendell. "We were trying to find them earlier today, and Lena never told us."

"Oh, they're about five miles up, over the north hill. Probably why you couldn't find them. They're kinda cut-off. Must've got here late for the winter work ... not that we have winters around here anymore." He chuckled.

"Thanks," I said.

Barrett shut the door. We were all ashen.

"Well, what do we do now?" said Ayla. We both looked at each other sheepishly. All our fighting about going up to Yanoda seemed petty now, while our audience was out of work, exploited and heat-sick.

"Oh, easy," said Barrett. "We go over the hill and play."

"But the Phantom . . . " said Wendell.

Barrett, and I'll never forget this, said: "It's not the bus, man. It's the people inside." He added, getting louder, "And if this is our last gig, let's blow it out. Make it our last stand."

Wendell broke into a wide, goofy grin. He looked at Ayla. "We need a vote?"

"Motion's on the table," said Ayla. Her whole body had started to relax again.

"All those in favor," said Barrett. "Vote by the usual sign."

"Aye!" we all said.

We packed up our gear. We lost Ayla for a little while; I'd figured she'd stormed off, mulling over whether she should be pissed at us or not. When she came back, there was a wad of paper in her hand. But she just strapped on her guitar and picked up an amp and said nothing.

A little after noon we started off for the hill. It was hell, getting all our gear over that thing—the heat was like a chain around your throat—but we made it there.

The old neighborhood was there, just like the guy had said, all circled like covered wagons around a central patch of dirt.

We found Lena's trailer. It was a little beaten, an old, electrified Ford Ranger truck with living quarters off the back. None of us could stand up in there, but Lena was short enough that she could and not touch the ceiling.

Through the door, Wendell said: "Lena, we're ready to play!"

There was rustling in the trailer. "I told Franz to find you," she said as she opened the door. She was wearing a house dress and a robe, even with the heat. A blast of cold air blew past her when she opened the door.

It was a long beat before she could talk again, after seeing us there sweating like pigs with all our gear. "I'm so sorry," she said on the verge of tears. "They shut the line down. We can't pay you."

"We didn't come to get paid," said Barrett. "We came to play."

Her eyes went wide. "But your rig."

"We came to play a picnic in the old neighborhood," said Wendell. "That's what we're going to do."

Lena hesitated. Then she pushed her gray hair off her face and went back inside. There was a rustling in the trailer, and when we saw Lena again, she was wearing an old print dress, and she had an old aluminum lawn chair in her hand.

She came down out of her trailer, and it was easy to tell how weak she was. But she was shouting for everyone to come out, get out.

And the neighborhood did come out. They were ragged, squeezed of everything. They couldn't dance, because of their knees, and they couldn't yell too loud, but they were *there*.

We played like hell. All these songs Wendell had taught us. He was out front, having the time of his life. He was beaming, having too much fun, making his accordion do incredible things.

Ayla said to Wendell: "Hey, can we take a detour?"

"What's up?"

"I got a song. We can play it to the Argonne polka, if that's all right."

"When did you write a new song?" said Wendell.

She pulled out her wad of paper. "You can read it before, if you want."

Wendell's eyes scanned the page quickly, jumping from one word to the next. When he finished, he grinned. "Well, all right," he said. "Let's do it."

Ayla took up the mic and sang something new.

She sang about sorting bins and moving lines, aching hands

and busted knees, terror and joy. She sang a polka about Yanoda Fulfillment and what we'd seen in our time at the site.

It was one of the best songs I've ever heard come out of the band. The crowd cheered as much as they could. They were feeling it. They knew Yanoda was screwing them. They knew that they were sitting in their trailers, heat-sick, while the fucks on top were so callous they'd fuck a whole neighborhood because of a broken heat exchanger. She'd made something new, out of all those old songs. And the old neighborhood loved it. They understood.

After we played our set list, and our encore, Barrett said, sweaty and happy: "We've been the Lena Yankovic Band! Tip your veal and eat your servers!"

And we broke down our gear and left.

When we came back, there was a notice on the Phantom that explained, because of our work status, we would need to vacate within twenty-four hours, or begin paying a rental fee, which would accrue interest for each day not paid. It didn't say anything about getting impounded, but we knew that was the logical conclusion.

"Must not like polka," said Barrett.

The engine was still dead. Wendell made one last-ditch effort to try and get the engine to turn. Nothing. We resigned ourselves to our fate, and ate the last of the crickets in the farm, frying them up. I wasn't as sick of them then.

We turned in for the night, fat and happy. Early the next morning, there was a knock on the bus door. I opened it, expecting some Yanoda goons.

But it wasn't.

It was the mechanic, the one that had given us the tow.

"Hey," he said. "Can I have a look at your engine?"

"We can't pay," I said. "All we got is a little scrip and a bus full of junk."

"It's all right," he said. "I heard what you did for Lena. She's a sweetheart."

"Yeah," I said. "She is."

The mechanic spent most of the day working. He and Wendell lorded over the engine, poking and prodding, making things move and not move. A little more coolant, a good flush, and a ton of patching polymer later, the engine coughed to life.

Wendell whooped. "She's alive!" he said. "She's breathing again!"

We made it out of there just as the Yanoda deadline was passing.

I wish I could say we lasted forever after that. I mean, the cracks were already starting to show, even then. But we made some beautiful stuff together. We're scattered all over the place now, but we still keep in touch when we can. We're still even friends.

That friendship is what made this album you're now holding. *You Can't Kill Polka, You Bastards*! was a lot of fucking work, so I hope you enjoy it.

More than that, though, I hope you have an old neighborhood. If you don't, I hope you can find one.

It's not the bus, it's the people inside.

- Samara Kuybyshev
The Lena Yankovic Band

ABOUT THE AUTHOR

Steven Assarian is an author and librarian. He was in the band *Whiskeyocracy* and is currently in the band *Cephalopods, Motherfucker!* You can find his writing on *Cracked.com*, *The Modern Rogue*, and *Workers Write! Tales from the Cafe*. He blogs at *Masterlibrarian.com*. His wife is his greatest editor, partner, and ass-kicker when necessary. Without her, he would be completely screwed. He believes in the good fight.

ABOUT THE EDITOR

Born in Salem, Mass., **Steve Zisson** grew up in the late 1970s when punk was exploding on the Boston music scene. Zisson is a science fiction writer and editor, whose speculative fiction has appeared in *Daily Science Fiction, Nature's Future, One Night in Salem,* and *Mad Scientist Journal,* among other places. Zisson is also a biotech journalist and publisher who for many years was editorial director of a Boston-based clinical trials publishing company, CenterWatch, and senior editor at BioSpace.com. He was previously president of Carlat Publishing, whose books and influential newsletter, The Carlat Psychiatry Report, provide independent continuing medical education free of pharmaceutical company influence for psychiatrists and other mental health professionals. He got his start in journalism as a newspaper reporter in the Boston area. He now lives on the North Shore of Boston.

ACKNOWLEDGEMENTS

Thank you to all of the writers, the dreamers, who contributed stories to this book as well as to the writers who submitted stories. Many fine stories didn't make it into *A Punk Rock Future*.

We want to give special recognition and a big thank you to all of our Kickstarter backers without whom this book would still be a dream.

Josh Fisher, Jürgen Neuwirth, Cindy Zisson, Samantha Henderson, Beckett & Gibson Rountree, Sam Whitmore, Chris George, Kelly Robson and Alyx Dellamonica, Zach Bartlett, Job Tooth, Tom Foster, Sean Cohea, Aoife Walsh, D Franklin, Ellie Campbell, A Grue, Matthew Pedone, Ande Davis, Patricia McNally, Lesley Conner, John Winkelman, Grace Vibbert, Jessica Reisman, Dan Bloch, Richard Jinks, Alan Snow, Karyn Korieth, Charlie Heaps, Melissa Nazzaro, Virginia Zisson.

Kerri Regan, Angus Abranson, Thea Flurry, Chris Brant, Dagmar Baumann, Peter Beckett, xerode, Spence Fothergill, Aidan Doyle, Kaiqua, Alan & Jeremy VS Science Fiction, Susie Munro, Owen and Oliver Davidson, Corey J. White, Mike Bundt, AJ Fitzwater, Lukas Myhan, Erin M. Hartshorn, Maria Haskins, Dan Hill, Sam Stilwell, Frances Rowat, Phoebe Barton, Ryan Harron, Benjamin C. Kinney, Matt Hope, Silvia Molina.

Alyssa Hillary, Tom Prasch, Matt Harris, Lance Jonn Romanoff, Jen Gheller, Heather Valentine, Jennifer Priester, Terry Somerville, Kathy Schrenk, Fenric Cayne, M. V. Ho, Ivy A, Patrick Miller, Richard Wilkin, Nachtwulf, Sean Parson, Lexie Carver, Rosemary D. Do, Edward Greaves, Allison Matthews, Elisabeth Fillmore, Michael Vanden Berg, Baratz, Benjamin Hausman, Danni Brigante, Pat Foran, Jeremy Brett, Roberta Bononi, Rob Funk, Ether, Ceillie Simkiss.